THE YEAR OF
YELLOW JACK

Praise for *The Year of Yellow Jack*

"Simon has created an intriguing amalgam of oral tradition, historical fact, and plausible imagination. The result is a work of realism unafraid to confront the harshness of antebellum slavery and the many ironies of Old South race relations. Central to the work is the enslaved Haitian-born Félicité, who is often praised even today—in the real-life town of New Iberia—for her care of yellow fever victims, no matter their races, all those generations ago."

–Shane K. Bernard, author of *Teche: A History of Louisiana's Most Famous Bayou* and other books about south Louisiana history

"Anne Simon's captivating historical novel takes the reader back to the settling of South Louisiana by the colonists and their African slaves. Meticulous in her concern for accuracy of detail, Simon has recreated that world of cattlemen and sugarcane, families black and white, the ferries that crossed the waterways and the steamboats that plied them. Through two remarkable women it also examines the social structure that both a privileged matron and a woman of color would have faced. The Year of Yellow Jack *gives the reader a fascinating journey into a world from the past that has strong ties to the present day."*

–Ann B. Dobie, Professor Emerita, University of Louisiana, Lafayette

"The Year of Yellow Jack *describes nineteenth-century New Iberia and surrounding areas in such vivid detail that it's easy to forget this is a work of fiction. Infused with rich, believable characterizations of actual historic figures and events and three-dimensional depictions of enslaved men and women, Simon brings the period to gripping life."*

–Phebe Hayes, PhD, Founder & President of the Iberia African American Historical Society; and Retired Professor & Dean, the University of Louisiana at Lafayette

THE YEAR OF
YELLOW JACK

A Novel about
Fever, Félicité, and the Early Years
on the Bayou Teche

Anne L. Simon

University of Louisiana at Lafayette Press
2020

Front and back cover: *Duperier House in 1839* by Jerome Weber

ISBN 13 (paper): 978-1-946160-58-4

http://ulpress.org
University of Louisiana at Lafayette Press
P.O. Box 43558
Lafayette, LA 70504-3558

Printed on acid-free paper in the United States
Library of Congress Cataloging-in-Publication Data

Names: Simon, Anne L., 1931- author.
Title: The year of yellow jack : a novel about fever, Félicité, and the
    early years on the Bayou Teche / Anne L. Simon.
Description: Lafayette, LA : University of Louisiana at Lafayette Press,
    2020.
Identifiers: LCCN 2019058007 | ISBN 9781946160584 (paperback ;
acid-free
    paper) | ISBN 9781946160614 (ebook)
Subjects: LCSH: Frontier and pioneer life--Fiction. | Yellow
    fever--Fiction. | New Iberia (La.)--History--19th century--Fiction. |
    GSAFD: Historical fiction.
Classification: LCC PS3619.I56186 Y43 2020 | DDC 813/.6--dc23
LC record available at https://lccn.loc.gov/2019058007

Dedicated to all those who call the bayou country home.

TABLE OF CONTENTS

FOREWORD

For the past three years I have been on a journey with two amazing women: Hortense Bérard Duperier, the widow of the man who transformed a frontier settlement in St. Martin Parish (which became the town of New Iberia, where I now live), and Félicité, an enslaved Haitian woman who—using the traditional practices of her culture when medical doctors treated fever patients with leeches—nursed both enslaved and free persons through an epidemic of yellow fever that threatened to wipe the new town off the map.

The descendants of Hortense and her friends—the men and women who signed as witnesses to their baptisms, marriages, and burials—told me their family stories. The community of my second companion, Félicité, told me their family lore. I walked around the grounds these two women walked on, explored the house where Hortense raised her family and where Félicité worked. I saw a Duperier slave cabin similar to one where she slept. I canoed the waterway that was their means of travel—the Bayou Teche—seeing the same cypress trees and hearing the same kinds of owls call at night. I researched the many mysteries about how they might have handled the challenges of life on the frontier: what they raised to nurture themselves, how they kept warm in winter, what they did for fun. In the process, three little-known cultures in colonial Louisiana came alive for me: the French ranchers, the people they held in slavery, and the Native Americans whose land they appropriated as their own.

My journey began when a friend of fifty years, Penny White, pointed out to me a filing cabinet in the back of her garage crammed with letters, essays, photographs, and other remembrances sent to her by five generations of the prolific family of her great, great, great grandparents, Frederick and Hortense Duperier. The majority of the family still lives in the area. My first offer to my friend was to help her organize and preserve the treasure. I brought home a few files from the cabinet, but after a weekend dive into a mere sample I knew I would not live long enough to accomplish the task.

Yet the story of her ancestor's lifelong relationship with Félicité, an enslaved woman held by the family, took up residence in my mind. Félicité is buried in the Duperier family plot—a unique occurrence at the time. A plaque outside city hall recognizes her service during the 1839 epidemic of yellow fever, that mysterious scourge whose etiology would not be known until the end of the nineteenth century. She is the subject of a yearly celebration by a small group of citizens. Without verifiable research, her life story remains the topic of contradictory local lore and a footnote in the history of our town.

I did not believe I could find in the Duperier family papers collected by my friend any primary source material passed over by historians. Other than numbers or first names given by their masters, the tragic reality is that half the people who lived in our town during the years of slavery were officially invisible. But I thought I might write a story about the relationship between a privileged, widowed white matron of the early nineteenth century and a gifted enslaved woman who earned sufficient respect to be buried in the family plot.

A lawyer and judge by profession, I began my research in the record rooms of the parish (county) courthouses of the area that was the Poste d'Attakapas. In the basement file room of the clerk of court of Iberville Parish, I found a few crumbling pages of the original inventory of the succession of François Cézar Boutté, the maternal grandfather of Hortense Duperier. Listed therein: "Félicité a negro woman aged more than fifty years, estimated at three hundred dollars." On further research in the office of the clerk of court of St. Martin Parish, I found the following entry on a list of Boutté succession property located in St. Martin Parish: "une negresse nomée Félicité deplus de cinquante ans." Sale of the property from that succession took place at the home of Fréderick Henry Duperier, which still stands proudly on the shore of the Bayou Teche. A calculation quickly brought me to realize the possibility that I may have a primary source. This Félicité may be the "old slave" referred to in the Duperier family and Félicité community lore who, with the Widow Duperier, nursed the inhabitants of the town in 1839 and was buried in the Duperier plot. I became further persuaded by another barely legible document in French I found, in what the office of the clerk of court of St. Martin Parish labeled the "Original Succession Records." The family of François César Boutté signed a document promising that if the buyer of Félicité, F. C. Boutté, *fils*, did not pay her price when due, the family would do so. Apparently, they did not want Félicité to leave the family through a sheriff's sale. The records of the clerk of court of St. Mary Parish disclosed the ongoing financial troubles of F. C. Boutté, *fils*, that made that outcome a possibility.

This story also touches on the relationship between the early settlers and the Atakapa Ishak Nation, who are often referred to as the Attakapas. Another record in the St. Martin Parish courthouse—a deed from Bernard, chief of the Attakapas, to Hortense Duperier's paternal grandfather—opened the door to the relationship between the settlers and those whose land they came to occupy.

The story you are about to read is fiction. From the documents that are the fruits of my research, I proffer a plausible account of Félicité's life, including a possible answer to the question of whether she died enslaved or a free woman of color. In all, I have attempted to be consistent with the work of recognized historians and other experts listed in the acknowledgments and bibliography.

HISTORICAL NOTE

A brief explanation of the patterns of settlement and the complexities of administration of the location of this story, together with the map, may assist the reader in understanding the variations in the place names employed.

New Iberia is the only remaining town in Louisiana to have been founded by Spaniards, a remnant of the colonists who relocated in 1779 after a disastrous flood drove them from their original location downstream near the present town of Charenton. They called their home *Nueva Iberia*. The few Acadians already living in the countryside and the French grantees of large tracts up the Bayou Teche in the Poste d'Attakapas called the new settlement *La Nouvelle-Ibérie*. English speakers who came later called the settlement New Town. We do not know what the two Native American tribes, the Attakapas upstream and the Chitimacha downstream, called the settlement.

After statehood in 1803, additional French, Acadian, English, and American settlers (many with enslaved Africans) came to the Attakapas country, now renamed St. Martin Parish. *La Ville de St. Martin* or St. Martinsville, the older and larger settlement farther up the bayou, became the parish seat. Historians are unable to pinpoint an exact date when the name St. Martinsville morphed into St. Martinville.

By the turn of the century, the region was still a sparsely populated frontier. Cattle ranching was the predominant means of livelihood, followed by the farming of indigo and sugarcane. The towns developed as the centers for trade with New Orleans, either down the Bayou Teche or across the Atchafalaya Swamp and down to New Orleans on the "Big River," the Mississippi.

In 1811, the Louisiana legislature carved St. Mary Parish out of the eastern portion of St. Martin Parish, Vermilion Parish out of the western portion in 1823, and Lafayette Parish out of the northwest in 1844. Not until 1868 did the central area, now known as Iberia Parish, gain self-government, with the settlement now called New Iberia as the parish seat.

A resident living in the area during the frontier days heard a number of languages spoken: Spanish, English, French, Acadian French, and Creole. English and variations of French are still heard today, but rarely the Spanish of the earliest settlers.

The owner of the land on both banks of the bayou at the center of what became the town of New Iberia, Fréderick Duperier, used many variations of his name. My research indicates that his French-speaking parents probably named him Henri Frédéric Duperier. Orphaned by the revolution in Saint-Domingue, he spent his early years in Philadelphia. As a young man, English-speaking friends of the family brought him to St. Martin Parish. They or he partially anglicized his name. He most frequently used Fréderick Henry Duperier. The monument on his grave bears the name Frederick H. Duperier, without the accent. Historian Glenn Conrad used the name Henry Frederick Duperier.

Duperier married Hortense Bérard, a descendant of two original French ranchers—Jean Baptiste Bérard of St. Martinsville and François César Boutté of the area that became New Iberia. Duperier built a home on the east bank of the Bayou Teche and plotted out an area for town lots on the west bank. The town prospered as boats from New Orleans turned at the Duperier landing to make the return trip down the Bayou Teche loaded with the produce of the surrounding area. A few days before his death in 1839, Duperier incorporated the growing settlement as Iberia. In 1847, the legislature renamed the town New Iberia.

Félicité, a woman of color born in slavery, lived behind the Duperier house. She nursed victims of the 1839 yellow fever epidemic. She lies buried in the Duperier family plot in St. Peter's Cemetery, New Iberia. Little is known about her life, but her impact on New Iberia was profound.

GENEALOGY OF HORTENSE BÉRARD DUPERIER

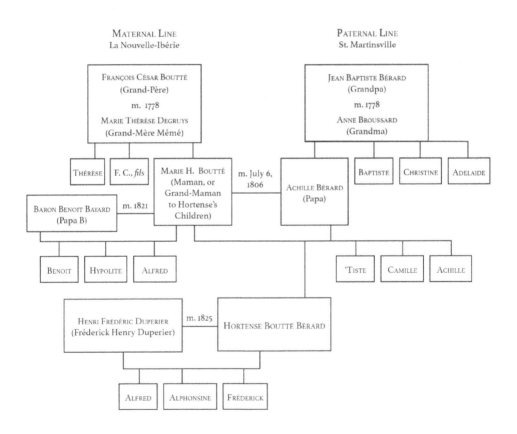

MATERNAL LINE
La Nouvelle-Ibérie

PATERNAL LINE
St. Martinsville

FRANÇOIS CÉSAR BOUTTÉ
(Grand-Père)

m. 1778

MARIE THÉRÈSE DEGRUYS
(Grand-Mère Mémé)

JEAN BAPTISTE BÉRARD
(Grandpa)

m. 1778

ANNE BROUSSARD
(Grandma)

THÉRÈSE | F. C., *fils* | MARIE H. BOUTTÉ (Maman, or Grand-Maman to Hortense's Children)

m. July 6, 1806

ACHILLE BÉRARD (Papa)

BAPTISTE | CHRISTINE | ADELAIDE

BARON BENOIT BAYARD (Papa B)

m. 1821

BENOIT | HYPOLITE | ALFRED

'TISTE | CAMILLE | ACHILLE

HENRI FRÉDÉRIC DUPERIER
(Fréderick Henry Duperier)

m. 1825

HORTENSE BOUTTÉ BÉRARD

ALFRED | ALPHONSINE | FRÉDERICK

BAYOU TECHE

St. Martinville
St. Martinsville
L'Eglise des Attakapas

Church
Crossing

Spanish Lake
Lake Tasse

Daspit
Crossing

Fausse Pointe

New Iberia
Nueva Iberia
La Nouvelle-Ibérie
New Town

Duperier House

The Shadows

Belle Place

Bérard
House

ATCHAFALAYA SWAMP

BAYOU TECHE

Charenton

5 miles

Franklin

PART I

September 1839

CHAPTER ONE

I rarely walked to the cabins behind our home by myself, and never after dark. The thick canopy of trees behind the animal yard blocked the light from moon and stars. My lamp provided only a wobbly break in the darkness in which to find footing on the path. Every breeze stirred the underbrush, the swish sending thoughts of scurrying critters shivering down my spine.

Normally when I needed Félicité for a task outside her usual work hours, I sounded the plantation bell three times. Her signal. When I needed Mr. Gordon, the overseer who stayed in the cabin past hers toward the quarters, I sounded the bell twice more. But summoning Félicité with the bell at ten o'clock at night would awaken everyone on the plantation and alarm my mother. I could add braving the darkness to the list of frightening things I had to cope with by myself since my Fréderick passed away.

I took a deep breath, straightened my back, and set out for Félicité's cabin.

Slowly, I took care not to set a foot one inch beyond the beam. I tried to close my ears to the buzz of mosquitos, the rustle of wind in the trees, the cry of an animal somewhere out in the bushes, but I tensed with every sound of the night. To my frayed nerves, the hint of breeze could well have been a gale.

"Open up, Félicité. I need to talk to you." I rapped hard, shaking the door on its hinges. When she didn't respond immediately, I rapped again.

"Comin', mistress." I heard the words through the door, in Creole of course. Félicité and I each spoke in our own language, but after so many years together, I could understand her well—when she did talk, that is. She wasn't one for long conversations. And she understood me, whether I spoke in French or English. I rapped again.

"Comin', mistress," she answered a second time, without a hint of impatience.

The wooden bolt scraped aside, and the door opened inward. Reflected in the light from my lantern, a stark white night slip stood by itself in the doorway. The head of the figure had vanished into the gloom behind. Spooked by the image, I reacted by quickly raising my lantern, restoring reality. Félicité's dark face appeared above the shoulders of the garment, two shiny spots marking her charcoal eyes.

Félicité was a small-sized person, even smaller than when I first met her so many years ago. I was not tall, but seemed so in her presence. Without her red tignon, the headscarf she always wore to work, clumps of grizzled hair sprang from her head.

When I stepped into the dark room, the toe of my short boot caught on the threshold. I stumbled forward. Félicité reached out. She saved my lantern with her right hand and steadied my arm with her left. She guided me to the one place in the room to sit—the wooden rocker Jacques had made for her last Christmas. I set my lantern on the floor next to the chair and sank down, perhaps the first time I'd been off my feet since morning.

Everything about me sagged—my bottom onto the seat of the chair, my hands over the arms, my chin onto my chest. Dust from my walk up the path from the house to the cabin encircled the hem of my skirt and clung to my shoes. Thick, dark strands of hair straggled from under my lace cap and onto my cheeks. I must have looked a mess. Dressed tip to toe in black, I still wore mourning clothes six months after my husband's death.

Without saying a word, Félicité crossed to a basin of cistern water set on a side shelf. She moistened a cloth and offered me relief from my obvious distress. The cool dampness on my face sent calm through my body. She knew me well.

"I'll be fine in a minute," I whispered. "I've had a difficult day." After what had been an even more difficult six months. I closed my eyes and pulled deep breaths into my chest to slow my heart rate.

I looked around at the sparse furnishings in Félicité's cabin: a simple bed, a barrel to one side for a night stand, a chest on one wall, a shelf holding the basin of water on the other. I couldn't remember when I had last been inside her cabin. I seemed to recall bringing her some soup a couple years ago when she had the croup. I slumped in the chair, closed my eyes, and almost instantly slipped into sleep.

Some moments passed before I opened my eyes. Across the cabin, Félicité watched me from where she sat on the edge of the moss-stuffed pallet on her bed. An oil lantern burned on the barrel. Her mosquito

netting lay open; papers littered her coverlet. No, my knocking probably
hadn't awakened her; she'd been studying something that looked like one
of Little Fréderick's school workbooks.

All day I'd been in town with my friend Eudolie Abbey. Mid-afternoon, I sent word home to my Maman, or Grand-Maman as the children
call her, saying I wouldn't be home for supper and would take the last
ferry across the bayou from town. I asked Maman to sit in my place at the
head of the table and report to me on the behavior of my children: Alfred,
Alphonsine, and Little Fréderick. She would have to put them to bed and
wait for the morning to catch a ferry back across the bayou to her house
and her own children, my stepbrothers, in the morning.

If she went home tomorrow, that is. I planned to ask her to stay longer.
I needed to return to my friend.

"Did supper go well tonight?" I asked Félicité.

"Yes, mistress. A covered plate of stewed chicken sits on the sideboard
for you."

"Yes, I found it. Were the children good?"

"Yes, mistress."

I smiled. "You always say the children are good."

"After dinner your mother told Alfred to go to his room to his lessons.
He went straight away. That's being good, mistress."

"Yes, it is. He has some catching up to do. In just two days he returns to
school up the bayou in Grand Coteau. What about Alphonsine and Little
Fréderick? Did they go off to sleep all right?"

"Yes, ma'am. Your mother played a game and got them ready for bed.
No trouble at all."

"I found Maman curled up next to Alphonsine, in her bed, sound
asleep. I hope the children didn't tire her out."

I sat in silence as I thought through what I had come to ask Félicité.
She folded her hands in her lap and waited. She was good at waiting.

"You know my friend, Eudolie? Eudolie Abbey, the wife of Dr. Abbey?" I asked.

"Yes, mistress."

"Dr. Abbey is very, very sick." My voice cracked.

"I'm sorry, mistress."

"Three days ago, this past Monday, he spent the day making rounds to
the Spaniards in the country. When he was done, he rode back into town,
straight to William Burke's livery to stable his horse. Mr. Burke came out
to fetch the mount. He found the doctor sprawled forward on the horse's

neck, close to unconscious. The doctor didn't even have strength enough to dismount. When the horse had been stopped for just a few moments, Dr. Abbey slid right out of the saddle onto the ground. Mr. Burke laid the doctor in a wagon, hitched up the mule, and carried him home. The doctor's been in bed ever since. Eudolie hardly leaves his bedside, day or night."

"I'm sorry, mistress."

"The rumors are flying, Félicité."

"Rumors of . . . ?"

I let a moment pass before answering. "The bad fever. It's because of what people are saying about Dr. Leonard Smith's nephew Raphael, who was buried last week. People over by the Big River say he had . . ." I honored the taboo about even speaking aloud the name of the fever. "You know the Smiths. They have the big plantation on the west end of town."

"Yes, ma'am. We had farewell dinner for Mr. Raphael when he left to take work over in Plaquemine." A smile opened Félicité's face. "The night the master sang."

"Oh, yes. Of course, you were there. I remember."

The memory warmed me. That night we had all the Smith family and our own around the table. Fréderick carved the roast pig standing up at the head. Before Félicité served the pudding, Fréderick raised his glass of blackberry wine and gave us a booming rendition of "La Marseillaise." Way off key, of course! Not one year ago.

Fréderick was never again as happy as he had been that night.

I caught myself pulling on the fingers of my left hand as melancholia crept back. I didn't have celebration dinners anymore. In fact, we rarely had company for dinner. I swallowed the beginning of tears. Raphael Smith got sick and died over there on the river. They shipped his body back for burial in the Smith family plot in the new cemetery. At the time, nobody said what it was Raphael died of, but it didn't take long for people to say he died of the fever. We really did not know.

"Dr. Abbey was one of the pallbearers for Raphael Smith." I paused. "You know about the bad fever, right? You've had experience?"

"I seen yellow jack, mistress."

Félicité called the bad fever by name.

"Do you think someone could catch it like that? From carrying a coffin?" I asked.

"Nobody knows how yellow jack spreads, mistress, if that's what you ask."

"But what do you think? Could someone catch the fever from fifteen minutes with the coffin of someone who died from it?"

Félicité pinched her heavy lower lip between her teeth, taking a moment before answering my question. She did so with more words than usual.

"Just my opinion, ma'am, but I don't think it possible someone carryin' a body across the road a short piece from the church into the cemetery could catch the disease a person died of. Not even yellow jack."

I sat back in the rocker. "That's what I think too. We've no need to jump to conclusions. Especially one so terrible. People get sick all the time. Why do we think it's some dread disease and we're all going to get it?"

An epidemic of yellow fever, or yellow jack as Félicité called it, was a frightening prospect. People lost reason even talking about it. We'd never had an outbreak in New Town, not one that I heard about anyway, but every summer we worried about the possibility.

I wanted to ask Félicité about the other rumor around town. Félicité appeared to be the only person I knew who had actual experience with the disease and might have an opinion worth hearing.

"People are spreading another story. When Mr. Raphael's body, sitting in a barrel full of rum, lay unattended in the Smith family sugarhouse waiting for the burial, people say one of the slaves tapped into the barrel and took a drink. Do you think it possible fever could come by someone drinking out of a barrel of rum used to preserve a body?"

Again, Félicité waited a moment before answering. "I don't think so, mistress. People are quick . . ." She stopped, but I could have guessed what she wanted to say. People were quick to fix blame for every bad thing that happened on a black man and a slave.

"I think there's not a bit of truth to the story, Félicité. Overseer Gordon checked with the overseer at the Smiths', and he says nobody's died there in over a month. Nobody's even sick. And at this point we don't know for sure we've *got* bad fever here."

I hadn't made a rare nighttime visit to Félicité's cabin just to pass on rumors of yellow fever. I inched forward in my seat—and toward my real reason for the visit.

"You've taken care of very sick people, right?" I recalled her care for my father when I was a child and for my children many times since.

"Yes, ma'am."

"My friend Eudolie is absolutely at the end of her rope. Since he came home on Monday, Dr. Abbey's gotten steadily worse. He's a doctor, of course, but his wife can't ask him what she should do because he's talking out of his head. She found his medical books on the shelf, and from the very first day she's followed the fever instructions to the letter. She closed all the windows to keep out the night air and she's given him nothing to eat or drink. When he hadn't improved after the second day, she sent for the doctor in Opelousas. He came yesterday evening and gave Dr. Abbey medicine for a purge. And he brought the leeches."

Félicité's chin dropped. "The worms," she mumbled.

"Yes, they bled him. My friend Eudolie watched the doctor make a slit on her husband's arm and attach the bloodsuckers." Félicité squeezed her eyelids together. "I understand you don't believe in bleeding."

"No, mistress."

"Why exactly is that? Doctors bleed people for most everything."

"That's their way."

"But not yours, I gather. Why?"

Félicité let out a puff of breath, but she didn't answer.

"Tell me why you don't believe in bleeding for the bad fever, Félicité. That and the purge are what the doctors do. It must work."

"I seen different, mistress. Worms are no good. That's my opinion."

"Tell me. Tell me what you've actually seen."

Félicité looked down at her feet. "When I was a little girl, I was sittin' on the porch of a house while my mother took care of a sick man. Yellow jack, they said. A doctor came with a glass case of wriggling, black worms. He stepped 'round me and went into the sick room. He stayed in there a good while. When he came out a piece later, the worms was double in size, puffed up like risen dough. Slimy and black as coffee, so stuffed with blood they couldn't wriggle anymore."

"But did the bleeding help the sick man?"

"No, ma'am."

"He died?"

"Yes, ma'am. The very next day. He died screamin'."

I swallowed hard.

"Miss Eudolie agrees with you, Félicité. People are telling her she needs to have the doctor from Opelousas come a second time, but she can't bring herself to put her husband through the bleeding again. After the doctor came last night, after the purges and bloodletting, Dr. Abbey got worse. Now he's talking out of his head and throwing up bile."

"Crazy talk is not a good sign, mistress."

"No?"

"All fevers go like that, not just yellow jack. Crazy talk come near the end. I'm not sayin' he's got yellow jack, you understand."

"Good. I just hate to think about it."

I sat up on the lip of the rocker, getting to the point of my visit.

"Miss Eudolie's been taking care of her husband by herself, night and day, ever since Monday. She won't let anyone help her. In fact, she won't let anyone into the bedroom, not even Dr. Abbey's brother who came all the way here from over on the Big River. Pointe Coupée Parish, I believe, where the Abbeys come from. This afternoon when she went into the doctor's room, I disobeyed her instruction and ducked my head in behind her." I clutched the arms of the rocker. "Félicité, Dr. Abbey looks absolutely dreadful."

"Tell me how he look, mistress."

"He's flat on his back with his eyes closed, skin drawn tight across his cheeks and pale. His mouth open and dry. His breathing is quick, shallow. Kind of like panting. And the smell!" I rubbed a finger under my nose.

"Did he look yellow, in the eyes or his skin?"

"I didn't notice. It was dark in the room. Eudolie shooed me out. To tell the truth, I was glad to have reason to leave before I got sick." I paused and looked Félicité in the eye, pressing my lips together and swallowing hard. "Félicité, I have something I want to ask you."

"Yes, mistress."

"I'm hoping you can talk to Miss Eudolie and help her decide what she should do."

Félicité dropped her chin. "Miss Eudolie has to do what she thinks best, ma'am."

"Of course, she does. The decision is hers, but . . ."

"Can you get a hold of Dr. Neal, mistress?" Félicité asked. "He may know somthin' different Miss Eudolie can do."

I shook my head. "Dr. Neal's been in New Orleans for over a month. He's due back on the next steamboat, but no one knows when the boat'll actually arrive. The ship entered the lower Teche, we know that, but we haven't had a report in a while. Dr. Neal will be staying with us when he gets here, at least if Jacques finishes building the new room in time. Actually, I want Dr. Neal to stay with us even if I have to give him Alfred's room. Alfred can bunk in with Little Fréderick for a few days until he goes back to school."

Félicité did whatever I asked her to do, but when she didn't readily agree to help Mrs. Abbey make a decision, I offered an alternative.

"Jacques tells me you make visits to the sick cabin back in the quarters when they need you."

Félicité again dropped her chin. "Yes, mistress. You mind I do that?"

"No, no. I don't mind. You make Overseer Gordon happy. Your care is free. The doctors charge us every time they come."

Félicité's expression eased.

I continued. "Maybe you could go with me to the Abbeys' house in the morning. You could stay with the doctor for a few hours. A rest might give Miss Eudolie strength to continue. I'm just asking, Félicité. I wouldn't make you go into a house that might have the bad fever if you didn't want. And Miss Eudolie may not even let you stay, she's so not wanting to expose anyone. But if you came . . ."

I didn't say she might know if he had the bad fever when she saw him.

"I'll go, mistress. I'm not afraid of yellow jack. I've taken care of people with the bad fever and never caught it. People say I can't. Maybe I had it as a child in Saint-Domingue and don't remember. People don't get it twice."

Maybe the old wives' tale was true—black-skinned people didn't get it so bad. And I clung to the hope we weren't dealing with yellow fever at all.

"I'll tell Miss Eudolie you can't get sick from it. That might help her accept the offer."

"But I don't say I got the real knowledge, ma'am. Not that anyone does, although the doctors got all kind of explanations."

"I understand. I'm just asking you to lend a hand."

"I do whatever you say, mistress."

I stood up to leave. "Thank you. The ferryman is back on the other side of the bayou for the night now, but he says he'll be at our dock in the morning at first light. We can go across together, and Jacques will go with us. I can't ask Jacques to take us in the skiff because he might need to meet the steamship and offload the boards for our addition. I'll take him from the building project for now. We're held up anyway until the shipment of cypress comes."

At the mention of Jacques, Félicité had a question. "Can you tell me about Jacques, mistress?"

"What about Jacques?"

"Is he sold?"

I didn't want to answer Félicité, but she'd just agreed to help Eudolie. I owed her. I sat down again. I didn't trust myself to keep my composure talking about the sale that took place at the house ten days ago. After Fréderick passed, the state of his affairs had been a complete shock to me. I knew nothing about his business. Our lawyer told me I had to sell off some belongings to pay what he owed people. The Henry Fréderick Duperier

Family Meeting—a meeting of only the men of the family, of course—decided who and what would be sold.

The day of the sale, I sent the children to be with my mother. I told Félicité to stay in her cabin and catch up on her sewing. I closed myself up in my room. Out front, buggies lined up on both sides of the road. I recognized many of the men who came: Judge Briant, several lawyers, my stepfather, and some of my cousins from here and from St. Martinsville—the people who were in charge of my business. Men of the family made the decisions; I had no say.

Mid-afternoon, I went to the well for water and overheard a conversation between two men smoking cigars on the back gallery. *I never realized Fréderick had such debt,* one said to the other. *I do believe everything's under the hammer except the Widow Duperier herself. Town lots, land, slaves, equipment, household goods.*

No, not quite. Fréderick left me income-producing property, but the rest had to be sold. I didn't want Félicité to worry. Since she'd agreed to help me, she deserved an explanation about the sale.

"We're not going to be planting cane anymore, Félicité, so the men decided I no longer have need of slaves young and strong enough to work the crop. Jacques qualified for sale. Although payment is due in installments, the buyer could come for him at any time, or not. I don't remember exactly the terms of the sale." I could see Félicité's face darken and a worry line appear between her eyes. "But in the case of Jacques, the buyer says he can stay at least long enough to finish the addition. And you know, you don't have to worry about yourself. You belong to me, not the master, and I'm not about to lose you." I stopped to keep my emotions in check. "I don't want to talk any more about selling."

"Yes, mistress. I'll be ready in the morning whenever you call me. I'll need to fix breakfast for the family—"

"No, no. Forget about the cooking for now. My mother will see to the kitchen. I'll ring the bell when I get up and the three of us will cross the bayou together."

CHAPTER TWO

Before dawn, I laid out bread, butter, and fig preserves on the sideboard. I stepped off the back gallery into pitch dark and heavy fog. I rang the plantation bell to summon Félicité and Jacques. Fog was a harbinger of fall. September was still hot during the day, but in the early morning, relief from the heat and humidity seemed a possibility. I looked forward to the end of the days when the least exertion stuck these black clothes to my body.

A tall figure emerged from the direction of the quarters. Jacques. I sent him to the well to fetch water. Shortly after, Félicité came across the field from her cabin behind the big house. I wished her a good morning.

"I called you early, Félicité. I didn't sleep well. Come inside and have a bite to eat. Jacques will be back in a minute and we can head down to the bayou. Dawn will be here shortly. We can walk to our dock to wait for the ferry."

When we were ready, Jacques carried the lantern low as I picked my way on the path to the bayou and over to the dock. At the dock, Jacques raised the lantern to locate the half-barrels set out for anyone who might have to wait for the ferry. For anyone except slaves, that is. They were expected to remain standing. I sat down; Jacques and Félicité stood by my side. We didn't have long to wait.

Accompanied by the song of a waking mockingbird, the splash of paddles resonated on the surface of the water. The front edge of the ferry pierced the fog, and we made out the figures of the ferrymen, their backs curling and straightening with each stroke of their paddles. A few feet from shore, the ferryman on the port side positioned his paddle in the water as a rudder and the ferryman on the starboard stroked to maneuver the boat parallel to the dock. With a steady arm, Jacques handed me and then Félicité aboard. I sat on a plank at the stern. Félicité looked at me, her arms hanging straight down at her sides. Her thick eyebrows pinched together.

"You're the lightest," I said. "Sit here with me." Jacques stood up front.

We were halfway across the bayou before the sun creeping upward behind the trees broke through the fog to reveal the cluster of buildings on the other side.

Before we married fourteen years ago, Fréderick bought all the land before me and behind, two forty-arpent tracts, one on each bank of the Bayou Teche, including the dock and buildings of the landing where we headed now, from the succession of his guardian, Hester Pintard. He and his Tante Hester, as he called her, weren't actually related. Fréderick told me his father had died in the Haitian Revolution and his mother died in childbirth, leaving Fréderick and his new baby sister Alphonsine orphaned. My son Alfred claimed his father told him he was himself in the revolution in Saint-Domingue, but I wasn't so sure. His mother's family originally came from France. Alphonsine went into a convent up north and friends of the family, Tante Hester and Henry Pintard, brought Fréderick down to Louisiana. Now that was a lucky day for our little town!

I regretted I never knew Tante Hester. She could have told me about when Fréderick was a boy.

When they arrived, there were only a few houses on the right bank of the Bayou Teche between the bigger tracts that bookend New Town. Downstream from town was the Weeks tract, and a little farther, the property of my mother's parents, Grand-Père and Grand-Mère Boutté. My parents built a house on a piece of their land. Upstream was the Darby Plantation, which we passed on the way to St. Martinsville where, as a child, we went every Sunday to church and to visit my father's parents, Grandpa and Grandma Bérard.

Many settlers—Acadian, French, English, and American—started coming to our town. Everyone was excited when Fréderick cleared the woods and had the land on the right bank surveyed for lots. He reserved a whole block for a church and started to raise the money needed for a building. Once we had St. Peter's Church, we no longer had to make the long trip to St. Martinsville to go to Mass. That church made us a real town, people said, and Fréderick began talk of ending administration from St. Martinsville. Growing our town—and ending our dependence on St. Martinsville—was the usual topic of discussion when he and his friends gathered at our dining table.

Just to please me, Fréderick had the surveyor leave an empty strip of land between the church site and the bayou. From the lovely house he built for me on the left bank, I could see straight across to the steeple of our new church. Every time I did so, the pain of losing Fréderick bit again. And every time I made the ferry trip, I missed him even more.

Pintard's Landing, across the bayou from the house, was a source of income for me. I rented to the post office, to the storeowner, and to the tavern keeper. Above our town, the bayou was narrow and full of snags, too treacherous for all but a few shallow-draft vessels to maneuver their way to St. Martinsville. Boats from down the Teche turned in front of our house and stopped at Pintard's Landing before restocking their supplies and making the return trip downstream, carrying crops to market in New Orleans.

I wished Fréderick could watch how the settlement he dreamed of was growing. His development on Tante Hester's property motivated others. Just six months after his death, each time I crossed the bayou I saw a few more houses had been built. I was grateful he lived to see the church, but I choked up thinking he would not see what we became.

A wave of concern drifted in. What *would* we become if we found ourselves dealing with the bad fever? I shook my head to banish an unwelcome thought.

The ferry let us off at Pintard's Landing. We crossed the dock, the Old Spanish Trail, and turned to walk up Petit Anse Road. We passed the church, Madison Street, and two neat frame houses still shuttered for the night. That's what people would do when there was sickness, shut out what they called "the bad night air." Beyond the two shuttered houses, a gathering spilled from the porch of the house next door.

"That's Dr. Abbey's house," I said to my companions.

Immediately, I knew we were too late. Father Joseph stood on the porch, his cassocked arms encircling the shoulders of my friend Eudolie and her children. A dozen men and women gathered in the yard, whispering to one another. A woman I didn't recognize rushed over to me to make a sad report.

"He's gone, Madame Duperier. The doctor's gone." I closed my eyes and made the sign of the cross. "Miss Eudolie says that early this morning the doctor fell into some kind of fit. After she got him calmed down, she fell asleep in her chair by the bed. When she woke up, the doctor wasn't breathing. She brushed her fingers across his face to close his eyes and felt him cold, cold. Father Joseph is with her now."

I wanted to go to my friend Eudolie, but the messenger kept chattering.

"Miss Eudolie folded her husband's hands on his chest and sent word to Father to come administer the last sacrament. The sexton already took the body. Miss Eudolie will be going over to the church to make arrangements."

I looked the woman straight in the eye and asked my question. "Do they know what—?"

She wouldn't let me finish, interrupting to whisper in my ear. "Hush, now. Don't say the word. But you know, we've heard a rumor a Spaniard out in the country has come down with a suspicious fever."

I broke away from the messenger and ran up on Eudolie's porch. I gave my friend a quick hug, telling her I'd be back in the afternoon. I beckoned Félicité and Jacques to join me, and we started walking down the road to the landing. Next to me, Jacques mumbled.

"Should we do somethin' mistress?"

Hearing the low rumble of Jacques's voice made me realize he hadn't said a word since we met at the house this morning. That's the way he is around white people, even me. Eyes down and silent.

"Do what, Jacques?"

"Do somethin' for our people, ma'am. About the sickness."

"I don't know what we should do, and I have no one to ask. Overseer Gordon hasn't been around for days. He's planning to leave on the next steamboat to New Orleans and is thinking of little else. The assistant overseer at the Smith plantation is supposed to be in charge of our quarters, but I haven't even met him. I'll go find him as soon as we get back."

A cool breeze blew across us, bringing with it the dreadful smell of the tannery on the bayou bank. Beside me, Félicité coughed.

"Pretty dreadful, isn't it? That smell is the price the town pays for any break in the summer heat. When the wind shifts to the north, they're favored with the stench of the curing barrels. I'm glad we live across the bayou."

The ferryman had dropped us off less than an hour ago, and since then, the area around Pintard's Landing had come awake. Well, not completely awake. Opened one eye would be more accurate. Enough activity that I concluded people expected the steamboat to arrive from New Orleans sometime soon.

Three wagons perched along the road on the back side of the dock. The wagon beds held barrels, crates, and black and brown backs—slaves from the plantations and small farms who could offload cargo. Three white drivers leaned on the hatch of the first wagon, now and then raising their heads to check out their surroundings. Something might happen, they appeared to signal, but not much and not any time soon.

The few half-barrels on the dock usually available for sitting had been cleared away in preparation for the arrival of cargo from the steamboat. The innkeeper at the tavern, expecting the occasion to bring him an increase in customers, set out a triangular board announcing the special of the day: fried catfish. Where could we be comfortable waiting for the ferry to take us home? Jacques put his head down when he saw me looking in the direction of the tavern.

"Don't worry, Jacques. None of us is welcome in there."

On the front of the dock, at the water's edge, a bare-chested negro coiled heavy ropes around a stanchion, taking direction from a white man who recognized me. I knew him as the town busybody.

"Ah, Madame Duperier!" He walked toward us. "I understand you have cypress beams coming from the sawmill in Centerville. The steamboat docked in Franklin yesterday. You'll have your beams today, but probably not till quite late. I guess your nigger here will pick them up."

I winced. Jacques's face showed no reaction to the busybody's choice of words.

"Jacques will be helping me," I answered.

Once our overseer Mr. Gordon grumbled to me that he couldn't believe I had Jacques's muscles doing nothing more than hitting a nail with a hammer. Most plantation owners wouldn't allow a strong young body like his to be spared from work in the fields. I had reason to keep him at the house. I needed Jacques's carpentry skills to construct an addition I could let out for extra income. My house was big, and roomers would help my finances, but I wanted strangers to sleep separate from the family.

Which made me think about where Jacques would be when everyone connected to any sugar plantation around here, male and female, had to go to the fields to cut cane. Gabriel Fuselier, who bought Jacques at the succession sale, said he could stay with me to finish the addition, but where would he be after that? And that made me think about Eliza and their children. They were sold to Dr. Neal. Where would they end up? Jacques might never see his children again.

I supposed the family meeting did the best they could to get Fréderick's creditors paid. I had to agree that I had little need for sugarcane workers or more than a few to help in the house, but I wished a widow had some say in her own business affairs. I needed Jacques for heavy work and I hated to see a family separated.

I tried to block tragic thoughts from my mind.

"We're not here for the steamboat," I told the busybody. "We came over for something else, but we're ready to go home now. We're waiting for the ferry."

"That will be a while, ma'am. The ferrymen just went downstream. They have to make a special crossing from the Weeks house."

"No problem. We'll wait."

I nodded my head to Félicité and Jacques to signal we needed to move away from the busybody. I had to be careful. That nosy man always tried to pick up some bit of gossip he could pass on to the next person who came along. I made a good target for his prying. He knew we heard a lot of important information about the town at our dinner table. At least we used to when Fréderick was still with me. I sure didn't want to give the busybody any information about Dr. Abbey. Maybe he hadn't yet heard of his death, or what people suspected he might have died of.

"Let's go inside where we can sit down," I said to Jacques and Félicité.

Jacques dropped his eyes to the ground. "I can't go there, ma'am."

"What? Of course, you can. Not into the tavern, I know. I can't go in there either. But the post office and the customs house are public space. You have my business to complete, and the last, I knew I still owned the Landing, just rent it out to the tenants. Follow me." I caught myself. "Wait a minute. Do you have your pass?"

"Yes, ma'am." Jacques patted his pocket. "I picked it up from the sideboard this morning."

"Good. That's all we need. They know Félicité has standing permission to do my errands in town."

We entered the post office door and eyed a couple benches against the wall. Before we had taken steps in that direction, we caught sight of someone we all recognized in an instant—our six-foot tall overseer, Mr. Gordon, delivering a loud and angry tirade to the top of the postmaster's head. Next to me, Jacques stiffened. He dipped his chin and turned to the door. He mumbled something about giving a hand to the men outside. Félicité spun around and followed him out the door.

Mr. Gordon spotted me.

"Ah, Miss Hortense," Mr. Gordon boomed out across the room. "You're just the person who can solve a bit of a problem we have. Our harbormaster, Mr. Aborn, is about to do something idiotic. He's proposing to turn away the steamboat."

I was trapped.

The poor harbormaster, who was also our postmaster, had sewn a few brass buttons on his work shirt in a ridiculous attempt to look as if he had a uniform. He puffed his chest like a pigeon. Appropriate. Mr. Gordon gave him about as much respect as he'd give to a dirty bird at his feet.

"I am the harbormaster of the Port of New Town," Mr. Aborn squeaked. "I have taken an oath to abide by my duties and enforce the laws of the land."

Mr. Gordon rolled his eyes. The harbormaster flushed, but he drew up as tall as he could and made a pronouncement.

"One of the laws I'm sworn to uphold sets out my duty to report to any approaching ships the presence of an epidemic in our town. That's exactly what I'm fixin' to do. I'm sending a courier from Burke's livery to the harbormaster at the port in Franklin to inform him we have suffered a death from yellow fever."

Mr. Gordon exploded, splattering the harbormaster's head with spittle. "And I say bullshit! Sorry, Miss Hortense. Yes, you have a duty to report an epidemic, Mr. Aborn, but one death is no epidemic! And anyway, we don't really know what Dr. Abbey died of."

The harbormaster turned to me. "Madame Duperier, you've just come from the Abbey house, I believe. Hasn't Dr. Abbey succumbed to the fever?"

Mr. Gordon interrupted before I could respond. "I'm as distressed as anybody about the death of Dr. Abbey, but your reaction is uncalled for. One person got sick and died. *A* fever? Yes. *The* fever? We don't know. Epidemic? No! No! No!"

"But—"

"No! You know as well as I do how critically important it is for the future of our town that we receive this ship. Barges being slowly dragged upstream aren't going to cut it in modern commerce. If we're not open to receive steamships, all the bayou trade will stop at Franklin. Franklin will do to us what we did to St. Martinsville just a few years ago."

Mr. Gordon paused only to catch his breath.

"We haven't had a steamboat from New Orleans come up here for months. We're damn lucky the state snag boat finished cleaning out the debris from the spring rains, and doubly lucky we had a wet summer. Right now, the water level in the bayou is high enough for a steamboat to make the trip up here. We probably won't have favorable conditions again until next spring."

The harbormaster stayed on message. "Can you answer my question, Miss Hortense? Did Dr. Abbey die of yellow fever?"

I had nowhere to hide, but I thought of an evasion.

"He died, all right, but I'm not the one to say what he died of. The doctor who came from Opelousas to treat Dr. Abbey is the one who should answer your question."

I didn't want to allow the dire diagnosis to take space in my head. It might be several days before they could get hold of the doctor from Opelousas again. He had a large area to serve.

Mr. Gordon stomped his foot like a three-year-old having a tantrum. "You see, she doesn't know any more than anyone else. And even if Dr. Abbey had the bad fever, one case isn't an epidemic. Dr. Abbey had been all over creation the day he got sick, and not one other person has any sign of a problem. Whatever the doctor had, it isn't spreading to anyone else."

Apparently, the rumor about the Spaniard in the country hadn't reached Mr. Gordon. I wasn't going to tell him.

Turning to the harbormaster, who would, after all, be the one making the ultimate call, Mr. Gordon took his tirade down a notch. He tried reasoning with the little man.

"Steamboats have given life to our town. Stop them, and in no time, we'll go back to where we were ten years ago: three big brick plantation houses, a few wooden ones, and several littler wooden dwellings. In town we had but a half dozen warehouses, a bakery, and a tannery."

"I know but—"

Mr. Gordon interrupted. "See those wagons out there? The farmers from up the bayou are already bringing us the last of their summer crops. They can't wait. Turn this ship away and they'll find another way to send their harvest through the maze of bayous over to the Mississippi and down to New Orleans. And we need what's on that steamboat. The courier from the city brought us bills of lading for a dozen arriving crates. To top it off, the Smiths are expecting four slaves they bought for this year's harvest."

The harbormaster wasn't giving an inch. He moved his feet farther apart, balancing himself to withstand Mr. Gordon's tirade. He knew he'd have the last word. "I have my legal responsibilities, sir."

The overseer got personal.

"I need to be on that ship. I have sugar contracts to negotiate for three plantations. I have only a few weeks until I have to be back here for grinding. I sure as hell don't want to ride all the way to New Orleans and conduct important business with only what fits into two saddlebags."

Aha! The real cause for his anger came to light. If Mr. Gordon took a horse to the city, he'd miss a few days sipping cognac and juleps and playing many a good hand of poker. He wouldn't be cutting much of a figure in the salons of the city wearing dusty riding clothes!

The harbormaster couldn't hide his smile.

"Mr. Gordon, here's what I'm gonna do. I'm sending the courier down the bayou to Franklin with two letters, one letter for the harbormaster and one letter for the captain of the steamboat. These letters will state the exact situation. Dr. S. F. R. Abbey came down with a fever. He died. We don't know of anyone else who has signs of a problem. The captain of the steamboat can decide whether he wants his ship to come here. The harbormaster at the port in Franklin can make the call about whether he'll allow any other ships to travel in this direction."

I resolved to adopt the harbormaster's limitation on drawing conclusions.

My best guess? We wouldn't be seeing the steamboat tonight or any time until next spring.

I was wrong.

CHAPTER THREE

After supper, as I made the rounds to put our house to bed, checking that all the tall windows and the doors were secured, my ears picked up a jumble of unfamiliar sounds from the direction of the bayou. I opened the door to the gallery and stepped outside to investigate. From downstream, daggers of light sliced into the darkness. The steamboat!

I ran through the house to the side yard and rang the plantation bell, for the second night in a row disturbing Félicité after she had retired for the night.

My mother, Alphonsine, and Little Fréderick appeared first. Félicité, wearing a smile that showed her bright white teeth, followed right behind. My oldest child Alfred joined us a few minutes later. The citizenry of the town had spilled out of their houses and clumped up on both banks, the largest crowd directly across from us on the broad dock of Pintard's Landing.

Fire and smoke lit up the trees on both sides of the bayou as a steamboat came around the bend. The sight quite literally took my breath away. Flaming baskets mounted on poles protruded five feet from the side decks of the ship. On the surface of the water, reflections of the flambeaux sparkled like a blanket of diamonds. The captain well knew what excitement he engendered. He stood like a triumphant warrior at the most forward point of the bow, his stiff right arm reaching high in a salute, his left hand holding a megaphone to his lips. He slowed the steamboat to draw attention from the gathering crowd.

"Ahoy, there, good citizens of New Town! Ahoy! The steamboat *Logansport* approaches."

Grand-Maman pressed her fist to her mouth. Alfred stretched both of his arms into the air as if he had crossed a finish line.

"Can I go, Mama? Can I go down to the dock to see the steamboat come in? I've never seen a ship lit up like that. Please, please. Let me go! Let me go!"

"To tell the truth, son, I haven't seen a ship lit up like that either. Pick up a couple lanterns from inside the door and we'll walk down to our dock together for a front row seat."

Although I had spent the afternoon consoling my grieving friend, my mood soared at the display.

My mother looked down the dark path and shook her head. She found a chair and settled down to watch the goings on from the gallery. The rest of us were on for the full show.

Alfred handed off a lantern to me and another to Félicité. He ran on ahead. Imagine, my oldest child, thirteen years old, and as tall as I. Holding a lantern in her left hand, Félicité carried Little Fréderick, just six, on her right hip. His long legs dangled almost to the ground. He'd be shooting up to be another tall dark-haired child in no time. Alphonsine, my middle child, clutched my fist.

It had been a long time since I'd heard my children bubbling with delight. Not Alphonsine. She didn't bubble. She never did. She walked beside me smiling but silent. Although only ten, she liked to wear her hair tight on her head, not flowing like that of a little girl.

Alphonsine hadn't known her aunt, after whom she'd been named. My Fréderick told me long ago that Tante Hester said his sister never had the Duperier personality. Did the name Alphonsine come with the power to make one timid? No one had contact with his sister Alphonsine anymore. She probably didn't even know her brother had passed.

The eight-man crew of the *Logansport* stood at attention, four hands on the port deck, four on the starboard. The ship passed up our dock and backpedaled to a halt at the upstream boundary. She maneuvered back and forth at the cut dug in the bank to accommodate the length of a turning ship. Every variation of the course drew applause from the crowd. A prolonged cheer sounded across the water when, bow pointing downstream, she pulled up alongside Pintard's Landing. We joined the ovation, Alfred's voice the loudest of all. My husband's outgoing personality had definitely passed to my oldest child.

"All ashore who's going ashore," the captain bellowed through his megaphone. "Be on notice, one and all. It is now late to find a night's lodging in town. All passengers of the *Logansport* may disembark for one hour and return to the ship to pass the night. One hour and one hour only. I will sound the ship's bells when it is time to board. The gangplank will come up, and I will set the watch." The captain paused to take a breath, and for dramatic effect. "All hear. In one hour, I will secure the ship for the night. We will unload the cargo and load up for the return trip in the morning."

Alfred danced by himself at the front of our dock. Next to him, Félicité put down her lantern and held the hands of my two younger children. I stood behind them. We watched as a lanyard was tossed from the ship and secured around a stanchion on the dock—under the direction of the busybody, I believed. Tonight, the busybody probably gathered a storehouse of news to pass on to anyone who might have missed the show.

Two crew members lowered the gangplank. Another member of the crew turned a crank to drop the anchor at the stern of the ship.

A giggling gaggle of passengers picked careful steps down the slats of the gangplank to the dock with the assistance of men in jackets, cravats, and wide-brimmed hats. Several ladies needed more than just a hand to maneuver the descent in sky-high heels. Beads sparkled on the bodices of their low-cut dresses. The tavern would do a fine business tonight, at least if the pockets of the passengers hadn't been stripped bare in the poker games legendary on the steamships from the city. My store would do a good business in the morning as the steamship laid in supplies for the trip back down the bayou to New Orleans.

One passenger stopped at the base of the gangplank, turned in our direction, and waved.

"That's Dr. Neal," I said to Félicité. "He appears to be joining the festivities at the tavern. I think his signal means he'll be coming to us tomorrow, not tonight. We'll ready Alfred's room for our guest in the morning as soon as Alfred leaves to go back to school in Grand Coteau."

After we watched the passengers disembark and endured too many mosquitos to ignore, I suggested we make our way back to the house. Félicité, carrying Little Fréderick, led our procession up the path. Alfred and Alphonsine came behind her. I took up the rear. Just before reaching the gallery, I glanced back and saw two large cages being unloaded from the ship and onto a wagon. I recognized the overseer from the Smith plantation supervising the operation. I knew what the cages held: the four slaves Mr. Gordon said the Smiths bought for this year's cane harvest. That brief glimpse cast the only shadow on the evening's adventure. I think no one in the family saw the cages but me, and the passengers had already entered the buildings on the landing.

When I reached the gallery, the ship's bells sounded for the passengers to come aboard. Félicité thanked me for calling her to see the steamship arrive.

"You are quite welcome. I wouldn't have missed this show for a full plate of Louisa's bread pudding." I sniffed the night air. "Do you smell the sweet olive, Félicité? That fragrance is a sign of fall, but I think we have another few weeks of heat."

Watching the steamboat lit with torches had been good family fun, which the children had too little of lately. Joy was good medicine for hard times.

When I turned to go into the house, Jacques appeared from the shadows.

"You startled me, Jacques. Did you see the steamboat?" I asked him.

"Yes, ma'am."

"Quite a spectacle, I'd say. I've never seen anything like it."

He said something I couldn't understand.

"What's that you say, Jacques?"

"Fancy ladies gettin' down from the boat."

I laughed. "Fancy ladies, indeed. Yes, I saw them. Net stockings, red shoes, hair piled up on the top of their heads."

Maybe our overseer Mr. Gordon would get lucky on his trip to New Orleans, I thought. Then perhaps he'd leave Caroline, another slave of mine who was part redskin, alone. Félicité had told me Caroline had just turned fifteen and Mr. Gordon had started sniffin' around. He turned my stomach. One good thing about not growing cane was we no longer needed an overseer to manage the slaves.

I stopped and looked Jacques in the eye, "I'm sorry about the sale. That wasn't my doing."

"I know, mistress."

"I guess you also know Eliza and the children will be going to our neighbor's plantation."

"I know, ma'am. Children under eight go with their mother."

What could you say to someone who had to live under our slave law? I looked at my faithful Jacques and felt shame. How could the family meeting separate a man from his children and the woman he loved? I sputtered out the only solace that came to my mind.

"For right now, you're all together here with me."

Jacques closed his eyes and hung his head. He shifted the lantern to his left hand. He didn't make any sign of leaving.

"You have something on your mind, Jacques?" I asked

"Yes, mistress."

Getting Jacques to talk was not easy. "What is it, Jacques? Do you need to tell me something?"

"Yes, mistress. We got somebody sick."

"Somebody's sick?" Fear cut through me. "How sick? Who is it? Tell me."

"It's Patrick, ma'am. The old one. Caroline came tell me he took to his bed with headache. He's so weak his legs won't hold him up."

"Oh my God. Does he have fever?"

I turned to Félicité. "Do you think . . . ? Have you seen Patrick?"

"No, mistress. We could have a problem. Headache's an early sign of the bad fever. Maybe we take steps."

"Like what? What can we do?"

"Set him apart from the others."

"Like in a separate cabin?"

"Yes, mistress. Where we can tend him more easily. Watch him close. Keep him cool. Give him lots of water to drink."

"Okay. Let's do that. Jacques, do we have an empty cabin we can move Patrick into?"

"We got plenty empty cabins, ma'am. It's not like it used to be. Nobody's in the first cabin across the path, other side o' the woods."

"Fine. Move Patrick there. If he falls sick, you'll need help caring for him. Is there someone who could stay with him?"

"Eliza's still here, but—"

"No, no, Jacques. Eliza needs to be with the children. Do we have anyone else?"

"Louisa or Caroline. Either one would stay with Patrick. They love the old man. They're heartsick he's been sold."

"Louisa and Caroline both come to the house to cook. I need them, especially since Dr. Neal will be staying with us. But if Patrick won't need to have someone steady, they could share checking on him during the day. And—"

Jacques spoke up. "I stay the nights, ma'am."

"You can do that?"

"Yes, ma'am. I want to do that. Félicité will tell me what to do, right?"

"I'll do my best," Félicité said. "Simple enough. Keep him cool and give him water to drink. Wait to see what develops."

"What should Jacques be looking for?" I asked her.

"Well . . ."

"Tell us. We need to know."

"If it's yellow jack, after headache come fever, mistress. Then *vomito negro*, and then crazy talk. Delirium, they call it. But we don't know that's what it is."

"Let's pray not." I stopped and did pray. "Fine. We have a plan. Jacques, first get Patrick moved to the front cabin. Félicité, give him time to do that, then go on back."

Jacques looked down at the ground and shuffled his feet. I knew the signs. He still had a problem.

"What is it, Jacques? You don't like what I said?"

Jacques frowned, his face even darker. "Félicité shouldn't be goin' back to the quarters in the dark, mistress. The quarters are through woods and as far again as here down to the dock. I'll come get her when I have Patrick settled."

"Nonsense, Jacques," Félicité interjected. "Maybe not in the old days, like a few years back when we had lots of men there, comin' and goin' from the master's farms at Isle Pivert and the Segura brothers' fields. Do we have any men living in the quarters now except you and old Patrick?"

"'Bout it. And who knows whether in a while there'll be anybody left." Jacques looked at the ground. "Mistress, do you know what's to become of me? When I'm goin' away?"

"My cousin Gabriel Fuselier . . ." I choked on the words. For a moment I couldn't go on. "But he says you can stay for a while, until you finish the addition for sure. And who knows? I'm talking to my family to see if anything can be done. For sure, you aren't leaving any time soon."

"And me?" Félicité asked.

"I've told you. You belong to me, Félicité. You aren't going anywhere."

* * * * *

Before turning in for the night, I wanted to take a look at two folders my uncle F. C. Boutté had brought to the house while I was in town with Eudolie. Since Uncle F. C. told her they were important, Maman placed them on Fréderick's desk in the parlor. Taking my lantern, I sat down at the desk to check them out.

The first folder, entitled *Final Report of the Family Meeting of Fréderick H. Duperier, Deceased*, held a packet of a dozen long legal-sized pages: an inventory and appraisal of the assets and liabilities of Fréderick's succession and a report of the items sold to satisfy his debts. The sale listed the names of the persons who bought the assets and for how many *piastres*, or dollars, the persons were to pay within a year. The last page bore the signatures of members of the family. Men only, of course; husbands signed to represent their wives. I guess that meant we were done with the legal proceedings. From then on I would manage my own income and expenses. Both a good and a bad thing. I opened a drawer where Fréderick kept legal documents and placed the packet inside.

I opened the second folder. Inside were two notebooks. The cover on the first read *Property of Marie Hortense Bérard*. The cover on the second read *Property of Marie Hortense Bérard, Book II*. My long-lost journals! I hadn't put my eyes on those notebooks for over twenty years, probably since the day my father died. Where had they been hiding all this time?

I opened the first notebook and barely recognized my own childish hand. I read the first page—a tale of a goat who flew into the spirit world at night. I didn't notice tears soaking the page until the ink began to run. I closed my eyes and sat back in the chair to gather myself. I opened the second notebook in the folder. *After dinner today, dressed in our Sunday best, we gathered on the floor in front of Grandpa. "I wasn't born here in Louisiana like you were," he said.*

Where had Uncle F. C. found these notebooks? Not now, I told myself. I cannot read them now.

I opened a drawer and placed the notebooks inside with the folder of legal papers. I turned the key to lock the drawer and put the key onto the ring I carried with me always. I went to bed.

Dreams disturbed my sleep. In the morning I couldn't reconstruct any of them.

Chapter Four

As I came down the stairs from my bedroom the following
morning, I was startled to see Jacques standing on the back
step. I thought he'd been waiting for me. Wide black eyes fixed
on my face; the pink palm of his right hand slid down the side of his pants.
He didn't speak until I did.

"Good morning, Jacques. How is Patrick?"

"He still got the headache, mistress, but nothin' else."

The tightness across my shoulders eased. "So far, so good, although I
guess we won't know for sure for a while yet. Waiting is hard."

Jacques nodded his head. "Louisa and Caroline are checkin' him regular, mistress."

"Fine. You can go on with your work."

Jacques picked up an empty water pail and carried it outside to the
yard where Bessie stood patiently waiting to be milked. She mooed her
greeting. Jacques stroked her back as he set the stool. "Easy, Bess. Go easy,
girl." He kept talking to her, but I couldn't hear what he said.

Caroline appeared next, carrying a basket of eggs she'd gathered from
the chicken yard. She stepped into the kitchen, put the basket down, and
began to lay out plates and silverware on the sideboard for the family's
breakfast. Then came Félicité.

"Do I wake the children, mistress?" Félicité asked.

"Only Alfred for now. He needs to get off to the Weeks house as soon
as possible. I don't think he'll give you any trouble this morning. He has
a long wagon ride ahead, but he's anxious to be back with his friends
at school. If he gets himself put together, he can cross the bayou when
Jacques goes to unload the cypress beams from the steamboat."

"And your mother? Should I wake her, ma'am?"

"No need. I've heard her stirring. I wish she'd sleep in. The only schedule she has to keep is her own. Ben goes out with the herd now and the younger boys pretty much take care of themselves. But she's anxious to get on home."

An hour later, Alfred stood in the parlor ready to go down to the dock to wait for the ferry. He'd put away a big serving of cured meat, eggs, and biscuits. I couldn't eat but a few bites. Alfred looked all grown-up in his long pants and jacket. I wouldn't see him again until Christmas.

"The ferryman has his instructions, son. He's to drop Jacques off at Pintard's Landing, then go on downstream to take you to the Weeks house. He'll return to the landing to pick up Jacques and the beams and boards."

Alfred tolerated hugs from his younger brother and his sister, and a quick pat on the arm from Félicité. A wet spot glistened on her cheek. I was grateful Alfred could leave with Jacques. I'd embarrass him if I teared up in front of another family.

Later in the morning I said another goodbye when Félicité and I walked down to the dock with my mother. I turned to Félicité as soon as the ferry pulled away with Maman on board. Félicité looked as gloomy as I felt.

"Let's go tackle the garden. We need to clean out the remains of the summer vegetables and plan for the fall."

We'd both feel better after a stretch of physical work. Alphonsine came out and joined us. As my mother trained me when I was a child, my children began the day doing chores. Little Fréderick was supposed to pick up our leavings, but when he saw a proper stick, he threw it out into the yard for his dog to fetch. I took a short break to make a few throws also. Activity worked its magic and smiles returned.

Late morning, Félicité and I still bent over our vegetables, considering which plants should be pulled out and which had the possibility of more yield. Jacques and a helper he'd picked up in town came across the yard carrying a long beam on their shoulders.

"How many more beams do you have, Jacques?"

"Three more, ma'am."

"That one looks fine."

"They fine, mistress. All of them."

The sounds of a wagon pulling up out front reached back to the garden. I straightened up and spotted a sleak buggy perched at the front of the house. A tall black man sat on a plank behind the mule, holding the reins.

"My friend Susanne must be here, Félicité. Pick up my tools for me. I'm going to send Caroline to open the front door for her while I clean up."

I asked Caroline to settle Susanne in the front parlor and tell her I'd join her in a minute. When I came to the parlor, Susanne sat on the edge of the divan. She twisted a little white handkerchief in her fingers. Her thoughts tumbled out through trembling lips.

"It's here, Hortense," she sniffled.

"What's here, Susanne?"

"The fever's here in town."

"Oh my goodness. Tell me."

"I know some of what people say isn't true. I first heard that Antoine Broussard, who lived out at Fausse Pointe, died of it. Now I know he fell from his horse, for goodness sake! But the family of Salvadore Migues, the Spaniard out in the country who passed last week, is now telling what Sal looked like when he died. Bright yellow eyeballs!"

"Oh my God! But that's out in the country."

"There's fever in town, Hortense. Our overseer says William Burke at the livery is sick. He may have caught it last Monday when he got Dr. Abbey down from his horse. What are we going to do?"

"What do we do? First, we stay calm. Panic is no help. I'll call Félicité to come talk to us. She has experience with yellow fever. While she's cleaning up, I'll make us a cup of tea."

When Félicité came a few minutes later, I asked, "You recall my good friend Madame Decuir? From Belle Place?"

Félicité nodded. "Yes, ma'am."

I sank down on the divan next to my friend; Félicité remained standing.

Susanne pulled on one hand with the fingers of the other, but she was elegant always, even in her fidgets. I used to wear clothes like Susanne had on, and I knew I looked better for the bit of color. Imagine! Ten children, the last but three years old, and she still looked like a page from *La Mode Parisienne*.

"Tell Félicité what you've heard, Susanne."

Susanne repeated her report, daubing her eyes with her handkerchief. "They tell me you know about . . ." Susanne mouthed the name of the feared disease. "Do you think it's here?"

Félicité took a minute to respond. "Perhaps, ma'am. We've a man in the quarters with bad headache. Headache's not a good sign. But so far that's all he has, and it's been two days."

"Where's Mr. Gordon, anyway?" I mumbled to no one in particular.

"At Pintard's, mistress," Félicité answered. "But he'll be on the steamboat when she pulls out. We can't be countin' on him."

"Fine with me. What can he do anyway? I'm ready to forget about the overseer. Where's Dr. Neal? He's supposed to be coming to stay here and we haven't heard a word from him since the steamboat docked. Alfred's room is ready. Jacques brought the doctor's suitcase when he came with the lumber."

"I can answer that," said Susanne. "Mr. Dart, our overseer, says the doctor stayed with the Burkes last night. Mrs. Burke went to Pintard's to fetch him from the steamboat. The doctor's been makin' calls all day. A lot of people think they're sick."

Susanne turned to Félicité. "Here's what I want to know from someone who's had experience with yellow jack. If somebody feels bad, how do we know whether it's the bad fever?"

"At the beginning we can't know for sure, ma'am. That's why it's hard to get overseers to take men out of the field."

"What do you think we should do for someone who has headache or just feels bad."

Félicité pressed her lips together.

"Tell my friend what you told us to do for Patrick, Félicité."

"Put him to bed and make sure he drinks water, ma'am."

"You don't think he has to be isolated from everybody?"

"Not necessarily, ma'am, unless it's easier to care for him in a sick cabin—to make sure he gets rest. I don't see that yellow jack spreads from one person to another by touch, or by someone who has it breathing on someone else."

"So how does it spread?"

"It's a mystery. Husband get it and not the wife. One child but not another. Yellow jack goes where it wants."

"Then it must be in the air, Félicité," I said.

"Yes, ma'am."

Susanne pondered what this information might mean. I gave her my opinion.

"If that's the case, there's no reason for us to hide. We can go on living. We do what needs doing, even if what we do exposes us to a person who's sick. There's no way to keep safe. If someone's going to get it, he gets it. Right, Félicité?"

"That's what *we* say, but not the doctors, mistress. They'll tell you different. They close the sick up tight."

"I've seen what happens when you follow their advice. Poor Dr. Abbey."

Susanne had another question for Félicité. "If we can't keep from getting it, what do we do for someone who does get it?"

"I'll tell you our ways, ma'am, but you may not want. We treat yellow jack the same as we treat any fever. Rest. Keep air comin' in the room and water going into the body. Fever tea is good. If the fever comes, bring it down by fanning wet cloths on the chest."

"Not purges and bleeding?"

"No, ma'am."

"What's that fever tea?"

"We make it, mistress. Lots of my people do. I don't have all the ingredients I wish I had, but I can come close. We make it with herbs."

"I'm scared to ask this question, Félicité. Does anybody who gets the bad fever recover?"

"Oh, yes, ma'am. Often the fever breaks and the patient gets through. Not always, though, I got to say." She paused. "But you know, that's not how the doctors treat yellow jack. You may want the doctors' ways."

"You mean like close the house up tight, give the patient a purge, and send for the leeches?" Susanne asked.

"Yes, ma'am."

I had something to say about that. "That's what they did for Dr. Abbey and it was no help at all. Made him worse."

"From what I seen, ma'am, the purges and bleeding make people weak. Then without anything to drink, everything inside a body stops working. They dry up," Félicité said.

Susanne put a clenched fist up to her mouth. I took a few deep breaths. We sat silent for a few moments.

"I don't know about you, Susanne, but I've made up my mind. I'm ready to follow Félicité's ways."

My friend nodded. "I am too."

She sat back on the divan, closed her eyes, and sighed. "Of course, if it comes to it, I'll have to check with Max."

Of course, she had to. The men in a family expected to make all important decisions. For just a moment I felt glad I didn't have to wait around for someone to tell me what I should do. I could decide for myself.

Félicité stepped from one bare foot to the other. "If that's all, ma'am, I need to help in the kitchen."

"Before you go, tell me how Jacques is coming with the construction," I asked. "I see he took the plans off the sideboard."

"Yes, ma'am."

Félicité was good with numbers. I knew she helped Jacques. Although it was supposed to be against the law to teach slaves to read, write, and do numbers, sometimes I let Félicité join the children for lessons. She needed numbers to help run this house.

Susanne folded her hands and bowed her head. "Dear Lord . . ."

"Yes, Susanne. One thing we know we can do is pray."

Suzanne stayed for lunch.

* * * * *

After supper, while still light outside, Jacques brought another report. Patrick still had only headache, but he'd turned restless and couldn't seem to get enough water to drink.

"Félicité, I'd like to go see him for myself. Would you come with me?"

"If you want, mistress."

I picked up a lantern just in case.

I drew in a deep breath and followed Félicité into the thicket. I hadn't been through the woods and back to the quarters since early last winter, and then Fréderick had been with me. Tonight, we passed up Félicité's cabin and the cabin for Mr. Gordon. We walked to the woods.

Lush summer growth had narrowed the passage through the trees, re-minding me we lived in the tropics. I jumped when an errant vine whipped against my face, and I came close to losing my balance when I stumbled on something I couldn't identify. I lowered my lantern to check it out. Just a root. If we should have need of a sick cabin in the quarters for any length of time, cleaning up and widening the opening through the woods would be a priority. A task for Jacques.

What about when Jacques had to leave me? How could I manage this place without him? I shook off what I couldn't do anything about.

We emerged into the clearing and saw faint light in the first cabin of the quarters. I raised my lantern and mounted the steps. At one time a whole family lived in each half of this divided structure, the entire cabin the same dimensions as the one Félicité had behind the big house for herself alone.

Patrick lay flat on his back on a blanket-covered layer of moss spread on one of the two wooden bedframes in the room. He reached from one end to the other. Bare-chested, he wore only loose, tattered pants. His eyes gaped open, but he didn't react to my presence. Jacques did, jumping to his feet from one of the two half-barrels set next to the bed.

"You shouldn't come back here, ma'am," Jacques said to me.

"Well, I'm here. I'd forgotten how big Patrick is," I said.

Beside me, Jacques smiled. "Big all right. And heavy. Had to get a litter to tote him."

Félicité leaned down close to the still figure and spoke softly. "It's Félic-ité, Patrick. How you feel?"

Patrick groaned and closed his eyes, which told me he didn't feel good.

Félicité felt his forehead. "Maybe a bit warm. Tell me what hurts, Patrick."

Patrick still didn't have words. Félicité touched his throat. "Quick pulse," she mumbled.

"*Vomito negro?* Has he vomited?" Félicité asked Jacques.

"No. At least not since I got him. All he says is headache's bad, bad."

"I don't remember what we gave people for bad headache in New Orleans, probably because I just went to the herb store and asked for the headache potion."

"And water," Jacques added. "He says he wants water."

Félicité reached into the pocket of her dress and drew out a bottle with a stopper stuck in the mouth. She pulled out the stopper, raised Patrick's head, and put the bottle to his lips. His eyes closed to a slit. He took one sip, and another. "That's good," she said. But when his lips went searching for still another sip, her face stiffened. She stepped back from the bed so Patrick couldn't hear her words.

"That worries me, mistress. The big thirst come before the fever. But it's good he's drinking. As I say, fresh air and drinking water. Get cool air into the room and give him plenty water to drink. That's the first instruc-tion for fever, no matter what kind it is. Treat fever early and most times it break. We're more than early. He only seems a bit warm and it's been a hot day."

"Let's get on it," I said. "Jacques, open the shutters front and back. We want to let in as much air as we can. Go get a supply of drinking water from the well."

"And a pail of cistern water too," Félicité added. "If the fever comes, we cover him with wet cloths and fan him to keep him cool."

The doctor from Opelousas who came to treat Dr. Abbey ordered the shutters closed and that the patient be given nothing to drink. Five minutes on the job and we'd already violated conventional medical practice, twice.

Thank God the overseer hadn't been here the last few days. He might have made Patrick clean up the cane fields for the new owners. But even if Mr. Gordon used the lash on him, in his present condition Patrick would just fall smack down between the rows. At the mill, he'd end up in the crusher.

Patrick faded in and out. Félicité leaned down again and spoke in his ear. "You've gotta drink and drink, Patrick. We'll be waking you up tonight to give you water." She supported his head and coaxed down a few more swallows.

Jacques drew me and Félicité from the bedside. "I'm going for the waters. When I get back, I'm taking you home, mistress. Félicité and I'll take turns watching. We'll rest on the other pallet. If the fever rise, we'll start the cool baths."

"Tell me what Patrick's been doing the last few days," I asked. "Where has he been working?"

"At Miller's Mill. What's left of our cane's goin' there this year. We have to help get the mill ready. You know where Miller's is, ma'am?"

"I do. Just past the Weeks house."

If this fever was yellow jack, Félicité was right. This fever made no good sense. Raphael Smith got sick way over on the river; Dr. Abbey spent the day in the country where Salvatore Migues got it; Patrick worked in town at Miller's Mill. Four probable cases popped up in three different places and struck four people who had no contact with each other. It had to be in the air. But what made some people get it and not others?

While Jacques went for water, Félicité and I sat by the bed. There was something about sitting by a sickbed that gets the mind to thinking about past times.

"Do you remember when you first came to help us out?" I asked Félicité.

"Yes, ma'am. You were a little girl."

"The scene just popped into my head! Isn't it funny how all of a sudden you get a picture from a long time ago you haven't thought of for years? You came across the field from Grand-Mère Mémé's house when we were getting ready for a trip to St. Martinsville to visit my father's parents, Grandpa and Grandma Bérard. I don't think I even talked to you in the beginning. If you talked to me, I couldn't understand a word you said. I'd never heard Creole before."

"You saw me before, mistress. When your Grand-Mère was sick."

"I don't remember that. I do remember later, when Maman started popping out those baby boys, Grand-Mère Mémé left you with us more and more." I chattered on, caught up in my own remembering, oblivious to the fact that Félicité wasn't saying anything. "Do you remember when you were a young girl?" I asked.

Félicité tilted her head and closed her eyes part way. She stood up, turned her back to me, and crossed the room to the other bed frame. She picked up the pallet, turned it over, and threw it down.

"I don't do remembering."

Her words dropped hard. She didn't call me "ma'am" or "mistress." I felt she'd thrown that pallet in my face. It had totally slipped my mind that long ago she told me her memories were difficult. I could have kicked myself for being thoughtless.

Jacques returned with the water.

"I walk you home now, mistress," Jacques said.

"Good night, Félicité."

Félicité had her mouth set and didn't say a word.

Chapter Five

The following morning, we had two visitors before we finished breakfast. First, I heard rapping on the tall front door and Dr. Neal appeared on the porch. Ordinarily immaculately turned out in jacket and cravat, he looked this morning as if he'd slept in his clothes or not slept at all. The latter, I soon learned. He held the arm of a tall, dark negro who carried his medical bag. No bright blood in that one, my Maman would say.

"Madame Duperier, if I'm still welcome, I'd like to lie down." The doctor's voice rasped like a crow.

"Of course, Doctor. Your suitcase is already upstairs in Alfred's room."

I pointed the way. Dr. Neal headed straight ahead to the staircase. He stopped, turned his head, and spoke over his shoulder. "My man Charles here, can he bunk in your quarters?"

"Of course, Doctor. I'll call Jacques to make accommodations. When you get to the top of the stairs turn right, and right again. Alfred's room faces the bayou. I'll come up behind you to be sure everything's in order."

Dr. Neal looked dreadful. Beard untrimmed, dark pouches hanging beneath bloodshot eyes. He stumbled on the first step of the stairs. Charles caught his arm and held onto the newel post until the doctor steadied. Struggling to think how I could help, I asked the doctor if he might like a cup of tea.

"Just sleep, ma'am," Charles responded for the doctor. "He needs a good sleep."

I followed them up the stairs. "How did you find Mr. Burke at the livery?" I asked when the doctor paused on the landing.

"Just a passing malaise, ma'am."

"The word in town is he has the bad fever. Is it not so?"

"A little calomel did the trick. He's sleeping comfortably." Dr. Neal turned and resumed his climb, puffing air with each footfall.

"Are you sure I can't get you anything? I could bring you a breakfast biscuit."

"Nothing ma'am," the doctor answered when he reached the top. "The more Mrs. Burke worries about her husband, the more she cooks." He entered the room and sank onto the edge of the bed.

The doctor fell back onto the covers fully clothed, mumbling something about all of us needing to be careful not to give way to panic. Charles followed me out the door. I doubted the doctor heard the latch close behind us.

"The doctor looks exhausted, Charles."

"He has good reason to be tired, ma'am," Charles said as we descended the stairs. "Mrs. Burke fetched us from Pintard's as soon as the steamboat landed. We examined Mr. Burke and we've been making calls all over New Town ever since. A few people are sick, but it's just overreaction to rumors of fever."

I summoned Jacques from the back of the house and asked him to see to Charles.

Not a half hour later, our second visitor appeared: my stepfather. He tied up his skiff at the dock and came in without knocking. He walked straight to the kitchen where Félicité and I reviewed the day's chores. My stepfather knew our routines.

"Papa B!" I cried, choking up at the sight of him. Baron Benoit Bayard—my children and I called him Papa B—was a big bear of a man, six to eight inches taller than the men kin to me and outweighing them by a good sixty pounds.

After Papa B folded me in a long hug, he touched Félicité on the arm. She barely reached the height of his chest. A broad smile thinned her heavy lips. Félicité knew exactly what Papa B would enjoy. Without needing any instruction, she busied herself preparing the same breakfast she had made for my stepfather every morning for the half-dozen years he lived with us when he married my widowed Maman. That was before my marriage to Fréderick.

Papa B and I settled at a table on the back gallery. Félicité served him sausage, eggs, and her special biscuits. I had another cup of coffee.

"Dr. Neal is upstairs sleeping, not looking as if he'll need to eat any time soon. We plan to have Louisa and Caroline prepare a big dinner for two o'clock in the afternoon. They will turn off the fires in the outside kitchen, bring in the black iron pots, and set them on the braziers to stay warm. We'll save leftovers for a light supper in the evening. Please join us."

"I just came by to check on you," Papa B said. "Rumors of sickness are flying all over town. How is your household?"

"We have one man in the quarters with troublesome signs: headache and perhaps a slight fever. We're keeping a very close eye. I admit I'm concerned."

"I heard in town . . ." Papa B fixed his kind eyes on my face. "We have only two children at home now. Ben moved out, and the house seems positively empty. Any time you want to send Alphonsine and Little Frédérick to us, they are more than welcome. Hypolite and my Alfred miss their brother. They'd love to have company. And we have a new pony."

I raised my eyebrows. "Be honest, Papa B. Would Maman say the same?" My mother's impatience with her crop of overactive boys was a topic Papa B and I shared with each other, but not with her.

"My dear Hortense, you don't think I'd dare make the offer if I hadn't already checked! Your Maman believes the novelty of your children might keep our boys out of mischief for at least a day or two."

I told Papa B we had a shift checking on Patrick day and night. Most heartening, Dr. Neal arrived bringing good news from town—Mr. Burke's illness didn't seem to be the bad fever. We expected the tutor to come as usual today as the children needed to keep up with their lessons. "It's beginning to look as if all we're going to get out of this is a good scare," I said.

"I'll settle for that."

Just like old times, Papa B and I chatted about the cousins, the number of longhorns the Boutté ranch would have ready to send to market in New Orleans, and the political news of the village. Papa B picked up the sound of a hammer coming from the back of the house.

"I believe I hear your addition under way."

"Yes, indeed. Jacques is on the job. Actually, if you have a minute, you could go back and check on him. The cypress boards arrived on the steamship. Jacques is setting them now. They're unwieldy, and with Patrick down, we don't have another man to give him a hand."

Papa B jumped to his feet. "I'd be delighted. You know how I love construction. I should have been an engineer and not a rancher."

"Thank you, Papa B. You'll hear the bell when we're ready for dinner." Papa B headed to the back of the house.

* * * * *

When the tall clock in the front parlor read two o'clock, I rang the plantation bell to announce dinner. Alphonsine and Little Fréderick came in from the yard. The tutor hadn't shown up. Delighted with a reprieve from lessons, they had kept out of sight, hoping I wouldn't notice and supervise the lessons myself. Papa B reappeared wearing smears of sawdust and a broad smile.

"I'm having a grand time, my dear. If you don't mind, I'll go back to the project again after dinner. Jacques is a lucky find for you. He's a skilled builder."

The children ate quickly and disappeared. I gathered courage to share my concern about Jacques's future with my stepfather.

"You always ask if you can do anything for me. Perhaps so. A big something."

"Anything, my dear."

"Before he passed, Fréderick had settled up with Antoine Segura about the slaves they used on the farms. Only a few remained, but last week Jacques and most of the others were sold at the auction of Fréderick's assets. Uncle F. C. brought me the legal papers and I looked at them last night."

"I was an appraiser for the succession sale."

"Oh, yes. I saw that. I don't have a lot of understanding of these matters. May I ask you a question?"

"Of course, my dear."

"Gabe Fuselier bought Jacques for 1,728 *piastres*, payable one-half next April 1 and the second half April 1 of the following year. Two future payments. Does that mean nothing has yet been paid?"

"I think that's right."

"My question is this. Do you think there's anything we could do to cancel the sale?"

Papa B blinked. "How can we do that, my dear? Gabe Fuselier bid high. I think Jacques was the most valuable slave of the half-dozen sold that day."

"I understand. You did your duty to set good prices to meet Fréderick's debts. We're out of the sugar business now and have no need for strong slaves like the ones Fréderick once had for the cane fields at Isle Pivert. But I have need for a man around this house. In fact, I don't know how I can manage the household without one. Maybe . . ." I gathered courage to make my request. "If Gabe hasn't yet paid the price, maybe there's a way the family can get together and come up with enough money to buy Gabe out. I could find some money, but not the whole amount. Nothing would help me more than being able to keep Jacques."

Papa B's two bushy eyebrows squeezed together. "Hmm."

I let him think a bit before I continued. "If Grand-Père Boutté were still alive, I'd ask him for help in a minute. And he'd do so in less time than that. He was very generous with me when Fréderick and I built this house."

In spite of the seriousness of this topic, a smile captured Papa B's face.

"Grand-Père Boutté was generous with you for a reason, my dear. I'm sure you've heard the story. Your Maman caused a big dust-up when her father appeared in that Jean Lafitte costume at the *bal masqué* in St. Martinsville. Grand-Père Boutté tried every way he could to get back in her good graces. In vain. She never forgave him. Can you imagine, bearing a grudge against your own father to the day he died? And all over a Mardi Gras costume he wore to a ball?"

"My Maman? Yes, I *can* imagine. I've known her longer than you have. Maman always considered the rumor her father was a relative of Jean Lafitte, or maybe even the pirate himself, the ultimate humiliation for our family. She won't hear talk of it. Even today, almost twenty years after that masquerade ball, the mere mention of pirates causes her to see red."

I was just a child at the time. My brother 'Tiste and I attended the parade that caused the rift, not that we recognized Grand-Père Boutté behind his feathered mask, wearing a wide-brimmed black hat with a tall feather stuck in the band and a sword at his waist. Everyone else did—and ever after wouldn't stop bringing up the topic.

With a mischievous twinkle in his eyes, Papa B continued. "You know, my dear, your mother has one flamboyant piece of jewelry—a gaudy ring your St. Martinsville cousins say once belonged to Lafitte. She doesn't ever wear it. One day I saw it in her jewelry box and asked if your father bought it for her. Her cheeks turned the color of fire. She said no. A gift from Grand-Père, she said. I knew not to connect the dots and suggest maybe we now had proof of the identity of the head pirate."

Now that was interesting. I had never heard about a ring.

I thought of another argument I could make for saving Jacques from being sold, one that would touch Papa B's soft heart.

"You know Eliza and her children were bought by Dr. Neal. If I kept Jacques, I'd make sure he would be able to see his family. That won't be possible if he has to go off with the Fuseliers."

Papa B ran a hand through his curls. "I'll see what I can do, my dear." Papa B had a postscript. "Let's keep this just between us, Hortense. Your Maman doesn't need to know about our conversation."

Good. There was hope. Papa B returned to meet Jacques at the addition.

*****

In late afternoon, Jacques and Papa B appeared wide-eyed at the front of the house. Louisa had come from the quarters with a report we didn't want to hear. Patrick looked flushed and felt hot to the touch.

I took a deep breath to clear my head. Although Patrick had been sold, I had as much concern for him as for any of the others in the quarters, maybe even more. If I couldn't deliver him to his buyer, I'd have to fund a replacement. I couldn't afford to do so. Even more serious, Félicité might not be correct that yellow fever didn't pass from one person to another. I felt I should safeguard the children. I accepted Papa B's offer to send Alphonsine and Little Fréderick to his house for a visit. Always happy to go there, they tucked a spare set of clothes in a carpet bag. Papa B packed the three of them into his skiff, and they took off.

I asked Félicité to inform Dr. Neal's man Charles there was food for their dinner warming on the braziers in the pantry. They'd have to serve themselves. I intended to be part of Patrick's care.

"Let's get going, Félicité."

Félicité stopped in her tracks. "You're not going back to the quarters, mistress. You mustn't do that. We can handle Patrick."

"I'm going."

As we walked out the door, Félicité picked up a bottle from a table on the back gallery and tucked it into the pocket of her shift.

"What do you have there?" I asked.

"The beginnings of a fever tea, mistress. I found bougainvillea, verbena, and portulaca in the garden. Mahogany bark is a critical ingredient and I don't have any. I don't believe anyone in New Town or St. Martinsville has been nursing a tree through the winter freezes. Perhaps you could ask your family in Plaquemine to bring me a branch when next they visit, but that may be a good while."

So, in spite of the optimism she expressed, Félicité had been getting ready for the fever. I made conversation with her as we walked back to the quarters, but anxiety crept up my spine.

"I've heard there's a new herb shop in New Town, Félicité. I'll take you to check it out when we get a chance."

"I'd like that, mistress. I need to replenish all my supplies."

"And we need to visit my friend Susanne Decuir. She has the finest garden around. She won't have a mahogany tree, I'm sure, but she might have other plants you could use."

We found Jacques standing by the wood bedframe where Patrick lay: eyes closed, flushed, breathing hard, tossing on the pallet. Félicité went straight to him, placing her hand on his forehead and then on the base of his throat. She set her lips against one another, nodded to Jacques, and mouthed one word: fever.

I had seen Félicité care for my children, and for my father years ago, but then she'd been under direction. Here in the quarters, she ruled. She issued commands. "Jacques, take the pan to the cistern and refill it. Take care to strain off any wiggly critters having a swim. Put the pan here on the barrel next to the bed." She unrolled a piece of cloth she had stuffed in her left pocket and ripped off a two-foot square. "Louisa, tear three more like this. You'll be dipping them in the water and laying them on Patrick's chest. Stand by to give him a sip of well water whenever I say. Caroline, be ready to spell anyone who needs a break."

I grabbed the first cloth Louisa ripped. "I'll fan over Patrick's chest."

All three pairs of eyes shot toward my face, and then to Félicité. As the one with the most connection to their mistress, Jacques, Louisa, and Caroline looked to her to deal with me.

"No, ma'am," Félicité said. "It's dark now. Jacques will take you back to the house when he makes his first trip to gather water."

I drew myself up. "No, he won't. I'm part of this project. I'm not going to sit in the house and worry myself sick about what's going on out here. I'm on the team. I'll fan over Patrick and be ready to replace anyone who needs to be spelled."

"But, mistress . . ."

"That is how it is going to be."

I don't know what possessed me to insert myself into a fever routine for a slave. Perhaps I reacted to a lifetime of being relegated to the background as decisions were made about my life. Perhaps I was just being ornery. I set my lips hard together and took a place in the line.

Dip the cloth in the cistern water, spread it on Patrick's chest, fan over him, coax him to take a sip of well water. Repeat. Dip, spread, fan, sip. Repeat again and again.

After an hour on the job, and a nod from Félicité, each of us moved from our original assignment to that of the person to the right. Félicité said change would keep us fresh. And after a dozen rounds, Félicité held up her hand for us to stop. Patrick still breathed hard and tossed fitfully on the bed.

"Let the cloth rest a few extra minutes to reach room temperature," she said. "I'll check to see if the fever has dropped."

It had not. We resumed the routine of wet cloths on the chest, fanning, and forcing Patrick to sip. Between my duties, I leaned against the barrel; Félicité smiled her approval. "Sit when you can, mistress. Likely we'll be at this through the night."

Félicité checked again several hours later. The fever raged on. Caroline came to take a turn in the routine, but I refused to be replaced. Louisa went to the other bed, dropped onto the pallet, and immediately fell asleep.

On the rotation a few hours later, Jacques insisted I go with him back to the house when he went to the cistern. I had to rest, he said. I agreed to take a nap, but on one condition.

"Come back for me when you break three hours from now. I know you want me to quit, but I will not. I'll have a snack of bread and cheese ready in a picnic basket to take to the crew. If you don't return for me in three hours, I'll come walking back here in the dark by myself. You won't like that at all."

I hadn't stopped to consider whether I'd be able to do so.

Jacques tipped up his head to the sky to judge the time by the position of the moon. At the house, I checked the hall clock. Three hours later, I stood on the right-side gallery with my platter of food for the crew. Jacques's lantern flickered into view from the path to the quarters.

Back at the cabin, I resumed my place in the rotation. I was at Patrick's bedside when dawn broke. Félicité held up her hand again for yet another test. She placed her hand on Patrick's throat to check his pulse and then on his forehead. Her face softened.

"His pulse is normal. His forehead's cooler. I'm hopeful the crisis has passed. We'll pull a few more rounds to be certain."

An hour later, Félicité declared victory. "The fever has broken, mistress. Now Patrick's got to rest."

"Did he have yellow jack?" I asked.

Félicité looked up sharply. "Of course, mistress." She leaned over Patrick and pulled down one lower eyelid. I saw yellow around the dark center.

Félicité assigned Carolyn and Louisa to divide the watch. She, Jacques, and I headed in three different directions but with the same goal—to sleep in our beds. I fell asleep before I could finish my prayer of thanksgiving.

CHAPTER SIX

"A very good morning to you, although it's actually afternoon. I hope you slept as deeply as I did," I said to Caroline and Louisa, who were standing in the pantry. Their faces brightened as I greeted them. Covered plates sat on the counter, probably the breakfast they had prepared but found no one to serve. Félicité mounted the back steps behind me. The sound of Jacques's hammer signaled his return to work on the addition.

"Has someone checked on Patrick?" I asked

"Oh, yes, mistress. He's resting quiet," Félicité responded. "I've just come from the cabin. We've been seeing to it he drinks water, and I just now gave him some chicken broth. He wants to get up, but I told him he must stay in bed for at least another day or two."

I looked into the face of each of the women. "I'm very proud of all three of you, and of Jacques. Under Félicité's direction, we pulled Patrick through yellow jack."

Caroline, the youngest, blurted out a response from the group. "And we're very proud of you, mistress."

I folded my hands under my chin and showed a small smile. I was actually quite proud of myself!

"I don't know about you, but I've missed at least three meals. I'm starving. I bet there are biscuits under the cover of that plate. Could you fix me a cup of coffee and the rest of a breakfast?"

"Yes, mistress. Should I get started on a special dinner for tonight?" Caroline asked.

"I think not for tonight, Caroline. We'll have a fine celebration in due time. I believe I heard Dr. Neal and Charles leaving early this morning. They'll be hungry when they return from making calls, but we can't know exactly when that will be. I think the best plan is to have a big pot of vegetable soup simmering on the fire."

"Yes, mistress. We can do that."

There could be no celebration that night, for a number of reasons. We needed Patrick himself to attend, and Félicité said he shouldn't leave his bed for several days. Dr. Neal, as a member of our household, should be included. And I wanted the children to be home to join us in the celebration. If we should have an epidemic one day—which I did not believe would be any time soon—Alphonsine and Little Fréderick needed to think of yellow fever in terms of recovery and not calamity. Most of all, I couldn't be absolutely certain the fever had left for good. We were all exhilarated by Patrick's recovery, but it was far too early to celebrate.

I didn't mention another concern I thought about that morning as I slowly awoke—how we *could* have a proper celebration of Patrick's recovery. I needed to think ahead. Was there any way to put on a party at which everyone in our household would be comfortable? After rejecting many alternatives, I considered a plan to have an informal picnic on the back gallery—the entire household welcome but no designated seating. To say thank you for stepping in to help, I would invite my Maman, Papa B, and their family to join us.

I asked Caroline and Louisa to think about cooking their specialty sometime soon. We all loved their chicken roasted with sprigs of rosemary. Delighted, Caroline and Louisa put predacious eyes on the saucy hens running around the chicken yard who were, of course, oblivious to the fate awaiting them.

Félicité cast about for instructions on how she should spend the rest of the day.

"Shall I notify your mother to return Alphonsine and Little Fréderick, mistress?" She asked.

"Not just yet. I'd like them to stay over a bit longer. Let them be. I have some reading I want to do while the house is quiet."

I knew Alphonsine and Little Fréderick never tired of riding the latest successor pony to the one their Uncle 'Tiste had when he was a child, and Papa B told me Maman appreciated the distraction of my children to keep her boys occupied.

Selfishly, I wanted to take advantage of a rare day without my boarder or my children. I planned to close myself off from all household distractions and take a deep dive into the papers from Uncle F. C.

"However," I continued, "Maman and Papa B deserve to know good news. I'll write a note for you to give to the ferryman to take to them. We didn't advertise what was going on here, but I bet the rumor is out. The ferryman will probably pry the good news out of Papa B and spread it to everyone at the landing! When you come back, I'd like you to prepare me a nice warm bath."

I expected no general acknowledgement from the townsfolk that our treatment had been responsible for Patrick's recovery. When they heard, some would say he really didn't have yellow fever at all. Others would say that a saltwater—that was what they called slaves born in Africa—didn't get the same disease, or that Patrick didn't catch it bad. Whatever people wanted to say would be fine with me, but I knew if anyone in my care came down with signs of yellow fever, I'd be certain we repeated the treatment we gave to Patrick. We'd strike early with rest and hydration, and fight fever with more water and wet cloths, not purge and bleeding.

With a quiet afternoon assured, I closed myself into the parlor and found a comfortable spot on the divan. I pulled out the papers and notebooks Uncle F. C. had delivered and prepared to remember my childhood self.

But I could not stop returning to our accomplishment. Our team worked as one, following Félicité's direction. I knew of her care for the sick, but this effort had been more complicated than anything I'd seen her do before. Perhaps we did not realize the capabilities of the slaves who served us.

When I was a small child, we had many slaves in our household. Patterning my behavior on that of my mother, I expected the slaves to do without question whatever they were asked to do, even when asked by a child. I could not recall any open discussion of their inferior status. Occasionally Maman corrected my behavior. She instructed me to be courteous at all times, not out of respect for the role the slaves played in our lives, but because courtesy was expected of people of privilege. I accepted the world I had been born into as normal. I gave little thought to the personal lives of those who lived behind the woods that separated us from them.

I was just nine years old when my father died. Maman went to pieces and Grand-Mère Mémé sent Félicité from her household to us. Our occasional helper slipped into a different role in the family. Maman disappeared from our daily lives and Félicité took charge. Even at that young age, I remembered that I sensed Félicité delicately maneuvering the conventions of slave and free. She was our servant, of course, taking instructions from our grandmothers. But even more, she gave gentle corrections to me and to my brother 'Tiste. When she helped us dress, her arm lingered around our shoulders. She held a hand at any opportunity. She stopped whatever she was doing to listen to our concerns. She mothered us.

And right after my father died and we spent that long time in St. Martinsville at Grandma Bérard's house, Félicité took care of us. She ate a bowl of mash from the quarters while we dined on succulent roasts. She slept on a moss-stuffed pallet on the floor by our soft beds. Our grandparents may have thought that was the way it should be, but the situation bothered me.

On our first brief return to our home, in what we then knew as La Nouvelle-Ibérie, I talked to my cousin and best friend Gabrielle (who I called Gabby) about the situation. As a child, Gabby had lived near my Aunt Thérèse in Plaquemine, on the Big River. She often came to visit. Two years older, she had already come to ask questions about why people with dark skin had a life different from ours. Gabby listened to my concerns but gave me a stern warning, based on her experience.

She said, "Forget about it, Hortense. I once brought up the subject of slavery with Grand-Mère Mémé. To this day I remember her reaction. Her sharp words sliced into me. *Never, never ask me about slavery again. For that matter, do not ask anyone in the family about slavery. And never, ever, ask one of the slaves.*

"Hortense, I was terrified," Gabby told me. "Grand-Mère Mémé was so angry I feared she wasn't going to let me stay with her any more. My advice to you is just don't talk about it."

I took Gabby's warning to heart, but being a bit devious as well as a curious young girl, I tried a round-about way to learn something about Félicité's story. I asked her questions about her life.

"Tell me, Félicité where did you live when you were my age?"

"Around eight? I lived in New Orleans."

"I thought you were born in Saint-Domingue."

"Yes, I was born in Saint-Domingue, but I don't remember much about those days," she answered with only a slight hesitation. "I was too little. I left there before I was three."

"Did you live with your Maman and Papa the way I do?"

I thought I could ask that question because I knew there were variations in family arrangements. Gabby didn't live with her parents. She spent most of her time next door at Grand-Mère Mémé's and not over in Plaquemine with her mother and father. Still following Gabby's advice, I thought I wasn't really talking about slavery. But I'd touched a nerve.

Félicité snapped up her chin and put those coal black eyes on mine. "I don't remember."

"What? You don't remember?"

"I try hard to forget the past. It's better that way."

I'd overstepped. I stumbled to an apology. The life of slaves must be just another facet of the incomprehensible adult world I couldn't know about until I grew up. Félicité did her chores. I played and went off to school. We didn't talk about her past.

But I was in charge of the family. Maman said my destiny was to be a good Christian woman and run a fine household. As such, what responsibility did I have toward a loyal slave who twice stepped up to play an extraordinary role in my life?

Now over sixty years of age, Félicité had her own cabin and I didn't assign heavy work for her to do. I knew that some slaves were set free, but to give freedom to Félicité at this stage of her life would not be kind. How could she support herself? Jacques, on the other hand, was young and strong. But I needed Jacques!

Was I any different from the sugarcane farmers my father once spoke of, whose very economic existence relied on the labor of the slaves in their fields and mills?

I wished my father were here to talk with me now. Serious discussions with my mother tended to end in confusion. Where could I turn for guidance? Perhaps I could talk with Papa B.

My mind flicked back to one day years ago in Mamselle's schoolroom when our teacher immersed us in studying a unit about the Greek and Roman gods and goddesses. When Gabby and I came into the classroom that morning, we found a drawing our teacher had made pinned up on the front wall. A large, muscular figure of a man sat upon a rock poised to thrust a bolt of lightning downward to a much smaller man below.

"What do you girls think is going on in this picture?" Mamselle asked. We offered suggestions: driving off an animal trying to attack him; trying to start a fire to keep himself warm. None of our suggestions satisfied her. She explained. "Throughout all literature, this image of the god Zeus symbolizes the flash of a brilliant idea."

Well, Mamselle, I had just received a bolt of lightning. I thought about the folders Uncle F. C. had delivered. At the time, I had read only a few pages of each folder before placing it in a drawer of the desk in the parlor. The first folder contained the legal papers, of course, but the second held notebooks covered with my own handwriting—the journals I kept as a child. Perhaps on those pages I might find indications of my father's wisdom. Perhaps I would learn more about the subject of my present concern—Félicité. I needed a period of undisturbed time, and a good measure of emotional strength, to undertake a journey back in time. Today I had the time. Buoyed by our success, I felt strong.

My solitude arranged, I pulled out the journals I had tucked into Fréderick's desk, and settled down on the divan for a slow read.

When I had first looked at those pages a few days ago, my childish letters brought tears to my eyes. I read of a world I did not know at all, people who lived in a country to which I had never been, at a time I could not remember. Now, as if watching fog lift in the early morning, familiar people, places, and thoughts emerged from the miasma.

In one notebook, I recounted the Sunday performances Grandpa Bérard in St. Martinsville put on to amuse his grandchildren. He told delightful stories but, I realized now, he was at the same time telling us the history of the Attakapas frontier. Before going on to the next notebook, I read the first one again. I plumbed a storehouse of memories I hadn't thought about until these pages brought them out of the recesses of my mind.

The next notebook recorded the fanciful stories I wrote to amuse my little brothers. The stories made me laugh out loud. What nonsense! Farm animals soared into the nighttime sky to travel to foreign lands. Water sprites danced in the streams that sourced the Bayou Teche. The sprites floated downstream to visit my two sets of grandparents: my father's parents in St. Martinsville——Grandpa and Grandma Bérard——and my mother's parents——Grand-Mère Mémé and Grand-Père Boutté next door to our bungalow in La Nouvelle-Ibérie. As I read the stories, memories of telling them to my little brothers crowded in. I pictured the make-believe boat I built in our backyard and the imaginary trips we made.

The other notebooks—the journals I kept when I was probably no more than seven years old and could barely write my letters—generated an entirely different genre of emotions. The very first page shamed me. I seemed to think the entire universe, every person free or slave, existed to provide a backdrop for my existence. I read all afternoon.

Late in the day, I stopped to have a bowl of Louisa's vegetable soup. I checked on Patrick. Still resting well. Yes, I believed we saved a man. If so, I would never look at life quite the same way again.

I lit a lantern to continue reading and remembering my childhood far into the night.

PART II
1814–1816

CHAPTER SEVEN

"Hortense, keep an eye on 'Tiste for me."

Maman called out to me over her shoulder. She gave me the same instruction almost every day as far back as I could remember, this time as she picked up a basket and a pair of scissors and headed down the back steps to the garden. "I'm going out to pick a few vegetables for the stew."

I liked what Maman called "keeping an eye on 'Tiste." She said all children had to do chores; I was happy when my chore was to watch my little brother. Since I was almost seven years old, she might have had me helping in the cookhouse. It was way too hot in there. The last time I had gone in I thought I'd faint.

My three-year-old brother 'Tiste, toddling around and into everything, needed to be out from under Maman's feet, especially when she had to go outside. I took 'Tiste by the hand and led him to the fenced-in play yard behind our house. I pulled two chairs from the back gallery and set one behind the other.

"Time for pretend, 'Tiste. Here's our skiff at the dock ready to take us up the Bayou Teche to town. *Tout le monde à bord!* All aboard!" We spoke French. I didn't learn to speak in English until much later.

I lifted 'Tiste and set him down in the front chair. "Let's make believe we're on a boat. It's a beautiful day for a ride."

I sat in the chair behind 'Tiste and called out instructions.

"Close your eyes now!" 'Tiste scrunched up his little face. "Uh, uh," I scolded. "No peeking! Keep those eyes shut tight." I reached my hands forward and placed them on his shoulders, gently moving his little body forward and back. "We're leaving the dock now. Wave goodbye to Grand-Mère Mémé who came from next door to see us off." 'Tiste turned and waved to the air. Giggles bubbled in his throat. We lived next to my

Maman's parents, Grand-Mère and Grand-Père Boutté. They owned a big tract on the bayou bank, reaching all the way back to the prairie. A *vacherie*, or ranch, they called it.

"Squank. Squank. Can you hear the oars creaking in the locks? We're headed straight toward the wall of green trees on the opposite bank. Can you feel the boat rocking on the water?"

"I'm rockin'! I'm rockin'!" 'Tiste called.

"Now we're making a turn to the port side. That's the left, you know. Papa is pulling the oar on the starboard to turn our skiff. Okay, now we're ready to go straight ahead. Settle back into the rhythm. Today we'll take the boat up to the turn-around in town."

'Tiste rocked his body on his own.

"Open your eyes now and put on your glasses." I curled my fingers into circles and pressed them to my eyes. 'Tiste did the same. "Let's look-see who might be hiding in the thicket watching us go by. Aha! I think I see a sneaky raccoon peeking through the trees. Mr. Raccoon has eyeglasses just like we do. Do you see him?"

'Tiste leaned forward in his chair, peering through his curled fingers. "I see him! I see him!"

"Watch that big turtle tumble off a log and plop into the water. Sploosh!"

I didn't tell 'Tiste about some of the bad things he might also see in the uncleared thicket on the opposite bank, like vines that make your skin break out in itchy, gooey sores, or a shiny black cottonmouth snake swinging from a low-hanging cypress branch. When a little boy playing on the bayou bank right in town died from a snake bite, Papa gave me a lesson in recognizing copperheads and water moccasins, and strict instructions to watch 'Tiste every minute, even when we were close to the house. Copperheads could be anywhere, he said.

"We're just going a little way today. Sunday we'll go to church in St. Martinsville."

Pretend boat rides were a sure way to make 'Tiste happy. The other was storytelling. I built make-believe castles (with pots and pans if we were inside, with sticks and pebbles if we'd gone to the play yard) and I told 'Tiste made-up tales about people who lived in them. I put on plays like the pageants at the church or the theater we sometimes went to when we visited Papa's family up the bayou in St. Martinsville. I changed my voice to play all the parts. 'Tiste liked my animal plays best, especially when I asked him to talk like one of them.

"How does the sheep ask for his breakfast?"

"Baa, baa, biscuits," 'Tiste answered.

"And the cow? How does the little cow ask his Maman for supper?"

"Moo-re m-m-milk."

We had a lot of our own animals in the fenced-in area between our bungalow and my grandparents' big house: chickens, sheep, a couple of milk cows, a pair of goats, some rabbits in a hutch, four hogs in their own sty. Even though 'Tiste begged and begged, we didn't let any animals come into the play yard. Animals made a lot of mess that Maman didn't want to have to clean up.

Until Papa bought 'Tiste a pony. Papa changed a lot of rules where 'Tiste was concerned.

I dressed up for some of my plays. When Maman took dry clothes off the line, I'd put them on myself. My costumes, I said. Maman fussed at me for that, but when she heard 'Tiste laughing at my antics, I could see her smile.

"Lordy, ma petite, you've got some imagination," she said. "How on earth do you think up your stories?"

Maman said I had a gift. I think I learned to tell stories from listening to my Papa and his father, we called him Grandpa. "You're right," Maman said. "The Bérards are a family of storytellers. My family—the Bouttés— can't hold a candle to them in that department."

Maman bragged about how I kept the little ones amused. I didn't like when she bragged on me. I thought I saw my St. Martinsville relatives pinch their lips together. Maman tossed her head and said I imagined things. When we visited, my aunts and my cousins over there didn't hesitate to hand over their young ones for me to keep track of along with 'Tiste.

I always got up in the morning in time to see Papa take off with our herd of longhorns. He gave me the same parting words every day. "Be good, Hortense, and do everything your Maman tells you to do." Papa and his top hand, Étienne, led the cattle parade stretching out as far as I could see, a half dozen dogs circling around them. They stayed gone all day, reappearing when the sun dropped low in the sky. When I saw the horizon wiggle and shimmer, I called to Maman. "They're coming, Maman. Papa's coming home with the herd!"

Maman stopped whatever she was doing and came out on the back gallery. She clutched her hands together under her chin. "A magnificent sight, Hortense, the men riding tall in the saddle, high above the prairie, the horns whipping up like white foam on an ocean of grass."

"One day I'd like to go to the ocean, Maman." I'd never seen any body of water bigger than the swampy lake on the way to Grandpa's.

Only in a saddle could you call Papa tall. He stood no higher than Maman. He had a dark complexion like me and a cap of black curly hair. Papa smiled all the time and loved to make jokes. Maman, on the other hand, had what people called "cool beauty." Everyone noticed her sparkling green eyes and her reddish hair. She was always pleasant but didn't see any need for small chatter. One time I heard my aunts in St. Martinsville talk about her "flinty" ways. I didn't know what they meant by that.

People said I looked like Maman, but they were being kind. I had olive skin. At least I got my Maman's green eyes. Both Maman and Papa insisted I wasn't small. Delicate, they said, and that was a good thing.

Papa walked funny. Maman said a bull had stepped on his foot. Yet he had no trouble doing whatever he needed to do. Every morning, after he hugged me and 'Tiste and kissed Maman goodbye, he threw one leg over the back of his horse and sprang right up onto the saddle. At branding time, Papa could wrestle a calf to the ground with the biggest of Grand-Père Boutté's herders. Maman said Papa believed that if you didn't dwell on possible problems, they were less of a bother; If you didn't worry about what might become a problem, it was less likely to happen.

At dusk, Papa, the herders, and the yapping dogs brought the longhorns back from the prairie into the fenced area behind Grand-Père Boutté's big barn. Cattle all tucked in for the night, Papa walked across the yard and climbed up onto the back gallery. He kissed Maman first, then lifted 'Tiste in the air and swung him around. He reached for me and hugged me, but he didn't swing me in the air like he used to. I was too big now, he said. Then he took Maman's hand and we walked up the back steps, crossed the gallery, and went together into the house.

"You know, my dear," Papa said to Maman one evening. "If Father Isabey held two Bibles written in Latin and swore to all the world that Jesus himself said there were no gods and goddesses living on Mount Olympus, I wouldn't believe him."

"Achille, what are you saying?"

"I'm saying I know better." Papa paused, and Maman stopped walking. "I know one little fellow slipped through the cracks."

"What?"

"Cupid. The naked little boy with a quiver of arrows on his back. I know Cupid still exists because the day I first saw your green eyes, Cupid pulled out an arrow of love and shot it straight into my heart."

Maman let out a snort. "Stop it, Achille! Don't let the children hear such nonsense."

Every night, Papa asked me if I'd been a good girl. Of course I'd been good, I always answered. I knew if Maman agreed, Papa would tell me a story before I went to bed.

"Papa, why don't you ever ask 'Tiste if he's been good? He gets to hear the story no matter what."

Maman laughed. "But not the end of the story. He falls asleep before Papa gets to *toujours, toujours, heureuse,* happily ever after."

Before dinner, we sat on the front gallery overlooking the bayou. Papa sipped a glass of blackberry wine. When mosquitos came, Martine served us dinner in the dining room. Martine was with us as far back as I could remember. Sometimes we had a special treat. If Grand-Mère Mémé had taken the wagon to the market in town, she'd come home with fresh-caught bass and share. Martine cooked wonderful dinners in the big black pots out in the cookhouse, but Maman didn't let Martine cook fish. She did that herself.

Papa told us what he'd seen out on the prairie, way beyond where we could watch from the house. He said horses ran wild out there, as did coyotes and occasionally a red fox with a bushy tail. Our cattle roamed free, which is why every longhorn in the herd had the brand of our ranch. When new calves were born, they had to stay in the fence until they'd been marked as our own. Papa told us he'd be branding later in the week. There were calves who needed to go out on the prairie with their mothers.

"And I'll be hiding in the farthest corner of the yard," I told him.

I watched the branding once. I saw Papa and Étienne throw a rope around the calves' necks and one by one drag them off to Grand-Père Boutté's barn. They seared a red-hot poker into the calves' shoulders. I could still hear the calves yowling. The smell would come back to me and roll my stomach. After that one time, on branding day, I hid.

"We can graze our herd anywhere on the prairie, Hortense," Papa told me. "If there weren't strict rules about cows having a brand and laws re-quiring witnesses at every slaughter, anyone could round up anybody else's cattle for themselves. Scoundrels would steal all our herd."

"The calves cry when you burn them, Papa."

"They get over it quick. We're proud of our brands. Both of your grandfathers have really old ones. My father, your Grandpa Bérard in St. Martinsville, has one of the oldest brands ever registered. He was among the first settlers to come from France to the colony of Louisiana. Back then the entire colony belonged to Spain. Grandpa's brand is famous—a circle with a cross inside."

In St. Martinsville, I never watched my Papa's father's herd taken out to graze. My Uncle Baptiste, my Papa's brother, led the Bérard cattle back beyond the trees. Indians lived back there, or so my cousins told me. They said Indians ate people.

At dinner, Papa gave Maman news of more people moving into our area. "English families have settled down the bayou," he said.

"Is that going to be a problem for us? We don't own the prairie where you and my father graze our herds."

"I'm happy to say the English aren't much interested in ranching. They're making a big investment in sugar, both growing sugarcane and building mills to crush out the juice. We'll still have the prairie pretty much to ourselves."

"My father says anyone can make money with sugarcane. Our friends the Darbys and the Grevembergs do very well, and my father says he's seen huge sugar plantations in Plaquemine and Pointe Coupée over on the river. On his next trip there, he says he plans to talk to my sister Thérèse's husband about raising sugarcane here."

Papa squeezed his dark eyebrows together. "Well, I'm not interested in growing sugar."

"No? We have the land for it."

Papa put down his fork—the signal he planned to say something we should listen to. "Growing sugarcane means managing a lot of slaves. Most of the year, when the cane's just growing, the slaves hang around and get into trouble. Then at *rolaison*, grinding time, the work for them is brutally hard. You have to have an overseer drive the slaves to cut the cane, take it to the mill, and feed the stalks into the grinder. They cook the juice down in kettles over an open fire, pouring the boiling molasses from one big kettle to another. It's all dangerous work. I don't see myself managing that kind of operation."

"My brother F. C. wants to grow sugar."

Papa scowled. "He'd better do that over in Plaquemine, where he so often goes. Here we're doing fine as it is. You know, with ranching, the cattle do the work for us. They feed themselves on the grasses. All we need are a few slaves and a half-dozen dogs to move them around during the day, lead them home at night, then catch and sell the calves they drop."

Maman smiled. "It's a little bit harder than that, Achille. You can't just tell a longhorn where to go. And how about being out on the prairie when the rains come, when the mosquitos swarm, or the cold wind blows? What about when you stay up all night with a sick mother cow, or get stepped on by a bull who has only one idea on his mind. Remember how you hurt your foot? Or for that matter, when my father gives you more advice than you want to hear? People say you can make money easily growing cane."

"There are considerations other than money, my dear." Silence. Papa looked Maman straight in the eye and changed the subject.

"This summer we're sending a big shipment of cattle down the Atchafalaya River and across the swamp to Plaquemine, then on down the Mississippi River to New Orleans to market. As soon as the barges dock in the city, we'll have a sizable number of *piastres* deposited into our bank account. We've already met our yearly expenses with our sales to the slaughterhouse in Vermilionville. The proceeds from the New Orleans sale will be mostly profit. I'm thinking we could buy some land in St. Martinsville and build another house over there. A bigger house. No more overnights at the Sunday house when we're caught after church by a turn in the weather."

A scowl grabbed Maman's face.

"What? You don't like my idea?" Papa asked.

"No, Achille. I do not."

"I thought you'd be excited. When you were a young bride, you wanted—and I guess you needed—to be next to your mother here in La Nouvelle-Ibérie. My mother over in St. Martinsville isn't the most domestic, and her Acadian accent takes a while to get used to. You've done beautifully with our household. You're entitled to a better house. And there's a lot more going on in St. Martinsville."

Maman tilted her head and took a moment before speaking. "I love my house, Achille. I'm happy right here."

I was too. I didn't like hearing about moving.

"But you're mostly here alone," Papa continued. "Half the time your father oversees his nephew's building projects in New Orleans and your parents are down there or in Iberville Parish visiting your sister Thérèse. And your parents are getting older."

Maman spoke very slowly now. "Exactly. When my parents are away, you have to take care of their herd as well as ours. If we lived in St. Martinsville, I'd be stuck over there next to your family while you'd be back here next to mine—or at least next to their herd."

Martine cleared the table and brought in bowls of fig pudding for dessert.

Papa kept pushing the issue of another house. "If we had a house in St. Martinsville, Hortense could go to school."

At the word school, Maman put down *her* fork. "And exactly where would that school be? There's no school in St. Martinsville."

"How about the tutor who comes to my father's house?"

"Haven't you noticed the tutor only teaches the boys? Girls are supposed to go off to the nuns to learn how to be proper young ladies."

"But maybe—"

Maman cut him off. "Stop that, Achille. Don't you go getting Hortense all upset with talk of going away to school. We've got a good while before we have to think about that. We're doing just fine. You love your work and I love my one-story bungalow. Enough said," she snapped.

Maman was right about one thing; Papa had worried me. Where would I go to school? I'd heard some girls got sent to a convent in New Orleans. I did *not* want to be sent away from home. And I didn't like the idea of nuns.

"I agree. Enough said about another house and enough said about growing sugarcane."

"Anyway," my mother said casually, "I guess my father makes the decision about what we do on his land."

I saw Papa's little beard quiver. "No, love. You make the decisions about the house, but I make the decision about what work I do. I'm dead serious about this. If you want to know about some of the consequences of the sugar business, talk to anyone who came here from Saint-Domingue, once the richest colony in the Caribbean and also the most brutal for the slaves who did the sugar work. Before the revolution, they had up to one hundred slaves for every white person in the colony. Some owners treated them cruelly to keep them in line. You know what happened. A bloody revolt. And you know who lost that fight."

"You wouldn't be cruel to slaves, Achille."

"When revolt comes, slaves don't care which white owner was kind to them and which wasn't. Every owner is fair game for sharpened cane knives. It could happen here, my dear. I'm just now hearing what took place on the Andry plantation over on the Mississippi. Slaves revolted and then got crushed by bloody retribution. Another thing, New Orleans learned the hard way that importing slaves brings yellow fever. They've shut the port to refugees from the islands."

Maman gripped the edge of the table. She stood up and gathered 'Tiste in her arms.

"I think it's time for this little fellow to get ready for bed," she said.

Papa stood up also. "We'll skip story time tonight, children. I'm going to go out with the boys to visit some friends."

I ate my fig pudding alone.

* * * * *

"So, where did you go on your so-called *visit to friends*?" Maman asked Papa the next morning at breakfast.

"Your brother F. C. and I rode up the road to town." Papa answered with a smile in his voice.

"You rode all the way to town in the dark? Was that a sensible thing to do?" No smile in *Maman's* voice.

"Well, I'll admit our mounts stumbled a few times, but we had Étienne ride ahead and hang a lantern out on a pole."

"And I suppose you met your friends at the tavern?"

"Yes, we did."

"Tell me, how much money did you leave on the poker table at Murphy's?"

"No cards last night, love," Papa answered. "Just a couple racks of billiards."

"Okay, Achille. How much did you lose at billiards?"

"I was a winner."

Maman flipped her long hair over her shoulder.

"Well, my dear," Papa said. "At least I won a lot of fun." He paused. "Let me be clear, love. As long as I'm alive and have two *piastres* to rub together, I'll be sure we live exactly where you want us to live. But what work I do? That's my business."

"But my father—"

Papa cut her off. "You promised to love and obey me. That's the way it is and the way it's going to be."

Silence. I hoped they'd end the talk with a kiss. I'd seen them kiss before. Not this time.

That was the last I heard about building another house up the bayou in St. Martinsville or growing sugarcane. I forgot about both subjects. But I didn't forget about school. Where would I go to learn to read and write?

Chapter Eight

Oone of the stories my Papa liked to tell was the one about the time I saved the family from being attacked by a bear.

We didn't have a church in the settlement of La Nouvelle-Ibérie. We went to Mass almost every Sunday up the Bayou Teche, across from Grandpa Bérard's house in St. Martinsville. One Friday night at dinner Papa made an announcement.

"This Sunday we're in for a special treat, my dears. Instead of the usual back and forth route across the bayou to go to church, we'll get into our wagon right at our own front door, go up the road to town, and then keep going all the way on our side of the Bayou Teche to Grandpa's in St. Martinsville."

Maman didn't believe him. "What are you saying? We can't do that. I thought there wasn't any road on the right bank of the bayou past La Nouvelle-Ibérie. We always cross the bayou on a ferry at Daspit, follow the opposite bank, and cross again behind the church across from your father's house."

"There *is* a road on our side," Papa said. "It's usually a muddy mess, impassible because of run-off from the swamp surrounding Spanish Lake. But this year the winter's over early and spring rains haven't begun. I rode it today. It'll be a bit bumpy, but for once the right bank is dry enough to handle the wagon the whole way. It's a shorter ride. We should take advantage."

Papa didn't mention any dangers we might encounter.

'Tiste piped up with a suggestion. "Boat, boat, Papa. Let's ride in the boat."

"We can't go all the way to your Grandpa Bérard's house by boat 'Tiste. The bayou makes a big loop between our town and St. Martinsville." Papa lifted his hand and drew a curving line in the air with his finger.

"It would take all day long to go on the water. We have to go by wagon."
'Tiste pouted. "But for once we can go straight there *like the crow flies,* as
they say."

We took our baths on Saturday night. Papa trimmed his beard. Sunday
morning, we put on our best clothes. I liked the new spring dress Maman
made for me—pink flowers and puffy sleeves—but I hated the silly, little
matching bonnet. Along with my shoes, I always took the bonnet off as
soon as we got to Grandpa's house for dinner after church.

When Maman got dressed up, she looked different. She pulled her
thick hair straight off her face, swirled it around tight over her ears, then
twisted what was left over into a fat roll at the back of her neck. Fixing her
hair took a long time. She put on a shiny dress with a full skirt and what
she called a "wasp waist." Wasps are really tiny in the middle. Other days
Maman wore a straight cottonade shift like my weekday dress, but bigger.

"Why don't you let your hair hang down on Sunday?" I asked her. "It's
so beautiful."

"And look like a loose woman?" Her green eyes flashed. "You can bet
your aunts would have something to say about that!"

Maman, 'Tiste, and I settled down on the second seat of the wagon
with Martine. Papa took a position on the board up front, the reins in his
hands, a shotgun at his right side. Étienne sat at Papa's left. Like Martine,
Étienne had always been with us. Maman said the pair were a present from
her father, Grand-Père Boutté, when she married. People did that—gave
slaves to their children as marriage presents.

Tall trees bursting with new leaves closed in both sides of the
road. How many different shades of green could there be? High in the
branches, white birds with curved red beaks bowed their heads down to
us as we passed.

"Can you see the birds nodding to us as we go by, 'Tiste? Let's nod
back." The nodding game kept 'Tiste busy for five minutes.

Farther up the road, we might set up a canopy to shield us from the
sun, Papa said, but during the first part of the trip, the shade from the oaks
and cottonwoods and a cool early spring breeze made it perfect for the
wagon ride. 'Tiste nodded off to sleep on Maman's lap.

I must have dozed off also. I woke with a start when I felt the wagon
jerk to a stop. We'd only made it to La Nouvelle-Ibérie. Not much of a
town compared to St. Martinsville. All I could see was a dock only a bit
wider than our own, a few grey cypress buildings, and one larger building
with the letters T A V E R N painted on a weathered sign. I'd learned my

letters but didn't know the words they stood for. I knew one building was a
tannery because it smelled bad, and one was a bakery because it smelled
wonderful. Papa tied the reins around a tree stump.

"We're pulling up here at Murphy's store," he said. "We'll lay on some water and a few supplies, but we won't be long. Everybody needs to take care of
personal business. The next good stopping point will be at the Darbys' house."
I didn't need to go to the public privy, another place that smelled bad.

We were on our way again. To our right, through the thicket of trees,
I caught views of the bayou. Five ugly back vultures circled high over us,
looking for a meal. The first snake I saw slithering across the road—probably a cottonmouth—sent a shudder down my back. To our left, a couple
alligators resting on the bank of a ditch at the edge of the swamp kept their
eyes fixed on a possum waddling by. Watch out, Mr. Possum! Shortly, even
the animals failed to keep my interest. I thought I might as well join 'Tiste
in slumber-land, until I caught sight of a huge black bear standing upright
on his hind legs, watching us go by. He had a snout bigger than on any dog
I'd ever seen. His arms dangled down past his fat belly.

"Psst, Maman," I whispered, pointing to the bear.

Maman followed my pointing, turned quickly, and whispered something to Martine. Martine scooted up to the front seat to reach Papa. Papa
pulled the wagon to a stop. He passed the reins to Étienne and picked up
his shotgun. He stood up and took aim. Pow-ow! My breath stopped in my
throat. Papa shot over the bear's head. Frozen for only a moment, the bear
dropped to all fours and lumbered off into the swamp. A flock of little birds
floating on the water rose in great swirls, the sun shining off the white of
their bellies. 'Tiste shook himself and mumbled something but went right
back to sleep. I breathed normally again.

Papa tipped his wide-brimmed hat to me. "You have sharp eyes,
Hortense. That bear could have destroyed our wagon and had himself a
tasty dinner."

Maman patted my leg.

We passed a few log cabins tucked in the woods between the road
and the bayou. Papa said there were a lot of Acadians coming into St.
Martinsville now, but they didn't stay in town long. They mostly passed
right through and settled in the country around the big oxbow loop of
the bayou Papa had drawn in the air for 'Tiste. Fausse Pointe, he called
the loop.

After Mass, when we went to Grandpa's for dinner with all of the Bérard relatives, Papa told everyone about how I saved our family!

Grandpa Bérard's *vacherie* stretched from the bayou to way back behind the woods. He owned the same amount of property across the bayou on the left bank and another tract farther upstream. Not many people had as much property as Grandpa. Maman said having a lot of land, being one of the earliest settlers and coming straight from France to the Poste d'Attakapas, mattered to people in St. Martinsville. And Grandpa had arranged for building the church, another reason people thought him important. Even Grandpa's name sounded special, Jean Baptiste Bérard, after John the Baptist, the man who told everybody Jesus was coming.

I thought Grandma Bérard talked different. When I asked Maman about that, she said Grandma was Acadian—her family one of the first of the other French speakers to come to Louisiana. Acadians came from Canada, she said. We didn't see many Acadians in St. Martinsville. Most everybody we spent time with came from France, some by way of "the islands." They called themselves colonials. Many of them hadn't planned to live here forever, but there was a revolution in France and another in the islands. They couldn't go back home. Revolutions must be bad, I thought.

Papa laughed off the idea that colonials were special. "Bunch of aristocrats, some think they are," he said. "Unless they work as hard as my father did, some of them will be in trouble after they finish cashing in their jewels. You can't eat your special lineage." I didn't understand any of that.

Funny thing, I thought Grandpa stood ten feet tall, but when I saw him with his friends, he was usually the shortest one. Uncle Baptiste, Papa's brother, stood taller than either of them.

"You can learn something there, Hortense," Maman said. "Looks like you're going to be small like Grandpa, but if you stand up straight, and speak up when you talk to people, no one will notice. I'm not telling you to talk when you have nothing to say. Just look people right in the eye and smile."

* * * * *

Once a year, maybe twice if we were lucky, we were able to have a long visit at Grandpa Bérard's. Maman liked to be there for Easter and stay about a month to enjoy the spring. I looked forward to seeing cousins, watching a show at the children's theater, and hearing Grandpa tell stories. Papa's parents set us up in a bungalow next to their house. We always had a lot of meals at Grandpa's, and Grandma sent us help for whatever we might need done.

Usually Papa couldn't stay with us straight through a long visit; he'd borrow a horse from Grandpa and come back home at least once a week to keep up with care of our own herd. In St. Martinsville, Papa went out with Grandpa's herd now and then during the visit. He'd been in charge of those longhorns before he married Maman and moved to La Nouvelle-Ibérie. Uncle Baptiste took care of the Bérard herd now.

We all had to pitch in to get the family ready for a long visit. That Easter, we made extra preparations. Papa said we might stay even longer this year. He said Maman needed a good break from caring for our household.

Maman must have gathered up everything we owned.

"Keep an eye on 'Tiste for me, Hortense," Maman called out when she was packing. Of course she did!

Maman passed me, carrying a bundle of clothes to a trunk set on the floor in the front hall. She leaned down and placed her load inside. Standing up, she wobbled a bit before she caught her balance. I thought she was sure to fall.

"Here comes the last load," Maman said, pointing to the burden carried by a small black woman who came up behind her. The woman placed her bundle on top of Maman's and stepped backwards. Head tipped down, she waited a moment for more instructions. When none came, she backed away.

Maman closed the lid of the trunk and brushed her hands together. "That's it," she said to the two negro men standing in the hall. "Carry the trunk out to the wagon. I'll follow behind and tell you where to set it on board."

My cousin Gabby, a visitor at Grand-Mère Mémé Boutté's next door, walked across the field to tell me goodbye. I asked Maman if Gabby could come with us to St. Martinsville. Maman said no. She couldn't take on anything extra right now.

While the packing went on, Gabby and I kept 'Tiste out of everybody's way. We set up chairs in the yard and played the game 'Tiste liked best—a pretend boat trip. Gabby took the chair between 'Tiste and me. She had a question for me. "Is Félicité going with you?"

"Félicité? Who's that?"

"The one helping your Maman. She passed you going down the center hall."

"Oh, that's who she is," I said. "When I first saw her, I thought she was a little girl, she's so small. I heard my parents talk about Grand-Mère Mémé bringing somebody new up from New Orleans to help take care of them. I've never seen her before."

"Actually, you have seen her—that time Grand-Mère Mémé was sick. She does nursing."

"I don't remember her."

"She's quiet and easy not to notice. She's small and looks like she can't do much, but she's strong. Her eyes are so dark sometimes I can't see she's looking at me."

"I said hello, but I couldn't understand a word of her answer."

Gabby laughed. "She's from Saint-Domingue and speaks Creole. I got used to her talk. She does everything Grand-Mère Mémé tells her to do. I think Grand-Mère Mémé sent her to you because she thinks your Maman needs more help."

"I just hope she's not here to take care of 'Tiste. That's my job."

I leaned forward so 'Tiste couldn't hear me and whispered in Gabby's ear. "Can you keep a secret?"

"Of course, I can."

"I think Maman's going to have another baby."

A big smile cracked open Gabby's face. She squealed and clapped her hands together. "Oh, I hope you're right." She caught herself and dropped her voice to a whisper. "I love babies. There probably won't be any more in my family. My brothers and sisters are old. This baby has got to be a girl because the last one your Maman had was a boy."

Gabby thought that's how it worked.

"They haven't actually told me anything," I whispered back, "but I can see Maman's not feeling good. That's how it begins, you know, with feeling sick. Just now Maman almost fell over. She mumbled something about needing nine months to fly by. That's how long it takes to grow a baby, nine months."

Because of 'Tiste, I thought I knew everything about babies.

We continued rocking along on our pretend journey. Gabby wasn't enjoying the trip the way 'Tiste and I were, but she loved the baby news.

"I'm going to miss you, Hortense. And what's worse, when you get back, we both have to face the business of going to school."

"No, no. Not right away. They're not even thinking about school until fall. We have the summer ahead of us and I'll be back before you know it. Summer's the best time of all."

I wished I hadn't said that. Gabby probably had to go back home to Plaquemine for the summer. She never seemed anxious to go home to her mother and father.

Boot heels clomping down the center hall and across the back gallery interrupted our game. Papa looked down on us. He watched our pretend ride for a few minutes before he greeted us, a smile taking hold of his face.

I said Papa greeted *us*. Actually, he greeted 'Tiste and just nodded to us. That's what he usually did.

"Are you going somewhere important, my little man? Where would you be traveling this morning?"

"To Grandpa's, Papa," 'Tiste answered. "We go to Grandpa's. It's a long, long trip. And this time we stay a long, long time."

"And how are you going to Grandpa's?"

"Boat, Papa. We go in a boat."

"Going to Grandpa's sounds like a wonderful idea," Papa said. "But don't you remember? We're going in the wagon; it's faster than boating around Fausse Point. We'll have only a couple ferry rides across the bayou. I wish we could go all the way by wagon the way we did once, but I don't think the road next to the swamp will handle our heavy load. The good news is I think I'll be with you on the trip. Let's go see how the packing is coming along."

Papa lifted 'Tiste onto his hip and carried him up the stairs. Gabby and I followed behind.

"You're coming with us Papa?" I asked. "I thought you said you couldn't, that you'd ride up later today, be there when we arrived, and come on back home in just a few days to deal with the cattle."

"I figured out a way to stay for most of the visit, Hortense. I turned the herd over to Grand-Père Boutté's new overseer. I'll check on the herd now and then, but Maman needs me to come with you."

Then I was sure there'd be another baby. I was particularly glad Papa would be on our trip today. Coming back home from St. Martinsville last Easter, our wagon broke down at the Daspit crossing. We had to unload everything onto the bayou bank and wait for help. We were lucky our friends, the Darbys, lived close by.

I said goodbye to Gabby. Maman, 'Tiste, and I settled in the second seat of one wagon with Martine at our side. Papa took his usual position on the board up front, the reins in his hands and a shotgun at his right side. From that spot he could give signals to Étienne, Félicité, and a couple of slaves from Grand-Père Boutté's who sat in the wagon that carried our trunks and what Papa called our "tra la la." Papa circled one arm in the air, as he always did when we were on our way to Grandpa's.

"Since it isn't Sunday, who's going to get us across the bayou behind the church?" I asked Maman.

"Grandpa has made arrangements. Just relax. You never fretted about such things before."

We passed the Darby plantation and at Daspit, took the ferry across. On the other side of the bayou, men from the Grevemberg place were waiting to help. In St. Martinsville, Grandpa's man Prosper handled the crossing behind the church. 'Tiste got cranky; all the moving about disturbed his naps.

We reached Grandpa and Grandma's house at dusk. After hugs and kisses all around, Grandma and Maman took 'Tiste and me for supper at the big house. I heard the men laughing in the parlor. After supper, Maman took us to the bungalow on a strip of land next door to Grandpa and Grandma's house and we settled in.

"Where are Martine and Félicité going to sleep?" I asked Maman.

"In the quarters, of course. Why do you ask?"

"Is it okay?"

"What do you mean, is it okay?"

"At Grand-Mère Mémé's, they stay in a cabin with just a couple other women. The quarters here are huge."

"They're bigger than those at home, but hardly huge. You should see the quarters at the cane farmers' plantations. They're really big. But we don't worry about what goes on there, love. They're slaves."

Her answer bothered me. She was right; I was starting to fret more. Or maybe I just noticed things as I grew older.

*****

The next day, for church and dinner afterwards, Grandpa dressed up in a white jacket with a sash and gold braid running down the front—a doublet, he called it. And he had a half dozen medals on his chest. He'd tried to slick down his hair, but it still looked like a bird's nest. Grandpa's sideburns were extra puffy, like he had the tail of a squirrel down each cheek.

Papa's sisters, Aunt Christine and Aunt Adelaide, and their families also came to Grandpa's for dinner. Uncle Baptiste's family and a few of Grandpa's friends came too. Aunt Christine had three girls about my age, but they didn't like to play games. They whispered to each other and opened up their sewing bags and worked on their embroidery. And although there were boys my age, they didn't want to play with a girl—until I made friends with Henri.

Henri was a year older than me and nice. He was related to me but I'm not sure how. He had a tuft of blond hair standing straight up from the crown of his head that wouldn't stay down, no matter how he tried to slick it. Henri always chose me to be on his team for the games.

Grandma Bérard didn't do the cooking at her house. In the winter, she sat in the parlor; in the summer, she sat on the porch, but always with a smile on her face watching the slaves come and go. We picked up a plate and served ourselves. Sometimes Grandma used a cane, even though Maman said she was a lot younger than Grandpa.

One boy who often came to Grandpa's was Dutch Grevemberg. He wasn't a cousin, but came with his grandfather, Grandpa's best friend. I didn't like Dutch. He said Indians lived with alligators in the swamps behind the woods where Uncle Baptiste took Grandpa's cattle to graze. He claimed that Indians ate people. Roasted negroes alive over an open fire, he said.

Henri reached up and pressed on that tuft of hair on top of his head. "He always tells me the way my hair sticks up proves I'm stupid."

"I hate Dutch."

"Don't listen to Dutch," Henri said. "He's a bully."

"What's a bully?" I asked.

"Somebody who doesn't feel good unless he can make other people feel bad."

"Well, he scares me!"

"On purpose! That's what he wants to do."

When I told Papa, he said Dutch probably teased me because he liked me.

"What? He likes me? He has a funny way to show it. Does he think scaring me about Indians is gonna to make me like *him*?"

Papa said one day I'd learn about boys; they just didn't know how to be.

Henri told me not to be worried about Indians. He said Grandpa Bérard knew the chief of the Attakapas and got along with him just fine. And anyway, Grandpa had a rifle he brought back from when he fought in the War of Independence. Henri showed me the rifle hanging on the wall over the fireplace.

"Grandpa's a hero, you know. He has medals and everything," Henri said. "He'll never let anything bad happen to us."

That Sunday, Grandpa took down the rifle and held it by his right side. He stuck his left thumb into the pocket of his jacket, striking a pose. All the boy cousins pressed around him, trying to touch the gun. Over the crowd of boys, I spotted the tuft on top of my friend Henri's head and wiggled my way up to stand by him. I figured Grandpa was about to tell one of his stories, and I wanted to hear what he had to say.

"We're not just a colony any more, you know. We've now become the State of Louisiana, one state in the United States of America. If Governor

Bernardo de Galvez calls me like he did when he was General Galvez and we belonged to Spain, I'll march off behind him quicker than you can clap your hands. The same if any commanding officer of these United States should need my service. I'll fight the bloody English any chance I get. I've fought 'em before and I'll fight 'em again." Grandpa raised his right arm to thrust the rifle over his head. "I'll take my trusty rifle wherever and whenever duty calls. She saved my life at the Battles of Manchac and Baton Rouge, and she'll save me again."

That night, after Papa told us a story, I asked him if Grandpa would go away to fight again like he did in the War of Independence.

Papa laughed. "Not a chance, ma petite. Not at his age. And thank God for that. But English ships are blockading the port of New Orleans, and they are doing their best to stir up the Indians. I guess we men could be called on to do our duty, but we hear Andrew Jackson and Jean Lafitte have everything under control. Lafitte's pirates are armed and ready."

Maman scowled at the mention of Jean Lafitte. "Hush about pirates, Achille," she snapped. I had no idea who Andrew Jackson was, but I'd heard about Jean Lafitte and his pirates. Henri told me my Grand-Père and Jean Lafitte were related.

"Related all right," Dutch said. "They're actually the same person!"

When I asked Papa about that, he said it was just a story. I should forget about it.

"What about you, Papa? You aren't old. Wouldn't you want to go off and be a hero like Grandpa?"

Papa scowled. "Grandpa talks about war as a wonderful adventure, my pet, but that's after it's all over and everybody you know is home safe. War is not a good thing. And anyway, one hero in the family is quite enough."

I liked Grandpa's stories. I wanted to remember them. I wished I could write them down. I wanted Maman to teach me to write.

CHAPTER NINE

A heat wave smothered South Louisiana on that Easter visit. The temperature soared twenty degrees in as many hours. The heat of the day lasted all night long. Trying to catch a breeze, I laid out my pallet on the back porch of the bungalow.

Midway through the night, the sound of drumming woke me up, not from the direction of Grandpa's quarters, but from past the woods. Thump, thump, thump—even and low. Not like negro drumming with rhythm to it. Each strike punched fear into my chest. Indian tom-toms? Did I smell roasting meat? I snatched up my pallet, scurried back into my room, and jumped into bed. I buried my head under my pillow and silently thanked the goose that shared its soft down.

I couldn't hear the drumming inside the house. What could I do? If I woke Papa, he would well tell me I imagined things. I curled in a ball, gripped my knees, and tried to fall back asleep. Impossible. Visions of redskins cooking dinner around a campfire swirled in my head. Would Martine and Félicité be safe?

In the nighttime, visions ruled. You couldn't confront them, argue with them, or order them to go away.

*****

"I think Grandpa heard the drums also, pet," Papa said in the morning when I told him what had disturbed my night. "I don't know for sure, but he sent word that today Uncle Baptiste and Prosper should take the herd up the line to graze on the property he bought from the Indian chief. I'm scheduled to go out with them today to talk to Prosper about how he rotates the grazing pattern for Grandpa's herd. I'll stop at the main house on the way in tonight to ask Grandpa about the drumming. My father knows his Indians."

"I told you Dutch said Indians eat people. Is that true?"

"And I told you Dutch teases you because he's sweet on you."

Papa didn't tell me what Dutch said about Indians was untrue, but he smiled when he answered my question. Maybe he wanted me to be a bit scared, to make me stay close to home. No problem about that. I wasn't going to step two feet off the back porch for fear I'd be snatched up by a redskin. And I'd slept inside from then on, no matter how I sweated. That evening, Papa reported Grandpa also heard the nighttime drumming.

"Grandpa told us to be patient. He knew we were uneasy. He said he'd look into the situation and talk to all of us on Sunday after church. That's day after tomorrow, Hortense."

* * * * *

"You know, I wasn't born here in Louisiana like you were," Grandpa said to the group of us sitting on the parlor floor after dinner the following Sunday, all dressed in our best clothes, the girls with curls popping out all over our heads, the boys with hair slicked down. Except Henri, of course. He couldn't get that top clump to go in any direction but straight up.

"You know, I came here from France, from the other side of the Atlantic Ocean. We'd been having a lot of trouble with the English over there. They blockaded our ports and hijacked our ships, which shut down any way for Frenchmen to sell to our neighbors. Then my family took another blow; our cattle came down with sickness. We got poorer by the day.

"I heard the Spanish were looking for settlers to live in their colony of Louisiana. They said all we had to do was cross the ocean, go see the governor in New Orleans, and he'd give us land and some money to get a herd started. They told us we might even find gold!"

"Gold?" A big whoosh rose from all of us sitting on the floor.

"They didn't promise gold, mind you. They said maybe. Well, we never found gold in the ground, not even by following the many treasure maps supposed to show where Jean Lafitte buried what his pirates took off ships making their way up the Big River to the port of New Orleans. You know, rumor has it that when the seas get rough out in the Gulf in the wintertime, the pirates take their ships up the Bayou Teche to hide out until spring."

That made me a little scared. But I loved Grandpa's stories. Everybody did, except Maman. She didn't want any mention of Jean Lafitte and his pirates.

"Over in France, I was a young man, just twenty-seven years old, with no ties to anyone," Grandpa said. "I couldn't make a living where I was, so

I signed up to come to the colony. After three weeks in a schooner on the ocean—sick as a dog, I was, but we won't talk about that—we came all the way across the ocean and landed in New Orleans. A foreign country, but I heard French spoken everywhere in the city."

Faraway stories were my favorites. One day when I was visiting Grand-Mère Mémé, she showed me a globe and pointed out the countries of France and Spain on the other side of the big blue water. Listening to Grandpa, I was reminded of that. I already thought Grandpa Bérard the bravest person I knew for being a hero of the War of Independence, but knowing he'd sailed across the Atlantic Ocean! In a schooner! Grand-Mère Mémé had also shown me pictures of schooners riding on waves that rose as tall as the masts of the ships. I wondered why the schooners didn't just topple over and sink to the bottom of the sea.

"The only work I knew was ranching and I couldn't do that in the city of New Orleans," Grandpa continued. "I went to the Cabildo to the office of the Spanish governor to see if I could move on to someplace else. He put me in touch with a group of men planning to settle in the back country. He gave us papers to go to the Poste d'Attakapas, the military station named after the Indian tribe here. He gave us each fifty *piastres* to buy supplies for the trip and, when we got to the Poste, to buy a few head of cattle to start a herd. We thought we were rich.

"One week later we were on a schooner again, this time sailing up the Mississippi River. We were through with the high seas, thank God, but we had a long way yet to go. We got off the ship in a place called Plaquemine."

"That's where my other grandparents are right now," I whispered to Henri. "I'm going to go there someday."

"We were young, strong, and stupid. We hired a guide who knew how to find his way across the big swamp, or at least he told us he knew his way. We paddled in pirogues, portaged across levees, paddled again, working our way west. Portage is when you go as far as one bayou takes you and then carry the pirogue on your back until you get to the next bayou. Sometimes the sun burned so hot in the day we chose to travel at night by the light of the moon. I had my doubts our so-called guide had any idea where we were. Bayous weren't where he told us they'd be. When he said we'd reach the Atchafalaya River in two days, it took six.

"We saw no human beings, but we were far from alone. Alligators, snakes bigger around than me." Grandpa raised his foot and put his hand around the stockinged calf of his leg. "Swarming mosquitos, marauding bears: you name it, we saw it. We saw incredible beauty as well. I remember to this day flocks of white egrets so thick they covered the sun and made a sunny day into dusk. A million stars dotted the night sky. I also remember lying in a tent trying to block out the night sounds: insects buzzing, animals howling, one of our men weeping with fright. Weeks and weeks it took us to cross the swamp. We ended up right here on the Bayou Teche. Attakapas Indian country, we'd been told, but we never saw any redskins. Our guide said they were out there watching.

"Later on, when I got to know the chief, I learned the Indians didn't call themselves Attakapas. They said they were the Ishak people. Attakapas means 'man eaters.' White men gave them that name."

"With good reason. They eat people." Dutch said.

"I can't say they never did, Dutch. They got very angry about settlers taking their land. Wouldn't you? And their people got sicknesses they never had before."

Grandpa strutted up and down in front of us. Even the adults gathered now. They'd heard Grandpa's stories many times already, but with the nighttime drumming going on, they wanted to learn all Grandpa knew about Indians.

"We were nervous, of course, but we hadn't run into any redskins on the way up from New Orleans or crossing the swamp. It was springtime in Teche country, and beautiful. The Garden of Eden, we thought. Untouched forests, not like the worn-out land we'd left behind in France. Oak, willow, and cottonwoods lined the bayous, giant cypress and tupelo trees thrived in the wetlands. Natural meadow spread to the west. We made camp on the bayou bank and cast nets to catch the fish we saw flashing in the stream. Poke a stick through a fish, hold it over an open flame, and you couldn't have a better dinner. After a couple days rest, we started to break up fertile black soil to make a garden. We made plans to penetrate the thick forests to hunt game, and cut trees for logs to build a shelter.

"We'd only been camped by the bayou for three days when we had a visit from four redskins."

A groan rose from Grandpa's audience.

"The redskins galloped right into our camp. Tall, tall men. Bigger than any of us. They had sloping foreheads, long noses bent in the middle, black hair pulled into two fat braids hanging way down their backs. They wore barely any clothes, but each one had a big knife stuck in a cloth tied around his waist. The tallest one, who must have been the leader, had the longest nose. He held one hand on a rope around his horse's neck; the other carried a stake with feathers tied to the top. We tried to talk to him, but he didn't understand our words, and we didn't understand his."

"Weren't you afraid, Grandpa?" A child's voice squeaked from the crowd.

"You bet we were afraid. We'd heard the Attakapas were cannibals, but don't think we were going to show them our fear!"

"What did you do, Grandpa?"

"We smiled at the tall one, and, as God is my witness, he smiled back!"

"That's all?"

"I swallowed hard and raised my hand in a salute. To my relief, he raised his stake in a return salute. He pulled on the rope, spun his horse's head, and dug his heels into his horse's belly. He galloped off. The other redskins followed behind."

"That was it? Did they come back?"

"Not for a long time. We knew they were out there behind the woods and up the bayou, and they knew we were down here. We just stayed away from each other. But after I came back from the War of Independence . . . Another story."

"Tell us, Grandpa. Tell us!"

"By then, your Grandma and I were married and had two little ones. We lived right here, in the beginnings of this house. We were doing pretty well. We had a herd of about a hundred longhorns we grazed up on the ridge. We had a half dozen slaves who helped us with the herd and the garden. We found out the slaves knew a lot about herding cattle from where they grew up in Africa. They taught us to move the herd according to the seasons. We grazed the cattle up and down the bayou and took the calves to the market in Vermilionville."

"Just like you do now," someone said.

"Yes. One day, a young redskin rode into our little village on a big spotted horse, right up to the back gallery of this house. He carried a stake like the Indian who came when we first got here, feathers tied on the top. Also tall, and I swear he had the same beaked nose. Was he the son of the first redskin we'd met? I thought that possible. This one spoke some French, not much but enough so we could make ourselves understood. He called himself Bernard, chief of the Attakapas village. Not an Indian name. A white man must have given him the name Bernard. He said he had land to sell and asked if we wanted to buy.

"Now Indians usually don't own individual tracts of land like we do; the tribe holds everything in common. When they want to move to a new hunting ground, they don't worry about selling the land where they are or buying where they're going to. They just pull up their huts, pack the pieces on a wagon, and set up camp in another clearing.

"We believed we owned our land already because the Spanish governor said it was ours, but I didn't want to take any chances. I told the chief yes, I wanted to buy some land. I said I'd pay him twenty *piastres*. As soon as I said that, Chief Bernard drew back, pulled on the rope, and galloped off. I had no idea whether he'd come back, or if he did, whether he'd come with a whole bunch of redskins and kill us dead!"

"What did you do, Grandpa?"

"Your Grandma and I gathered the children in the bedroom. I got my rifle down from the wall, and we settled in for a long wait. We sat up all night long."

Grandpa held every eye, children and adults. I liked to tell stories, but I could never talk to this many people the way Grandpa did.

"The next day Chief Bernard returned. He rode up on the same spotted horse, but with about ten more redskins he called his *guerriers*, his warriors." That word sent a shiver down my back.

"They were all older than he was but turned their heads to him whenever he talked. He was dressed up fancy. He wore a jacket just like the one I have on now. He had stripes of color painted on his face and beads and feathers around his neck. He carried what looked like the same stake with the feathers attached to the top. The whole Indian regalia. But . . ."

A long pause. Grandpa bent down to us and loud-whispered his next words. "Shu-sh. The bloody redskin had no trousers!"

Grandpa covered his eyes in mock horror of it all. The boys tittered. I felt my face on fire.

"What I remember most about those Indians," Grandpa said as he pinched the bridge of his nose, "was the stink. The chief got down from his horse and an awful smell wafted right at us. I thought I'd choke. Way worse than sweatin' slaves, and those redskins hadn't been working like the negroes do. I later learned they smeared bear grease all over themselves to keep off the mosquitoes.

"The chief pointed back to the woods. As I say, he spoke some broken French, but mostly he used signs."

Grandpa stopped to take a sip of his blackberry wine.

"I had papers for buying land all prepared, lacking only the description of what I was buying—I had no idea what he wanted to sell. I had my witnesses ready: my pal Ulysse and your grandfather, Dutch, were waiting with us at the house. You have to have witnesses when you do legal papers."

Grandpa turned to the grown-ups. "You all know Ulysse Grognieu and Bart Grevemberg. You can ask them if I'm telling the truth. Anyway, together with the Indians, we rode a ways up the bayou and then to the west. Chief Bernard pulled up by another bayou. He pointed with his stake and signaled to one of his warriors to ride a big circle—what I took to be the boundary of what he had to sell. I wrote on the deed and read the description to him. *Ten arpents of ground situated in Vermilion, west of the little river running a depth of forty arpents to Black Bayou.* The chief looked at his warriors and each one nodded. Chief Bernard signed with an X and we gave him the money. We saluted each other and off they rode."

"That was it?" someone asked.

"I took the paper to the courthouse. You can go see it registered. The X, the description, the witnesses, are all in the court records."

Papa spoke up. "And as I understand it, you never had any trouble with the Indians after that."

"Never. We graze our herd on that land today."

"Money well spent, I'd say. And afterwards you saw Chief Bernard now and then, right? You got on well."

"Right. Every once in a while, Chief Bernard rode in and we'd talk. He learned a lot more of our talk and I learned a bit of his. A couple times he took me back to where they moved, behind the woods. A bunch of little log sheds roofed with palmetto branches. It was sad, though. I think the Indians caught some real bad sickness and a lot of them died. I saw fewer huts each time I went to their camp."

A question from the back. "Other people had trouble with the Indians, didn't they?"

"Yes. The Acadians didn't have any trouble. Live and let live for them. But the sugar farmers had plenty trouble, and they still do. The Indians shelter runaway slaves and, of course, the planters don't like that. Slaves are worth a lot of money."

"The English like to get them stirred up," my Papa said.

"Yup. They do."

Uncle Baptiste spoke. "We don't have trouble with the redskins, but we know the Indians have been around. We have *griffons* in the quarters."

"Yes. We've had quite a few babies with a reddish hue." That caused more tittering from the older boys. "I just ignore their skin color. A slave woman has a baby, the baby is a slave. A *griffon* works the same as anyone else."

My uncle Baptiste spoke up again. "I've heard lately there's been another round of sickness in the tribe. I thought they might be coming in to see if we could help them out with medicine."

"No way. They have their medicine men and want nothing to do with our ways. But," and here Grandpa spoke over our heads to the adults behind us, "with that nighttime drumming going on now, I think it best we stay close to home. I have an idea what might be happening."

"What do you think's going on?" Uncle Baptiste asked.

"Chief Bernard would be a very old man by now, and . . ." Grandpa stopped. "Baptiste and Achille, I'd like to meet with you tonight. In the meanwhile, no hunting back of the woods." A groan from the oldest boy cousins. "In fact, no hunting at all until the drumming stops."

When Papa came home from Grandpa's meeting, he told us he and Uncle Baptiste were going to join their father for a visit to the Indians. Maman asked Félicité to put us to bed. Through the wall, I heard Maman and Papa talking late into the night.

*****

The next day, Grandpa, Papa, and Uncle Baptiste didn't take the herd out to graze. For the first time I ever knew about, Prosper and Étienne led the longhorns by themselves. Grandpa, Papa, and Uncle Baptiste mounted their horses and rode off in the direction of the drumming.

They were gone all day. Maman snapped at everyone.

At sunset, the trio rode in from the woods. Everybody came running out to meet them. Maman cried when Papa got down from his horse. He hugged her for a long time.

"Grandpa called it, everybody," Papa announced. "Chief Bernard has died. Every night, what's left of the tribe gathers around the campfire to drum for their chief. They laid out blankets for us. We got off our horses and sat with them for a while. They asked us to stay the night, but we said no. We wanted to get out of the woods in the daylight. They were really happy we came to honor their chief."

Now I knew for sure Grandpa was the bravest man on earth. And Papa and Uncle Baptiste came right behind.

Chapter Ten

O n that long visit, Papa had a special reason to saddle up and join his brother taking the Bérard cattle out to graze. He said he wanted to observe the rotation system Uncle Baptiste used to graze his herd. At dinner, Papa said he thought he and Étienne learned something they could put to use back home.

"My brother Baptiste has been grazing Grandpa's longhorns in different areas of Grandpa's land during different seasons of the year. When the spring rains flood the Atchafalaya wetlands, they take the herd out of the swamp and up to graze on the Teche Ridge, the higher ground formed thousands of years ago when the Red, Mississippi, and Atchafalaya Rivers flowed through here and left us the Bayou Teche. When summer heat dries out the grasses on the ridge, they drive the herd west and downslope to the grasslands of the back swamps. When the chill winds of winter blow in, they move the herd to the margins where the cattle find shelter and forage on cane leaves that stay green all winter long. Baptiste says the cattle put on more weight when the herders maximize access to new grass. More weight means a higher price at the market."

"Are you thinking you could do something like that with our herd?" Maman asked.

"Yes, I am."

"Here, your father has so much land and so many different types of land, Achille. Do the prairies behind our house have varied terrain like that? I've never been back there, but from what you describe, the prairie at home is all one level meadow."

"We probably don't have as much change in elevation as my father, but I've noticed we have different soils. We have red clay in some areas, rich loam in others, and even some sandy patches. There are differences in the grasses that grow in the soils the different rivers left behind. I've never paid attention to all that before, but I'm thinking I should."

"Where did Baptiste learn about the rotation system?" Maman asked.

"That's what's really interesting. He says he learned from Prosper."

"Prosper? The old slave?"

"Right."

"And where'd Prosper learn about herding?"

"He learned long ago in Senagambia, where he was born."

"Prosper's a saltwater?" I asked Papa. "He was born across the ocean?"

"Right. He came here on a ship from Africa."

I didn't have any interest in cattle rotation, but I was curious about Africa. I'd seen a big red area shaped like a ham on Grand-Mère Mémé's globe. She said Africa is not just a country, it's a whole continent with many countries.

"If Prosper grew up in Africa, he must have crossed the ocean in a schooner like Grandpa. Why didn't he get land like Grandpa?" I asked.

"Because Prosper's a slave, and . . ." Papa abruptly stopped speaking. "It's complicated, my dear." Papa tucked his neck like a turtle.

I thought I had this slavery business figured out. I'd asked Martine and Étienne where they were born, and they told me New Orleans. Félicité was born in Saint-Domingue. Prosper was born in Africa. No matter where you were born, if you were born black, or mixed red and black, you were a slave.

Maman and Papa looked at each other. Papa opened his mouth, but no words came out. Maman put her lips a funny way.

"This is a very complicated subject, Hortense. We don't have time to talk about it right now. I want to tell you about the special treat your Grandma Bérard has in store for you. She's going to give you a ride in her cabriolet."

"Wowee! In the cabriolet? The fancy little carriage? Oh, Maman, I would love that! When will Grandma take me for a ride?"

"Tomorrow afternoon."

In one second, I forgot all about Africa and slaves. I'd seen the cabriolet in a barn at Grandpa's, but never on the road. Henri told me Grandpa gave the little carriage to Grandma—a very special present for a very special wedding anniversary, he said. No one else in St. Martinsville had a cabriolet. In fact, probably no one outside the city of New Orleans.

"Will Grandma hold the reins? Can she do that?"

"Yes, she can. They just got a horse who's specially trained to pull a cabriolet. But I do think Grandma will have someone on the little platform on the back to help out if needed."

Whoops! As I remembered the carriage, the seat was tiny. How could 'Tiste and a driver sit in there with me and Grandma?

"That won't work, Maman. The cabriolet only holds two people. We won't fit."

"There'll be just the two of you, Hortense. You and Grandma."

"But what about 'Tiste?"

"Tiste is not invited. Grandma wants this as a special treat for you before we leave next week to go home."

The prospect of trotting around in the cabriolet drove every other thought out of my mind. "Where will we go on our ride?" I asked.

"That's part of the treat, pet. Grandma wants to take you for a little tour of St. Martinsville and then to visit one of her friends. You two are going to be the talk of the town!"

"'Tiste is going to be very upset not to go."

"Yes, I'm sure he will be. But this is Grandma's idea. She's quite impressed with what she calls your 'curious mind.' She's asked me again and again when I'm going to send you to school. Aunt Christine's girls are going to the Ursuline convent in New Orleans in the fall, and she wants you to go there also. I do not."

Thank goodness!

Not even bringing up school could lessen my excitement about a ride in the cabriolet. I'd seen the carriage looking forlorn in Grandpa's barn, the canopy folded back, wooden arms drooping sadly to the dirt floor. I'd never seen it at the ready, hooked up behind a horse. Then I thought of another problem.

"We'll be visiting one of Grandma's friends. I guess that means Sunday clothes—and shoes."

"Yes, love."

"Well, it'll be worth it."

* * * * *

Maman helped me dress and fixed my hair. Half an hour before pick-up time, I stood on the front porch peering down the path to Grandpa's. At one o'clock sharp, I heard the carriage coming—clip, clop, clip, clop, and then the jingle of a horse's harness. The nose of a most beautiful little horse came into view, a feather on his head bobbing each time his front right hoof hit the ground. Behind the horse, I saw the delicate shape of the cabriolet. Tucked inside the carriage, Grandma sat in the seat holding the reins, a bonnet on her head, a broad smile across her face. The canopy shielded her from the sun. When she pulled on the reins to stop the horse, I ran down the steps to meet her.

"Good afternoon, my dear," Grandma said. "Come right on up. We're going for a buggy ride!"

I looked at the little metal stirrup hanging on the side of the carriage but couldn't figure out where to put my foot.

"Philippe!" Grandma called to the mulatto boy standing on a platform behind the canopy. "Set the stool and show Miss Hortense how to step up."

That was the first time I'd been referred to as *Miss Hortense.*

The boy jumped down from the little platform. I stood on the stool. He placed my right hand on a bar on the side of the carriage. He reached for my right foot and lifted it into the stirrup. His left hand slipped under my left foot, and he boosted it up to the seat. Once I knew the trick to getting up on the seat, I'd be able to get in by myself.

Maman, Papa, and 'Tiste came out on the gallery to see us off. Maman had already told 'Tiste he wasn't included, but he couldn't believe she really meant it. At the sight of the carriage, he yowled like an angry piglet. Papa frowned. I offered to take 'Tiste on my lap.

Maman intervened. "No. This trip is just for Hortense and Grandma." She scooped 'Tiste into her arms and handed him to Papa. Thank goodness Papa stayed home today. 'Tiste in full tantrum was a challenge.

Grandma lifted the reins, snapped them down on the back of the little horse, and he pulled us away. Just as he did so, a wagon came up behind us. A driver and a man in a fine suit and felt hat sat on the front board.

"Maman and Papa have a guest. Do you know who it is?" I asked. I'm always curious.

"I believe that's Dr. Maugnier from New Orleans."

"A doctor? Is somebody sick?"

"Your Papa had a spell when you first came for the visit, but he's been fine since. Your Maman just wanted the special doctor to put his ear on Papa's chest. You know, doctors can tell a lot about what's going on inside a body just by listening at the chest."

Clip, clop, clip, clop. Grandma turned left and headed up Main Street toward the church square. Any momentary concern I'd had about Papa having a problem blew away in the breeze created by the cabriolet.

The church faced to the bayou. At the square, we passed up the back of the church, turned right along the side, right again into the street of markets, right again up the other side of the church to Main Street. Grandma pulled on the reins to stop the horse. She was pretty good at this business of handling a cabriolet.

News of a cabriolet on the church square must have flown through town. A dozen people gathered. Father Isabey came out of a building on the side of the church to check on the commotion. He raised his eyes and both of his arms to the sky.

"What a lovely surprise! Madame Bérard and her granddaughter Hortense have come to visit. Come on down. Let's go into the church and I'll ask the Lord for a special blessing."

Philippe jumped from the platform, placed a stool on the ground, and took my arm and then Grandma's to help us step down. I didn't get to use my new skill.

Grandma shook her finger at the onlookers circling around the carriage. "Look but don't touch!" she warned. It did seem as if a couple of husky boys could flatten the fragile vehicle to a pile of rubble if they merely stepped on board.

We walked up the path and into the back of the church. Father Isabey asked us to kneel on the cushion in front of the altar. He placed his hands on Grandma's head, made the sign of the cross on her forehead, and mumbled something. He did the same to me. He came around the cushions and helped Grandma back to her feet.

When we came out of the church, the crowd had doubled. Grandma shooed them on their way. We climbed aboard. Grandma turned the carriage around in the street, and we went clip-clopping off in the direction we'd come from. This time we passed up Grandpa's house and our bungalow and kept going to the shops on the next block. We pulled up in front of a sign I couldn't read.

"This is the joiner's shop, Hortense. Villeré and Mire. They're making a new table for our dining room. You can see our family has outgrown the table we have. I need to check on how the work is progressing."

We stepped through a wide opening into the workshop and were immediately greeted by a burly man in a leather apron. He bowed to Grandma.

"I am honored by your visit, Madame Bérard. Have you come to see your table?"

"Indeed, I have. Let me introduce you to my granddaughter, Hortense."

Mr. Villeré led us through a maze of work benches to a contraption on the side of the room. A leather-covered stone wheel as wide as my outstretched arms hung from a wood frame. A negro man turned a handle set into the wheel, buffing one side of a large piece of flat wood.

"Is that the tabletop?" I asked Grandma.

Mr. Villeré overheard my question. "Only the extra leaf, Mademoiselle. The top of the table is finished." He indicated a larger panel propped against the wall. Grandma went over and leaned in close to inspect it. She backed up and drew her fingers across the surface.

"It's lovely, Mr. Villeré."

"I had fine walnut planks to work with, Madame."

"Fine indeed."

"Now let me show you the legs for the table." Mr. Villeré pointed to a work bench where another man in a leather apron sat with a carving tool in his hand, wood shavings scattered at his feet. "Alphonse has finished working three legs for the table and has three more to go," he said.

"And the chairs?" Grandma asked Mr. Villeré.

"Six chairs are back in the warehouse ready to be delivered. Six more are in the works." He waved his arm around the workshop. "Your order is our priority right now, Madame. Everyone else must wait until your table and chairs are finished. We'll be ready to make delivery in less than three weeks."

"Wonderful! That's exactly what I wanted to know." Grandma turned to me. "We won't be having dinner at the table before the end of your visit, Hortense, but you'll probably be seated in our dining room when next you come."

When we were back in the carriage, Grandma raised one eyebrow and smiled. "I need to tell your Grandpa how soon he must gather his *piastres* to pay the bill. Villeré and Mire are the finest woodworkers outside the city of New Orleans, but their product comes dear."

On the road again, a cut-out of a boot hung from a rod over the door two shops farther. A shoemaker, I figured. When Grandma slowed the horse, I moved to get down. Grandma laid a hand on my arm.

"Not today, my dear. You'll soon enough need to be measured for school shoes, but I'm leaving that task for your mother. This trip is all for fun. Let's take a peek into the silversmith's, not that I have anything on order there. I believe the cabriolet is my present for the next three occasions."

I thought the silverware displayed in the shop not nearly as nice as what Grandma already had. She kept sixteen full place settings under lock and key, taken out only for Sunday and holiday dinners.

Grandma slowed down in front of the blacksmith. She didn't stop, thank goodness. I peeked inside as we passed and saw a red-hot fire and a rack of branding irons. Just the smell of the place rolled my stomach, reminding me of branding day.

Two shops farther down the road we stopped for Grandma to talk to the milliner, Madame LeFèvre. Gentlemen's hats lined shelves on one wall of her shop. On two other walls she displayed ladies' bonnets in a range of materials, from rough cottonade to fine silk. We had a hard time getting away from Madame LeFèvre. She was sure Grandma would fall for at least one of her new spring creations.

We passed two offices Grandma said were for attorneys and turned around at the big white courthouse.

"Let's stop at the bakery and pick up a treat to take with us to visit my friend Marguerite DeBlanc. She lives on the far side of the church, across the street that runs to the dock. Her friend Euphrosine Grevemberg may be with her."

"Grevemberg, Grandma? Like Dutch Grevemberg?" I asked.

"Yes, dear. The grandson of Grandpa's best friend. You see him at Sunday dinner."

Oh, my. I certainly had seen him. I hoped Dutch wouldn't be there.

"What pastry do you think we should take with us?" Grandma asked when we were inside the bakery shop looking at the display. "How about we buy a few *mille feuilles*?"

"Yes, yes, Grandma. There's nothing better!" Even dealing with Dutch would be worth it if I could have layers of puff pastry with creamy filling inside and chocolate dribbles on top. An apple-cheeked girl who spoke with an English accent packed a little white box with a half-dozen of the treats.

"Hand the box to Miss Hortense," Grandma said to Philippe when we had again climbed aboard.

"The baker comes from France," Grandma said as we pulled away. "A few of our shopkeepers these days are English." As she spoke, Grandma picked up her chin—her nose, really. "A lot of English settlers seem to be coming into St. Martin Parish."

We clip-clopped back to the church square. Two men on the corner hailed Grandma, and she waved back.

"Those are two of the Bienvenu brothers, Hortense. I hear they're going to open up a livery just down the street. The family came across the ocean from France to St. Louis, then down the Mississippi River. They settled in New Orleans. Seven brothers in that family, and they all fought in the war. Now they're moving to St. Martinsville. We're proud to have them."

We turned right and pulled up in front of a house not quite as grand as Grandma's, behind a calèche sitting at the edge of the road. Philippe helped us down. We walked up the path to the front porch. Two ladies in black taffeta dresses put down their embroidery to embrace Grandma and give me a quick hug. Two black crows! I recognized Dutch's grandmother, a tall woman with tall hair and a nose that would also be tall if it could sit by itself on a table!

"I'm so sorry Dutch isn't here this afternoon," the tall one said. "After lessons, he went home with a friend. He'll be disappointed he missed you, my dear. Perhaps rather more because he might have talked your grand-mère into giving him a ride in the cabriolet. You know how boys are."

Right. Papa told me. They didn't know how to be. I thought any disappointment Dutch might feel would be because he missed enjoying *mille feuilles*.

After we had finished our tea and were back in the carriage, Grandma praised what she called my "comportment."

"You were quite the lady, Hortense, complimenting my friend Margue-rite on her flower garden and Madame Grevemberg on her needlework."

"That wasn't hard. They were both lovely, Grandma."

I think I learned something. The way not to be shy was to search for something nice to say, and then say it.

"I did see you looking hard at the two pastries we left behind. Let's go to the bakery again on our way home and pick up a few more *mille feuilles* for you to share with your family. We'll circle the church so everyone can have another look at my granddaughter, Mademoiselle Hortense Bérard, riding in a cabriolet with her Grandma."

* * * * *

Before the end of our long visit, Papa rode home and brought Félicité back to St. Martinsville in a wagon to help us pack up and make the return trip. We crossed the bayou and followed the left bank to Daspit to cross again. On the way, Papa waved his hand in greeting to a tall white man in a wide-brimmed straw hat, on horseback, on a headland next to a sugarcane field. When we passed, I looked back and saw something I wished I hadn't seen. The tall man raised his right arm, unleashing a lash. He snapped it on the back of a black man running in front of him. The blow drove the man to the ground. Blood spurted from a long wound cut into his back. I cried out. Papa's face went stiff.

"That one won't get away," Maman mumbled.

"What did he do?" I asked.

Maman answered. "Looks like that slave didn't want to work today. The overseer will show him he has no choice in the matter."

Next to me, I heard Félicité breathing hard.

CHAPTER ELEVEN

"Marie Hortense, it's time we started lessons." Excitement shot through me. Maman was going to teach me to read! But wait. When Maman used my full name she usually said something I didn't want to hear.

"Lessons, Maman? What kind of lessons?"

"Sewing lessons, pet. Let's go into the parlor while 'Tiste is taking his nap. You need to learn how to sew."

"Why do I have to learn to sew? Someone comes to our house to do the sewing."

"I'm not talking about making important clothes, drapes, bedding, and such. I mean hand work, like embroidery and tatting. All ladies embroider and tat. Haven't you noticed?"

I had noticed, and I didn't like what I saw. On Sundays, after dinner, my girl cousins opened their sewing bags and bent over hand work, while I had fun running around the house and yard playing games with Henri.

"You know Maman, what I really want to learn is how to read and write. Henri knows how to read and write."

"Yes, yes, dear. It is time you and Gabrielle had schooling, but we have a problem. Girls are usually taught by the religious and we don't have a convent here or anywhere close. Your cousins in St. Martinsville always go to the Ursulines in New Orleans. None of us wants that. My mother, your Grand-Mère Mémé, is working hard to find someone close to teach you girls. We want you and Gabrielle to live at home for school. Be patient."

After lunch we went into the parlor where Maman laid out some of her hand work. I'd never before looked closely at what she had in her sewing bag. One piece caught my eye. Tiny stiches in different shades of pink created a bouquet of roses in the center of a stiff piece of cloth. The petals of the roses curled out like a cabbage. Maman turned the piece over to show me the back side, which was just as neat as the front. Amazing, really.

"I'll never be able to do that, Maman."

"Not right away, my dear. Eventually you will. We'll begin with learning how to thread a needle. Sit down by the table."

Maman handed me a needle and an arms-length of thread. She picked up a duplicate of the supplies for herself and demonstrated how to poke the thread through the eye of the needle, pull it through, then roll the thread between her fingers to make a little knot at one end. I tried to copy her actions. My fingers wouldn't do what I wanted them to do. I couldn't hold the thread steady enough to find the tiny hole in the needle. And I couldn't make that little knot on the end, either. Half a dozen attempts, and I still couldn't do it.

"Okay, love. Let me thread your needle. We can move on to practicing stiches. We'll give threading another try tomorrow."

Demonstrating stitching, Maman poked her needle into and out of the cloth, into and out again, many times, zip, zip, zip. She created a row of neat stiches. I took a deep breath. Twice I made a proper stitch, but the third time I stuck the needle in on the wrong side of the cloth. When I pulled the thread, the cloth bunched into a mess.

"That's a good start, dear. Let's try again."

Maman picked out my thread. I made a few more proper stiches on the second try, but then another mess. Maman came to my rescue one moment before the tears.

"You've made a very good beginning, Hortense. You'll do better when we try again tomorrow. For now, let me show you how to set up a tea tray."

"Set up a tea tray? Why do I have to learn how to do that? Martine sets up the tea tray for us."

"Because one day you'll be running a household and teaching the slaves how to do things."

For the first time, I thought maybe I didn't want to grow up to be just like my Maman. Was there anything a lady could do that didn't require embroidery and setting up tea trays? Every lady I knew ran a household. The one lady I knew who wasn't married kept a house for her father.

* * * * *

The next day we tried sewing again. Maman was right. I improved. After a few weeks, I actually enjoyed myself—until Maman said we'd be going next door to Grand-Mère Mémé's to sew with some of her friends.

"Oh, no! I'll be so embarrassed. I can't let anyone see how bad I am at embroidery."

"Grand-Mère Mémé needs you, dear. She's working with Gabrielle but making little progress. Gabrielle seems to be left-handed. Grand-Mère Mémé doesn't want to make her change. There's a lady in Grand-Mère Mémé's sewing group who sews left-handed also. Grand-Mère wants Gabrielle to watch her work. Gabrielle doesn't want to go without you."

I'd do anything to please Grand-Mère Mémé.

When I saw Gabby's sewing, I agreed with Maman. She was worse at embroidery than me. But Gabby could tat, even with her right hand holding the hook. She'd already made a lace collar to wear with her Sunday dress. Grand-Mère Mémé proposed I do tatting as an alternative to embroidery, at least when I sewed with her friends.

Grand-Mère Mémé gave me a crochet hook and showed me how to twist the thread on it just so. After only an hour at the task, my long string of heavy thread turned into a circle of lace. My circle needed to be bigger to be a collar, but I had hope. Whew! At least I could do *something* like a lady.

Wednesday became sewing day. The best part of the afternoon came when we were done. Grand-Mère Mémé called the kitchen to serve us *petits fours*—little cubes of white cake covered with sugar icing. I recognized the person who brought the tray: Félicité, the slave who helped us on our long visit to St. Martinsville. Félicité placed a small china plate with two little cakes right on my lap. She smiled and nodded an unspoken compliment about my tatting. She was nice.

On a different afternoon of the week, we had music lessons, also at Grand-Mère Mémé's house. Aunt Thérèse often visited from Plaquemine. She could play Grand-Mère Mémé's piano. Gabby picked up right away how to strike the notes in a pattern that made a melody. Not me. I couldn't remember the proper order. But when Aunt Thérèse asked me to copy the melody by singing *la la la la la*, she said I had the voice of an angel. Gabby sputtered with laughter. She said she hoped when she got to heaven the angels sounded a whole lot better than I did!

Monday became music day. We had *petits fours* on Mondays also.

In appearance, we were opposites. Where I was small and olive-skinned, Gabby had light hair and pale skin. And she was tall. Two years older than me, she looked down onto the top of my head. On the inside, however, we were very much alike, especially about learning. Gabby carried around a picture book with a few words in it. She turned the pages and spoke out loud the words on each page. The only lesson Gabby really wanted to have was reading. I wanted to learn writing just as much.

Gabby went back to Plaquemine in the summer. I missed her and was really glad when she returned. Supposedly she came back for school, but my parents said they still hadn't found a school for us to go to. Well into the fall, the only learning we had was lady lessons at Grand-Mère Mémé's.

Grand-Père and Grand-Mère Mémé seemed to make all the important decisions for Gabby. I met Gabby's parents when they came—separately—to visit. They seemed very nice. I was glad that Gabby lived at Grand-Mère Mémé's, but I didn't understand why she did. I asked Maman if Gabby's parents didn't love her and gave her away.

"Oh my, no. Her parents love her very much, but they have a difficult situation at their home right now. I gather Gabrielle hasn't told you anything about it."

"No, she hasn't, and I don't ask her questions. All I know is she seems happy at Grand-Mère Mémé's and gets sad when it's time for her to go back to Plaquemine."

"She'll talk to you about it one day. Wait until she brings it up. It's best for Gabrielle to be with us right now and to have you as her friend. You'll have each other for school."

"About school, Maman. You've taught me the letters of the alphabet. What I need now is how to put the letters together to make words that say something. Then I could read. I know you could teach me that. Gabby knows how to read."

Maman laughed. "Gabrielle can't really read, pet. She's learned to recognize those few words in her picture book. You both need to learn a lot of words. When you go to school, you'll read books that tell wonderful stories. I know you like stories."

"I also know stories. I want to learn to write them down. I don't want to forget them."

"Of course. And you need to learn history and languages, lots of subjects. Languages are very important. I can't teach you all you need to know. We need a real school."

"Languages? What languages do I have to learn?"

Papa, who had brought the herd in early because of a threatening storm, came into the room carrying 'Tiste on his shoulders. He took the question.

"You've noticed, I'm sure, that my mother, your Grandma Bérard, speaks a different kind of French. She's Acadian. Grandpa speaks regular

French, like we do. You'll need both. And you need to learn some German. Grandpa even knows a few words of Attakapas!"

"Indian language? Am I going to have to learn to speak Indian?"

Papa pretended to look serious, but I saw a smile trying to come out. "I was just kidding you about that, pet. You will *not* need to learn Indian."

"Creole? Do I have to learn Creole?"

Maman shook her head. "Of course not. Slaves speak Creole. But you will need to learn English."

"Oh no! I don't want to learn English. The English are bad people. Grandpa fought the English and he may have to go fight them again. He told us they are stirring up the Indians and threatening to march into the city of New Orleans."

"Now that Louisiana is one of the United States, we have to speak like Americans. As a matter of fact, your Maman and I are planning to speak more English at home. Anyway, it's decided. Grand-Mère Mémé has a plan for you and Gabrielle to go to school together."

I took a deep breath, which Maman taught me to do when I got scared. I sputtered, trying to come up with alternatives to being sent away like my cousins.

"We could stay at Grandma's and go to the academy in St. Martinsville?"

"No, no. The academy is only for boys."

"Henri goes to a tutor at Grandpa's house. Maybe Gabby and I could go to school there. That's how you learned, isn't it, Papa?"

"Yes, but I didn't learn all you girls need to know today. And the tutor at Grandpa's is also only for boys. Girls learn different subjects."

I felt hot. "That's not fair. Boys and girls should learn the same things."

"You might think so, but boys don't need to learn to run a household, and you don't need to learn about commerce."

A sob climbed into my throat. "I don't want to be sent off to a convent in New Orleans or anywhere else, even if Gabby goes with me. I want to stay home."

Papa put 'Tiste down and circled his arms around my shoulders. "You and Gabrielle are not going to be sent off to a convent in New Orleans. That is settled. Grand-Mère Mémé is working on a plan for someone to teach you two girls somewhere close. Be patient."

Well, they did have a plan. Somewhere close. I hoped it didn't involve being taught by nuns. Nuns made me queasy. I'd only seen nuns one time, at the church in St. Martinsville. Black robes clumped together way up in the front of the church. Just the robes—I never saw the faces between the white wings on the sides of their heads. The nuns bowed over their beads all during Mass. They didn't come around to visit with us afterwards the way most people did. The moment Father Isabey dinged the little bell to signal the Mass had ended, they stood up and glided out the side door of the church, and disappeared. Where did they go? If I went to nuns for my learning, would I disappear somewhere?

"Here's something you'll like to hear," Maman said. "The boys over in St. Martinsville stay in school until mid-afternoon. Grand-Mère Mémé has in mind that you two have lessons in the morning and come home for lunch. We'd even cut back some on sewing, music, and the other afternoon lessons about being a lady. You'd have time to play."

That was the second good thing I'd heard about the school they had in mind. Close and only until noon. I'd be able to spend afternoons playing with 'Tiste.

"Now go fetch your shoes like a good girl and I'll help you try them on. We may be needing some new ones for you to wear to school."

"Shoes? I'd have to wear shoes? Shoes have nothing to do with what goes on in your head when you learn."

"For school, you have to wear shoes."

My shoes came leftover from the cousins in St. Martinsville, and they never fit right. That didn't matter up to now. I stayed barefoot in the house and only wore shoes to church. Even then, as soon as I got to Grandpa's for dinner, I pulled them off and played barefoot.

But if I got truly new shoes, I'd be measured at the shop Grandma took me to in St. Martinsville. Maybe new shoes would fit. And maybe they'd come in a shoebox I could use as a prop for my plays. I'd already been collecting colorful pieces of paper, and I'd asked my aunts to save scraps of material their dressmakers might have to spare.

Wait. No paper box would make up for having to wear shoes.

"But what about 'Tiste?" I asked. "Who'll watch 'Tiste while I'm at school?"

"This little fellow is three years old! You've taught him to mind. He'll be fine at home. Think how happy he'll be to see you when you come back at noon."

Close and only until noon. Maybe I'd be able to handle this, but apparently not yet. I could hold onto the hope Grand-Mère Mémé wouldn't find a teacher, and Maman would have to do the job. I knew she could teach us to read and write. I could do without all that other learning they talked about, like history and languages.

Over the next few months, Gabby and I learned that grown-ups could keep secrets. The way Gabby put it, they could be sneaky. Brows furrowed. Conversations stopped dead when one of us appeared at a time they didn't expect. Something was going on, and they didn't want us to know about it. We figured it had to do with school, but if either one of us asked, we got the same response. "Be patient."

I noticed Maman giving me a bit of casual teaching. She'd ask me to bring her four place settings of our regular china. A little later she'd say she needed two more and ask me how many I had now. She'd ask me to note on her shopping list the color and number of spools of thread she needed to pick up on her next trip to Murphy's store. She'd ask me to bring her a certain jar of preserves when the only identification would be a word on the label. Gabby thought Grand-Mère Mémé was doing the same with her. I took it up with Papa.

"It seems to me Maman asks me little number and word questions while I'm helping her. Is she just going to teach me herself?"

"No, Hortense. Even though you two bright girls could learn a lot on your own, letting you just *pick up* the ability to read, write, and do numbers is not a satisfactory solution. Your grand-mère is nothing if not creative. She has a plan. You'll hear before too long."

If they weren't going to tell us the plan, Gabby and I decided we'd figure it out by ourselves. We collected clues.

The first clue came when Grand-Père Boutté's slaves began stacking up cypress beams on an open patch of ground between his big house and our bungalow.

"We need a little extra space for guests," Grand-Mère Mémé said in answer to Gabby's question.

"They don't need extra space," Gabby said to me. "They have three empty rooms upstairs. Let's keep our eyes on what's happening there."

When the boards became the framing for a building, we went to explore.

"I say it's a schoolroom." I said. "No, it's bigger than a schoolroom. Four rooms. I think it's a whole school!"

"Your Maman said school would be close. That's really close. Who do you suppose will be our teacher?"

Gabby uncovered a clue. Grand-Mère Mémé took three trips to New Orleans. She returned from the first two trips really grumpy. After the third trip, she wore a smile like it was Christmas.

"I think Mother Superior agreed to let a nun come here to teach us,"

Gabby said. "Grand-Mère Mémé can talk anybody into anything. I predict we'll have an announcement any day."

I groaned. Gabby was better than me about nuns. Oh well. Better a nun than no teacher at all.

But again, we heard nothing. Grand-Mère Mémé and Maman drank a lot of afternoon tea together. More than they normally did.

One night, I overheard a conversation between my parents. In the morning, I told Gabby I thought they'd found someone for the job, but there was a problem. Maman objected to the one Grand-Mère Mémé had chosen.

"Tell me!"

"Papa made an argument for hiring a woman recommended by the Mother Superior of the Ursulines. He said she's educated and has manners. Mother Superior said hiring her to teach us would be an act of Christian charity. She had no way to survive in New Orleans except to enter plaçage, whatever that is."

"I don't know either, but it must be bad."

"Maman raised her voice, so angry she wasn't aware how her words carried. She said she couldn't believe her father would move a woman of color into his household. People would say the woman was related to someone in the family, more likely her family than Papa's because Papa's family never went anywhere. She went on and on. She said she'd rather they sent me to stay at the convent in New Orleans!"

"Oh no! Do you think she meant it?"

"If she did that, Papa said, she'd be the only woman under our roof. She'd have to jump to attention for two men, one of whom still used baby talk. Can you believe Papa made a joke about this?"

"No. This is no laughing matter."

"Maman's anger took more than one night to fade. When I went out for my goodbye kiss from Papa the next morning, Maman didn't appear."

Gabby folded her hands together on her lap. "Hortense, they really are trying hard. We do have to be patient. Your Maman makes a lot of noise, but from what I see, your Papa decides. I predict we'll have our teacher."

We had another two weeks to wait before Maman, Papa, and I had an invitation to Grand-Père Boutté's for a special tea. Félicité served us *petits fours*. Grand-Mère Mémé dusted off her fingers with a little lace handkerchief and made an announcement.

"My dear girls, we have a teacher. She'll be here in a few days. Her name is Henriette DeLyon. You will call her Mademoiselle Henriette.

She's been at the Ursuline convent in New Orleans for many years, but she is, as a free woman of color, ineligible for holy orders. I met her in New Orleans and was quite impressed. On the way here, she stopped in Plaquemine and St. Martinsville. All the grown-ups approved."

Maman's lips were set hard together. For once, I was happy men made important family decisions.

"She will live in the bungalow we just built between our two houses. She'll teach you girls there."

"So, she's from the convent but she's not a nun?" I asked. "She won't wear a spooky black robe and wings on her head?"

"She won't wear a habit. I tried for that but did not succeed."

Grand-Père smiled. "Girls, your Grand-Mère has met someone with a head harder than hers! She made generous contributions to the Ursulines, virtually offering to fund a satellite convent right here in La Nouvelle-Ibérie. Mother Superior would not relent. Her sisters, still teaching or not, would never, ever, be allowed to leave the cloister."

"What if our teacher doesn't like us?" I asked.

Papa laughed out loud. "For anyone who enjoys teaching, you girls are a dream come true. Haven't you been waiting forever for learning?"

When they finally got around to explaining plaçage to us, an extra "marriage" some white men entered into with negro women, Gabby and I had something else to talk about, but only with each other. We both knew to keep touchy subjects to ourselves.

Mamselle, as we came to call her, arrived in October. From then, every weekday morning—with the exception of three weeks at Christmas—I walked across the field to the school bungalow and met Gabby. Three girls from town joined our school also.

Gabby and I might look different, but we discovered we were twins inside, especially when it came to reading. Six months after we began classes, Mamselle told us we were reading better than most girls two years older. And we could write paragraphs about what we had read, first on a chalk board, then in notebooks. I began to think about writing down my stories.

Chapter Twelve

I felt I'd been six years old forever. I got into my head that my next birthday would change my life. When I turned seven, I would no longer be shy. I would be bolder, prettier, and even taller. I was certain of it. Alone in my room, with the door closed of course, I rehearsed my new self. I experimented with different ways to fix my hair. Studying my reflection in the window, I tried on a new smile. I sat on a chair and placed one leg over the other. Should the crossing be at the ankle or at the thigh for the more sophisticated pose?

The first event of my new life would be my birthday party, the best birthday party ever. I had three new friends from school and another from town to invite. This year I wouldn't have just Gabby and a couple cousins whose mothers made them travel here from St. Martinsville. Grand-Mère Mémé planned to serve lemonade and a lemon cream birthday cake. There would be games and prizes—all to take place in Grand-Mère Mémé's parlor. The location eliminated my one cause of concern: I had not looked forward to inviting my friends to our bungalow where they would trip over the commotion of my brother 'Tiste.

Maman picked up on my expectations concerning my coming birthday and tried to make me understand reality.

"My dear Hortense, I hope your party is wonderful. Truly, I do. I want everyone to have a happy, happy time. Most of all, I want you to love every minute. But you must realize, my dear, that you are who you are. On the day after your birthday you'll be the exact same person you were the day before. That person is an amazing little girl."

I didn't believe her about either statement. Not in any way was I amazing now, nor would I be the same on the day after my birthday as I was on the day before. Just being seven would cause the first of the changes to take place. The second change would come on the following Sunday, two days after my birthday, when I would make my First Communion.

My party was wonderful. I did feel different the day after the party, but alas, my First Communion did not happen.

Gabby and I had attended the preparation class for the sacrament together. Although I was young for First Communion, Father said he would allow it since it was past time for Gabby. Several Sundays, Gabby came with our family to St. Martinsville for church. Father Isabey taught us to recite the catechism. Gabby's mother bought her a new white dress to wear for the ceremony. My dress was not new, but even more special. Maman had shortened her own First Communion dress, saved so carefully all these years, and created a new veil with matching lace she'd tatted herself. Grandma planned a reception at her house for our family and Gabby's family as well. They would come from Plaquemine to St. Martinsville for the event. We were ready.

The arrival of my second little brother destroyed all my plans. He decided to be born one month before he was due.

On what was supposed to be the day of the ceremony, I woke to piercing screams from Maman's room. I ran to her. She lay on her bed, writhing in pain, pale as the sheet she lay on, sweat pouring down her face. Papa leaned over the bed, swabbing up a mess of gushing blood with towels which, in frenzy, he pitched onto the floor. I was terrified.

"Maman, are you all right?"

She raised her head an inch. "Go for Grand-Mère Mémé, love. Run, run," she gasped, then fell back on the covers.

"Quick, go next door, Hortense," echoed Papa. "Tell them to come right away. And tell them to send a courier to St. Martinsville for the doctor. The baby is coming."

I was so caught up in thinking about my birthday and First Communion, I hadn't realized Maman's time was near!

I did as they told me, running as fast as I could across the yard to Grand-Père Boutté's house. I burst in breathless. I found Grand-Mère Mémé sitting in a chair next to their bed. Grand-Père lay flat on his back, snoring. Grand-Mère Mémé jumped up and led me to the kitchen where we found Félicité preparing porridge.

"You go back with Hortense, Félicité," Grand-Mère Mémé said. "I'll have Étienne ride to St. Martinsville to fetch the doctor."

I broke into tears. "Grand-Mère Mémé, I'm so scared. Blood is pouring out of Maman. Is she going to die?"

I'd heard grown-ups whispering about childbirth tragedies. Most every family I knew had lost a child, some many children, and I frequently heard stories of mothers not surviving having babies.

Grand-Mère Mémé threw her arms around me and hugged me tight. "Your Maman will be just fine. This business of having babies can be difficult, but your Maman has had two of you already without any problem. This baby is just coming a bit before we expected." Her hug hadn't wiped away my fears, but her next words did the job. She backed up a bit and placed her hands on my shoulders. "Mark my words, Hortense. You're going to have to keep a very close eye on this little child. We already see the character—headstrong, a mind of his or her own. Now run along home with Félicité. I'll be there in a few minutes."

Félicité took my hand to walk across the yard. When we got to my house, she went straight in to Maman. Papa took my arm and led me out of the room.

Within minutes, the parlor became a beehive swarming with women. The back gallery filled up with men: Papa, Grandpère, Uncle F. C., and some men I didn't know. Even though the day had barely begun, they lit up their cigars, puffing rapidly. Everyone spoke in whispers. I retreated to my room. My First Communion dress lay out on the chair, ready for me to slip on over my head.

I heard moans, murmurs, and mumbles through the walls, and occasionally a piercing scream. An hour passed. And another. Then quiet.

The howl of a newborn baby broke the silence. I knew the cry. I'd heard it when 'Tiste was born. Once you heard that cry, you knew it forever. I opened my door and ran to the sound. Félicité stood by the open door holding a bundle, a little bald head barely visible in the wrapping. Deeper in the room, Maman lay on the covers of her bed, pale but smiling.

"You have another baby brother, love," Maman whispered. "Achille Camille. We will call him Camille." Félicité placed my new brother at Maman's breast. "Thank God, Hortense. And thank Félicité. Call your Papa."

Within minutes the men and women assembled outside the bedroom door. Papa went in to Maman, then joined the crowd to give them a report.

"We have a fine baby boy. Mother and child are well."

Grand-Père took the floor. "Not now will the Lord take this holy woman and her child. Hail Mary, full of grace. The Lord is with thee. Blessed . . ." One by one everyone joined in saying the Rosary, then their own prayers of thanksgiving. They prayed for the new baby, but I thanked God that Maman survived.

No one came to take me to St. Martinsville for the ceremony. In fact, no one even mentioned my First Communion. The time for the service passed by. I looked at my dress, threw myself on my bed, and wept.

Gabby waited for me as long as she could, then took a place at the end of the line going up the aisle to the altar. She received the sacrament without me at her side. She and her family went to Grandpa and Grandma's for the reception. Gabby told me later a rider arrived from La Nouvelle-Ibérie with an explanation: the report of the birth of Achille Camille.

Throughout the next twelve months, I spent every communion service kneeling at the altar rail with my arms crossed over my chest. I received a blessing but no sacred host. At least I lived through the year. I didn't die while I was, I thought, not eligible to go to heaven. Soon I would be restored in the eyes of God. I started checking to be sure everyone involved knew I had to make this next scheduled First Communion ceremony.

"Maman, I know I've grown. Please go find my dress—your dress, I should say. I will try it on to see that it still fits. We may need to add another row of lace."

"Father Isabey, I went to last year's preparation class. Do I need to go through the training again? If I do, please let's start now."

"Grandma, will you have our La Nouvelle-Ibérie and St. Martinsville families over for a reception after the ceremony?"

No one seemed to take the occasion as seriously as I did. They just told me everything had been taken care of. And it was.

* * * * *

I continued to tell stories to 'Tiste, but began to give his favorite animal characters magical powers. They went on adventures more interesting than walking around in their pens talking to one another. When darkness fell, they rose on the nighttime breeze, sailed into the air, and met friends in the spirit world far above the earth. They rose even higher, crossed the big ocean, and visited the land where our grandparents were born. 'Tiste suggested the animals take a side trip to Africa to find Martine's and Félicité's families. He wanted the animals to invite them to come to our house for a visit. "They could ride here on the back of my pony," he said. "They wouldn't have to be tossed about on the waves in a schooner like Grandpa."

Yes, 'Tiste still had his pony, and Camille even had a turn on her back. Papa put him in the saddle and walked alongside, holding him. I'd never been allowed to ride the pony. Not one time. Not ladylike, Maman said.

After their adventures in the spirit world, the animals in my stories always came home. If I told the story at bedtime, 'Tiste ran to check the pens as soon as he woke up in the morning. The animals were all there, just as they had been before he went to bed.

"Our animals will always return, 'Tiste. They come home because they love us. Loving each other is very important." I didn't like sad endings.

I gave magical powers to the Bayou Teche as well as to our animals. Where trickles came out of the earth to join streams from farther north, I told 'Tiste and Camille that water sprites cavorted about with shimmering fish. The leader of the sprites decided which of them should travel down the bayou to visit us and which should stay at the headwaters to play.

"Keep a sharp eye out on our trips to St. Martinsville," I told 'Tiste. "You could catch sight of creatures with butterfly wings dancing in the stream."

I didn't know if 'Tiste actually believed my stories were true, but if he didn't, he put on a good show, which inspired me to add even more twists and turns to the adventures.

To write down my animal tales, or to record the stories I heard from Grandpa Bérard and the other old-timers, I needed paper, pen, and ink, all in short supply. I begged scraps of paper from anyone who could spare the blank backsides of anything. When I had a collection of scribblings, I gathered the courage to show a few of them to Mamselle. Her face lit up, and she clasped her hands together under her chin.

"My dear Hortense. I do believe you are a writer!"

"No, no Mamselle, but I want to be. Could you teach me to be a writer?"

"The best way to become a writer is to write every day. I'm going to find you a notebook, a pen, and some ink. And if you like, I'll give you a few exercises to help you develop your skills."

Before long, on reading and writing day, my seatwork—seatwork was what we called the lessons we did at our desks—had a special instruction tagged on the end. *Hortense, describe in detail an object you see in this room. Tell me where the object has been, and where the object will go next.* Or, *Hortense, tell me more about a person you heard about in the story we read today.* Or, *tell me how a longhorn mother feels when she has to leave her calf behind in the corral.* Once Mamselle gave me a really hard assignment: *Rewrite the story we read this morning from the way a different character would have felt about what happened.* I took that one home and worked on it for a week.

I spent a lot of my afternoons writing. I could look up from my efforts and find hours had slipped by. It took me a lot of thinking to make words say what I wanted them to say. Details for my stories sent me to Mamselle's bookshelves and back to my grandparents to ask them to tell me more. People I talked to liked that I cared about how things used to be, and they suggested other grown-ups who had stories to tell.

Maman was fine with my passion for writing—provided I had already finished my chores.

Gabby didn't care to write, but she begged every member of our families to let her borrow books from their libraries. Reading had opened up worlds for her to live in. Sometimes I thought she preferred other worlds to the one she had.

On Fridays, Mamselle asked us to stand in front of the class and give what she called "a report." I could tell a story. Gabby could talk about a book she had read. We became quite at ease in front of our friends and, soon enough, in front of anyone. Maman liked to see my shyness disappear.

And one day, quite by chance, Mamselle discovered Gabby had another talent. Gabby could draw.

Living right close to the school bungalow, Gabby often came early. She usually went to our little library and chose a book to read, but one day she passed up the bookshelves and went to the board. A little bird on the windowsill watched her; she watched the little bird. She picked up a piece of chalk and drew the shape of the bird's head, his round eye, the feathers of his breast, his knobby legs, his feet. She turned the chalk on its side and shaded in the shadow the bird cast on the sill. Intent on her drawing, she didn't hear Mamselle come into the room.

"Do you often draw, Gabby?" Mamselle asked her.

"I'm sorry." Gabby picked up the eraser to wipe the board.

"No, dear. Leave it. I'm interested in what you just did. I think you like to draw."

"I do."

"What do you usually use to make your drawings? Do you have any art supplies at home?"

"Art supplies? I use Grand-Père's quill pen. But it's hard. Chalk is better."

"Great artists discovered that long ago. Have you ever drawn with leads or a pencil?"

"What is a pencil?"

Mamselle put one hand on her hip. "My dear, I'm going to see to it that you find out very soon. When I'm next in New Orleans, I'm going to get you a sketching pad to save your drawings. And I'm going to bring back lots of paper for you, Hortense, and some notebooks so you can keep a journal."

CHAPTER THIRTEEN

Two years slipped by. Gabby and I loved our school. We had more students, which meant friends in town to visit. I filled a notebook with tales about them all. Gabby practiced drawing and created beautiful pictures.

As Christmas approached, everyone talked about the holidays. School recessed for a month. Mamselle and Gabby left for a visit to Plaquemine. They followed a different route this time, shorter and quicker. They took a barge down the Bayou Teche, across the Lower Atchafalaya River, up the river to Bayou Plaquemine, and then over to the Mississippi River. I'd never been to Plaquemine. It was a well-traveled route they told me, not like it had been for Grandpa when a pick-up guide maneuvered his band of settlers through the hazards of the swamp. When she reached Plaquemine, Mamselle planned to continue down the Big River to New Orleans to visit Mother Superior at the convent. I'd never gone anywhere farther than St. Martinsville.

The households of my new school friends also bustled with holiday planning. In our house, Félicité came over from Grand-Mère Mémé's to care for baby Camille. 'Tiste and I both invited friends over to play, but when I finished my morning chores, I preferred to sneak off to a quiet corner and write. Grandpa gave me my Christmas present early—a dictionary for children he bought from the St. Martinsville tutor for the boys. I could read and write for hours.

One afternoon, Maman went into her room to take a nap, and we three children were on our own. I held the baby in my arms and took the three of us out onto the south corner of the front gallery. Sheltered from the cold breezes that had sent our summer away, I rocked Camille on my lap and read to 'Tiste from *Les Contes de ma Mère l'Oye*, Mother Goose.

Startled by the pounding of hoofbeats on the bayou path below, I looked straight over the gallery railing to a three-foot tall feather waving before my eyes. Between the posts, I saw the broad-brimmed hat of a mounted courier. A sight from a storybook! The courier yanked on the reins of his horse and dug in his spurs. The horse reared up on his hind legs and snorted in our direction. The courier doffed his hat with a flourish, placed it back on his head, and swung his leg over the saddle to dismount. He dropped to the ground and stood before us in a costume entirely purple, green, and gold. 'Tiste watched, dazed and amazed.

"Mademoiselle Bérard," the courier called out to me. "I bring for your parents a message." He reached over his shoulder and pulled a gilded tube from a pack on his back. He withdrew a scroll from the tube, unfurled it, and read to us in a booming voice the farm animals next door at Grand-Père's could have heard. Silly man.

"Madame and Monsieur Bérard are cordially invited to attend a *bal masqué de Mardi Gras* on Tuesday, the fourteenth day of February, the year of Our Lord, eighteen sixteen, half after seven o'clock, at the boarding house in the town of La Ville de St. Martin." He handed the scroll over the railing. I took it from him.

Mission accomplished, the courier bowed to me, mounted his horse, and turned back to the path along the bayou. He thundered downstream in the direction of Franklin.

"Wow, 'Tiste. Can you believe what we just saw? Should I wake Maman?"

"Of course, you should. She always says we should call her if we see anything unusual. That sure wasn't usual."

It didn't take long for Maman to change from preparations for Christmas to preparations for a masked ball.

"First on my list is to select costumes for your Papa and myself. I know who I want to impersonate: Josephine Bonaparte. Because of her dress. Do you suppose your father will be willing to go to the ball as the Emperor Napoleon?"

"I'm sure he will, Maman."

Papa loved an adventure, even more so when Maman was on board for the fun. Not always the case!

"A Napoleon costume is not complicated. A few medals on the chest of his best suit and a sash around his waist will be all he needs. I'll have to locate a proper bicorn hat and sew on an edging of gold braid."

"Bicorn? What's that?"

"*Bi* mean two. Latin is another language you'll learn about in school. Two sides of Napoleon's hat turn up."

"I know where you'll be sure to find whatever hat you need. At Madame LeFèvre's."

"Madame LeFèvre? Who's that, my dear?"

"The hat maker in St. Martinsville. She has walls of hats. Grandma Bérard took me there when we went to town in her cabriolet."

"Wonderful. We can stay over in the Sunday house on our next trip. You can show me where to find her shop. Étienne will polish Papa's best boots to a high shine. When Papa tucks the fingers of his left hand into his jacket, he'll look exactly like the Emperor! Now me," Maman said, striking a pose, "I'll need a new gown. Perhaps one of the new Paris styles, the waist far higher than it's been, and falling straight to the floor. To tell the truth, I've been waiting for an excuse to put aside scratchy crinoline. And the dress should be green like my eyes! I really need to see the seamstress right away. She may have to order material from New Orleans. Would you like to go with me to the seamstress?"

I quickly accepted an invitation to go to town.

The day of our trip to the seamstress, Maman could not eat her dinner. We turned the boys over to Martine and climbed into the wagon.

In only two years, several new families had moved into La Nouvelle-Ibérie, many of them not French. Only a few brick buildings had appeared, but cypress bungalows popped up like mushrooms after a two-day summer rain. One was as likely to hear our town referred to as New Town or New Iberia as La Nouvelle-Ibérie, but our family continued to use the old name.

Madame Delphine lived at the back edge of La Nouvelle-Ibérie, almost in the woods. There was little to the house except her workroom in front and her bedroom behind. Maman said Madame Delphine and her husband came from France at the time of the revolution over there. They had planned to go back after the difficulties passed, but they couldn't when they heard what happened to the aristocrats. Poor Madame had very bad luck in her new country. Her husband died shortly after they arrived, and she had to figure a way to earn her living.

"She's landed on her feet, Hortense. She does very well with her sewing." I hoped I never had such a fate. I'd starve if I had to sew for a living!

We found Madame Delphine in her workroom, a little lady with a roll of grey hair twirled around her head like a sausage. When Madame turned aside, I rubbed my lip and mouthed the word *moustache*. Maman gave me a poke in my side.

Madame Delphine sat at a long table, bony fingers holding a large pair of shears. Before her lay a piece of shimmering silk with cloth pattern pieces laid out on top. I wasn't interested in the project on the table. A row of wooden statues standing sentinel along one side of the room drew my attention: lady bodies from small to large, with no heads and only sticks for legs and feet. Next to the bodies were two shelves of ladies' bonnets.

"Madame Bérard! What a pleasant surprise," Madame Delphine exclaimed at the sight of us. "And Mademoiselle Hortense. Which one of you ladies has need of a new frock?"

"I do, Madame," responded Maman. "For a Mardi Gras *bal masqué*."

"Aha! The word has reached me that St. Martinsville is to have such an event. I'm hoping to be very busy."

"Do you like her models, Hortense?" Maman asked when she saw my eyes bugged out at the bodies. "One of those statues along the wall is me! When Madame Delphine begins to make a gown, she fits a pattern on the shape, then places the pieces on the material selected. She cuts the material to the pattern and sews the pieces together to make the dress itself." Maman turned to Madame Delphine. "For this occasion, I want to be the Empress Josephine herself."

"Wonderful," Madame exclaimed. "Empire style. *Le dernier cri*, the very latest. I haven't yet made such a gown. Not to worry. I've seen pictures in a copy of *La Mode Parisienne* at Murphy's store." Madame tented her fingers and tilted her head. "I can create a pattern. You'll be absolutely lovely in that style." Madame consulted a notebook on the edge of her table. "We used figure six the last time I made a gown for you. There it is," she said, pointing to one of the wooden bodies along the wall.

"I've had another baby since then, Madame Delphine, and I'm sorry to say my tummy shows the effects. You'll have to ease out the pattern a bit."

"Which you know I can do. Actually, empire will be perfect. The high waist compliments the figure. The material will drop straight to the floor, covering a multitude of sins. Will you need a matching bonnet?"

"Yes, Madame Delphine. That will be very nice."

"Now we must choose a fabric. What do have you in mind?"

"Silk the color of my eyes. Do you have anything green?"

Madame tilted her head. "Oh, dear, Madame Bérard. I have no green silk on hand to offer you. We can check with my counterpart in St. Martinsville, but I believe the two of us have the same bolts of cloth."

"Could you order from the city?"

"The ships are not reliable in mid-winter." Madame scratched her chin. She leaned forward, knowing she stepped into a troublesome topic. "I know where I could acquire some magnificent silk. There is a smuggler tucked away—"

"No, indeed," Maman snapped, her green eyes sparkling. "I want nothing to do with the wares of those pirates. We will have to find an alternative."

"Perhaps an indigo blue?"

Madame stood up, went to the rack, and pulled down a tube. She laid it on the table and slipped out a bolt of material. Loosening a few yards, she held the material to Maman's face.

"Maman, your eyes have turned blue!" I cried.

"Wonderful! Blue eyes could be part of my disguise!"

Maman took the silk in her hands, caressing the folds. "Yes, yes, Madame. Magnificent. I have never had an indigo gown. But I've heard indigo bleeds. If we should have rain . . ."

"No ma'am. Not this bolt. Here, let me snip off a bit and prove to you the color is fast."

She trimmed a sliver of material and carried it to a basin of water, dipped the cloth, and laid it on a piece of cottonade. Not a spot of blue transferred.

Maman firmed up the assignment. She promised to come back in two weeks for a fitting.

"Next stop, Murphy's store. Hortense, I've heard Mr. Murphy is ill, but Papa tells me the store is open. They may have some masks we can decorate with feathers. You know, we're going to have to create magnificent masks to match magnificent costumes for a magnificent *bal masqué*!"

I loved to go to Murphy's. You never knew what treasure you might find stacked on his shelves. Papa would want us to bring home the latest copy of the *Bee*, the New Orleans newspaper, that he said had all the news.

Open, yes, but alas they had no masks. Maman wasn't worried. Maman was certain someone could create forms from their supplies: double crinoline, a pair of shears, and a hot iron could work magic. If we couldn't find supplies in La Nouvelle-Ibérie, we'd have a courier give our cousins the assignment of ordering mask forms from Madame LeFèvre.

And Maman knew where she would find what we needed to decorate the masks.

"These days, ducks are passing overhead on their way to winter across the water. Fortunate for us; not so fortunate for the ducks. Your cousins will be only too happy to bring a few down to give up their feathers to adorn our masks. I want feathers of every color of the rainbow, Hortense, and shiny black and snow-white ones for a mask for Papa."

"What about Grand-Mère Mémé? Will she be going to the ball?" I asked as we made our way home.

"Of course she will. I spoke to her just last night. She wouldn't tell me her costume, or Grand-Père's either. She wants them to be a surprise. She says once she went through an entire evening at a masquerade ball without anyone knowing who she was. She did ask me to see about getting forms for their masks and to share our feathers. I'll be happy to do so."

"I don't suppose children will be able to come to the ball."

"You know, my dear, I think there may be a pre-ball promenade to which children will be invited. I've heard they do that in the city now, and our hosts are trying to rival Mardi Gras in New Orleans."

"Who are the hosts, Maman?"

"Another secret, Hortense, but I can think of a few of our St. Martins-ville friends who are sure to have a hand in this."

At last, we had a project for the dark winter days.

*****

Foul weather rolled in with Christmas. Clouds took possession of the sky, hiding every inch of blue. On some days, rain fell all day. On others, *la brume d'hiver*, winter fog, veiled everything from morning through the night. Papa tried to keep charcoal burning in the heaters. The quarters had little warmth. Martine told me Grand-Mère Mémé let Félicité and a couple other slaves bring their pallets into her kitchen.

The animals' hooves churned the yard into mud. Forbidden to go beyond the galleries, our usually bouncy boys moped around the house and picked on each other. Papa, Étienne, and Grand-Père's overseer limited grazing to the nearest part of the prairie, and some days they kept the cattle at home, quieting their complaints of hunger with expensive feed. The longhorns lost weight, and the prospects for profitable sales dimmed. Everyone fell into ill humor. The grown-ups could not recall a patch of weather as bad.

Maman and Papa tried hard to be cheerful for the holiday, but being confined in La Nouvelle-Ibérie depressed them as much as anyone. Grand-Père, Grand-Mère Mémé, Gabby, and Mamselle had gone to Plaquemine. Deep mud closed the roads to St. Martinsville. Ferrymen raised the fee for crossings and frequently failed to keep an expected schedule. We couldn't even travel to church.

I had time on my hands, but wrote very little. My imagination failed me; I couldn't think of adventures for the animals or my pretend people in the spirit world. I remained faithful to my journal, however. To my surprise, I found the effort to describe the gloom diminished it. I counted the days until Gabby and Mamselle would come back and the routine of school begin again.

The day I expected them to return came and went. When a break in the clouds promised a few hours of respite from rain, Papa launched the skiff and paddled up the bayou to visit Murphy's tavern, the only place likely to have news of the world beyond. He brought home reports of dreadful conditions for travel. The bayous through the swamps had overflowed their banks. No one could cross the Atchafalaya or return from there for at least another ten days. Winter storms on the Gulf ruled out access to and from New Orleans by way of a barge down to the mouth of the Bayou Teche and out Berwick Bay. We were marooned—lonely, feeling sorry for ourselves, and as far from friends and family as if we lived on a deserted island. Papa had little to say; Maman snapped at our slightest mistake.

When Papa initiated talk of a house in St. Martinsville, Maman did not defend living in La Nouvelle-Ibérie.

"I'll think seriously about a home in St. Martinsville the next time we can get there," she said. "I don't want to spend another Christmas like this."

And although Maman and Papa again told me nothing, I could see that Maman had morning sickness. Imagine! Another baby on the way—and Camille not yet two years old.

Papa paid a price for his attention to the herd. After days out in the weather, he came down with a heavy cold. The sneezing and sniffling passed, but his cough lingered. Darkness came early in January. When Papa came back home in the evening, he often ate little, drank hot lemon water, and went straight to bed.

Thank goodness Maman had preparations for the *bal masqué* to think about. I heard talk that the hosts made arrangements for a Grand Promenade of maskers to which children would be invited. Transportation home for the children after the promenade and for the parents after the ball would be provided by the hosts, but our family could not take advantage. It was too treacherous to travel by wagon and ferry in winter darkness. We would all spend the night in St. Martinsville.

During another brief afternoon break in the winter rains, Maman engaged Étienne to take us in the skiff to Madame Delphine's for a fitting of her costume. When we walked into the workroom, one wooden lady wore a magnificent indigo blue silk gown.

"Number six has been waiting patiently for you, Madame Bérard."

Madame Delphine removed the gown from the form and led Maman to an area separated from the workroom by a curtain. In a few moments Maman emerged resplendent. The material gathered directly under her bosom, then flowed softly to the floor. Her rounded tummy, which I knew came not from past babies but from another on the way, disappeared. Maman stepped up onto a stool. Madame pulled a cushion of pins from the roll of grey hair on her head and proceeded to make a pinch here and a tuck there and to mark the hem.

"I need but a few days to complete the gown, Madame Bérard. Return whenever you are able."

"Indeed, we will."

Anticipating the evening of the Mardi Gras ball brought the only smiles I saw on Maman's face through the wet and lonely season.

One sad note, however. When we left Madame Delphine's workshop, we found a black wreath hanging on the door of Murphy's store. James Murphy had passed, but a passerby told us the store would live on. A man named Henry Pintard, recently arrived from Philadelphia by way of Opelousas, planned to buy the entire operation at the landing from Mr. Murphy's widow. The store would reopen in a few days. Thank goodness. We couldn't make it without our store, and I believed Papa would not make it without the tavern. We sought out Mr. Pintard to inquire about Mardi Gras masks. The stock boy, a teenager named Fréderick Duperier who came from the north with Henry Pintard, consulted the inventory and told us there were no masks on the lists of goods to be transferred with the sale of the store.

When we had a short spell of good weather, Maman thought we could make the trip to St. Martinsville. I believe she was more interested in visiting the milliner than getting to church. Madame LeFèvre shrieked with delight at our appearance.

"Madame Bérard, I am saved from a winter slump. Masks are flying off the shelves as fast as freshly baked bread. Some customers buy the forms and complete their own designs; some give me instructions. I thank you all for finding a new product to tide over my sales until the ladies of St. Martinsville take an interest in new spring bonnets, in this weather they're about as appealing as another deluge of rain."

When we returned home with the forms, Maman set up a table in the parlor and turned her attention to the creation of masks to match the costumes of Josephine and Napoleon Bonaparte. She dumped out a bag of bird feathers our cousins had harvested from their fall hunting and set me to organizing them by color. Swallowing thoughts of the sacrifice the birds made for our decoration, I first picked out white and black feathers for Papa's mask, pure white feathers from great white egrets and shiny black ones from boat-tailed grackles. I next separated the blue and green feathers and arranged them lightest to darkest, short feathers to longest, for Maman's mask. Maman's nimble fingers attached each feather, one at a time, to the surface of the forms. Embroidery had trained her fingers well.

"What's the sticky stuff, Maman?" I asked.

"Glue, my dear. The tannery has a side business. They make glue from the hooves of animals. As you see, I keep the jar tightly closed. Glue dries rock hard. The feathers will be so well stuck, they won't come loose no matter how fast we spin and twirl on the dance floor."

For her own mask, Maman began with two long blue jay feathers pointing out from the upper corners of the form. She curved the yield from greenheads and *gros becs* over the cheeks. Quite a few teal gave up the patches on their flanks for the perfect color to encircle the openings for her eyes. From time to time she paused to hold the mask to her face for my review. A work of art. Through the holes, Maman's eyes sparked like blue-green diamonds. For Papa's mask, the long tail feathers of a boat-tailed grackle cleverly disguised his beard.

Grand-Mère Mémé came over for instruction on how to attach feathers to the forms, but she didn't create the final product at our house. She took the forms, a pot of glue, a bag of feathers—black and white for Grand-Père, an assortment of colors for herself—back home. She would make their masks in secret, she said, quite convinced she and Grand-Père would again pass the entire evening of the ball without anyone knowing their true identity until the unmasking at midnight—including her own daughter, Papa, and the grandchildren as well.

Papa was sure the weather would break soon. And it did.

Mamselle and Gabby returned to town at the end of January, bringing with them a box of books for the school library and a good supply of notebooks for me. In New Orleans, Mamselle found a special treat for Gabby: a set of pencils and a sketch pad. Mamselle believed she had located an artist tutoring the Durand children who would come from St. Martinsville to La Nouvelle-Ibérie to give Gabby art lessons. Although we then had more students in our school, clearly Gabby and I received the most attention.

As her tummy rounded a bit, Maman began to feel better. Only Papa did not bounce back to his usual good humor. His cough persisted, and a touch of the winter chill came with him whenever he walked into a room.

CHAPTER FOURTEEN

T he day of the ball dawned clear and almost warm, perfect for the spectators and the maskers alike. Our winters could be like that, giving us abrupt change anytime. Taking no chance of travel complications, Maman and Papa left for St. Martinsville on Lundi Gras, the day before the ball. They sent a wagon for 'Tiste and me on Mardi Gras itself. We left Camille home with Félicité.

The local children were already there when 'Tiste and I arrived, running around in front of the grandstand set up on the back lawn of the boarding house that would be the location of the festivities. I spotted the tuft on the top of Henri's head. He still had it! He ran to us from the pack.

"I've got seats for us on the very first row, Hortense, right off the red carpet the maskers will walk in the parade. We're not going to miss a moment."

When the band began to play, we took our seats. The Grand Marshall—I believed he was the courier who delivered our invitation—entered from the left on his magnificent black horse. He pranced his mount across the carpet and cried out for the festivities to begin. I put my hand on 'Tiste's knee to still his dancing feet.

One by one, couples passed before us. Each gentleman doffed his hat and held a hand to his lady, who folded into a deep curtsy to the right side of the grandstand, to the center, and then to the left. There were kings and queens, Cleopatra and her Roman emperor (who wore what Henri told me was a toga), pirates and princesses, jesters and jugglers, gods and goddesses, and fairytale characters galore. We applauded each couple. I thought I spotted Madame Grevemberg, the only woman tall enough to be Mrs. Jack with her beanstalk. In truth, in all the promenade, the only people I could identify for sure were Maman and Papa, and only because I had seen their outfits laid out on their bed. I thought them the most magnificently costumed couple in the entire procession.

One of the pirates dropped his chest of doubloons and almost fell over trying to scoop them up. "I believe Jean Lafitte has been sampling his supply of rum," Henri whispered in my ear.

Following their bows to the crowd, the couples climbed the stairs to the upper gallery and disappeared into the house for dinner, dancing to follow. I'm sure all had enjoyed a few cups of rum punch. I'd overheard Papa saying some of the sugar farmers who came from Saint-Domingue had begun making rum from their own crops.

We children had a picnic supper on the lawn, and then played a variety of games. Every participant received a prize doubloon as a souvenir. At eight o'clock, we climbed into a wagon to be taken to the Sunday house to spend the night.

Maman and Papa came home from St. Martinsville with us the next morning. I expected Maman to be buzzing around our house prattling about who wore what costume and who succeeded in being anonymous until the unmasking at midnight. She said nothing at all, her lips pressed tight against one another. Her eyebrows came close to meeting between her eyes. Something about the evening must have gone wrong. I sought out Papa for an explanation and found him sitting in a chair on the back gallery, his head in his hands. He said he was waiting for Étienne to bring his mount so he could go out to help bring in the herd.

"Are you okay, Papa?" I asked him.

"Of course, pet. Just up a bit late last night." He ended his response with that deep cough he'd been having for weeks.

"Maman seems to be mad about something, Papa? Is it you, me, or the boys?"

"She's mad, all right. But not at us."

"So, who's she mad at?"

A deep sigh. "Her father, I'm sorry to say."

"Why is she mad?"

"If you can believe it, Grand-Père Boutté came to the ball dressed as the pirate Jean Lafitte."

"Really? Maman hates to hear mention of the man. Tell me, Papa, why is she like that anyway? When Henri told me Grand-Père is related to Jean Lafitte, you told me it was just an old story and I should forget about it. But even mention of the name upsets Maman. Even if Grand-Père is related to him, what's so terrible about that?"

"Okay, pet. It's kind of a long story, but I guess I ought to tell you what we know. Apparently, the story is going to follow you around the way it follows us." Papa sat up straight and took a deep breath.

"There's an island at the mouth of the Mississippi River, down below New Orleans, in Barataria Bay. The court records in New Orleans show two brothers, Hillaire and Jean-Baptiste Boutté, bought the island in 1805, right after Louisiana became part of the United States. Since the deed of sale is a court record, I guess we have to say we know that fact for sure. And another fact we know for sure: our Grand-Père is another one of the Boutté brothers. He and your Grand-Mère visit Hillaire's family on their trips to New Orleans. Their oldest son is an architect, I believe.

"A third fact we know for sure is that a band of pirates makes a practice of intercepting ships coming in and out of the port of New Orleans. They raid all along the coast. They did, and probably still do, some other pretty bad things. Not even helping Andrew Jackson defend New Orleans from the English restored their reputation. Okay, that's where what we know for sure ends. Are you with me so far?"

"I think so. We know Grand-Père's brothers owned an island and we know pirates hang out around there."

"Right. Now from here we slip from fact to rumor. People say the head of the pirates is named Jean Lafitte. Is that his real name? We don't know for sure. Some people say Grand-Père's brother Jean-Baptiste Boutté is Lafitte himself. True? We don't know. Could be a mistake made between two similar names: Jean-Baptiste Boutté and Jean Lafitte. We would like to think he's an entirely different person, or Jean Lafitte is a name given to any pirate who marauds in the area, or is totally imaginary."

Papa paused and made a funny twist of his mouth as if trying to decide whether to tell me more. He must have decided to do so.

"And then there are those who say Grand-Père is himself Jean Lafitte."

"Grand-Père a bad pirate? That's crazy!"

"Yes, it is. But people can be mean. They don't have any proof, but they keep saying it anyway. When Maman hears people say her father is a pirate, she goes crazy."

"What does Grand-Père say? Can't he just tell everybody he has nothing to do with pirates?"

"He says of course he isn't a pirate, but then he laughs. I guess you can imagine how Maman felt when he came to the ball dressed as a pirate."

"Why did he do that, Papa?"

"He was playing a joke, he says. I sure wish he'd thought first about how Maman would take it. She burst into tears at the sight of her father in that costume, or maybe I should say blew up in weeping fury! I had a time getting her out of there. She's convinced Grand-Père has humiliated her, made her a laughingstock, and totally ruined the family reputation. She says she'll never speak to her father again."

"Papa, that will never work."

"No, it won't. We live right next door to each other. We are in and out of each other's houses all the time. My goodness, Grand-Père, your uncle F. C., and I run the B2 branded longhorns together. Our total financial wellbeing is intertwined."

"Did Grand-Père apologize to Maman?"

"Yes, he did, but he did so in front of everybody at the ball, down on bended knee, doffing his big hat. Maman took his apology as additional ridicule of her position."

"Oh, dear. What can we do, Papa?"

"We just have to give Maman time to get over this. She's not going to forget the evening for a while—and frankly, my dear, neither am I. She made quite a spectacle!"

He started coughing before he finished his sentence.

Papa's cough hung on. For the past week, through the wall separating my room from theirs, I heard sound grating and grinding in his throat off and on all night long. Maman's usual remedy for a cough—honey, lemon juice, and a dash of rum—didn't seem to help.

That afternoon, Papa came in early and went straight to bed. The following morning, when I looked for Papa to tell him goodbye, I found him under the covers, only his wool winter hat peeking out the top.

"Find Maman," he mumbled to me. "Ask her to bring me a glass of water. Check around to see if there isn't a window open somewhere."

Maman instructed me to go to the back gallery and, when Étienne brought around Papa's mount, tell him Papa wouldn't be going out with the herd today. He needed to sleep in and see if he could shake his cold.

When I came home at noon, things had gone from bad to worse. Papa had a fever. He was sweating and then shivering with cold at the same time. He said he saw lizards climbing the walls, lavender growing at the foot of his bed, a wolf chasing his dogs—crazy things I never even thought of for my stories.

Maman swung into action. She told me to go next door to Grand-Mère Mémé's with instructions for her to send a courier to St. Martinsville to fetch the doctor and send Félicité to give us a hand. We had called on Félicité whenever the baby was sick. Papa was *really* sick.

When Félicité arrived, she asked me to heat some water on the brazier and bring her a cupful. I expected her to lance Papa's arm to let blood come out. That's what doctors did.

"Oh my, no. I don't do bleeding," Félicité said. She drew a bag out of the pocket of her dress and poured some powder into the cup of water.

"What's that?" I asked.

"As close as I can come to fever tea. I wish I'd started giving this to your Papa days ago. He's burning up."

Maman helped Félicité hold Papa up so he could sip the tea. It scared me to hear him straining to pull in enough air to breathe. Maman took me into the kitchen.

"I just don't understand," she said. "The doctor who came from New Orleans once had a new instrument to listen to the sounds coming from Papa's chest. He told us Papa had a funny sound in his heart, but this is something entirely different. Papa can't breathe, and he says he feels a heavy weight on his chest."

The doctor from St. Martinsville came around suppertime, and indeed he applied the leeches. He said Papa had a problem in his chest, but it was his lungs not his heart. He gave Papa a drink that put him to sleep and said he'd return in the morning. The fever should be broken by then.

Maman asked me to put the boys to bed, tell them a story, and stay with them until they fell asleep. She said Félicité would be with her at Papa's bedside for the night.

When I went into Maman and Papa's room the next morning, I found Maman in bed next to Papa, her arms entwined around his shoulders. Félicité jumped up from a chair by the bed and led me out of the room to the parlor—but not until I had a glimpse of Papa lying there, pale as the sheet he lay on. When he heard my voice, he opened his eyelids just a slit. Thick liquid oozed out onto the darkness spread under his eyes. His mouth gaped like the opening of the well. He struggled for breath.

Félicité put her arm around my shoulder before she spoke.

"Your Papa is very sick. He didn't rest until your Maman lay down beside him. The fever has not broken. I'll help get the boys dressed. Take them next door to your Grand-Mère Mémé, and ask her to give them breakfast and keep them for the day. Ask her to send someone to St. Martinsville to tell your Grandpa about the sickness. You go on to school. I'll be right here with your Maman and your Papa until the doctor comes."

*****

Back in my home in the year 1839, I turned the page of my journal. I confronted blank paper. There's more, there's more! I knew there was more. I turned empty pages to the end of the notebook. The pages trembled in my hand. There must be another notebook. I went back to Fréderick's desk in the parlor and searched through every drawer. No, no other notebooks. I know I probably didn't write in my journal daily for the next month or so, but I'm certain I took up writing again. Perhaps Papa B would have an idea where another notebook might be.

Later, Papa B searched every cranny in what used to be my house. He found none. He asked Uncle F. C., who told him he found the journals he had given me in an old armoire—the kind that can be taken apart and stored or shipped flat. Just for me, Papa B emptied the armoire, took it apart, and found nothing.

Although certain I had resumed making daily entries about my life, I had to accept the fact that at least one other journal had disappeared. I had only my memory to rely on.

My memory might be good enough. I closed my eyes, relaxed my body from toe to top, and emptied my mind of all thoughts of the present. Near a meditative state, I asked my brain to take me back to the summer I was eight years old, turning nine. When I recalled all the confusion of those days, it was not surprising my journals went missing.

From the miasma, I coaxed buried memories into the light. The physical world I lived in took shape first. My grandparents' big house down the Bayou Teche from La Nouvelle-Ibérie, our bungalow next door, the play-yard, and the animal pens. The people emerged next. My Maman, my brothers 'Tiste and Camille, and Félicité who cared for us during the crisis. I let the pain of loss and confusion come up from the depths and occupy the present. The sight of my Papa's face that morning came back again and again, a knife repeatedly thrust into my gut. Pale gray skin, dark beneath oozing eyes, his mouth a black hole emitting puffs of air.

*****

Following Félicité's instructions, and with her help, I got my little brothers dressed to go to Grand-Mère Mémé's. Félicité and I walked the boys across the field. Grand-Mère Mémé met us on the front gallery. Félicité lowered her head, dropping her gaze to the ground, and moved her head from side to side. I heard Grand-Mère Mémé draw in a quick breath.

"The doctor will be coming from St. Martinsville soon, my dear. I'm sure your Papa is going to be fine," she said.

I didn't believe her. Grand-Mère Mémé hadn't seen Papa's face.

Grand-Mère Mémé turned the boys over to the kitchen slaves and, as requested, dispatched a rider to St. Martinsville to deliver the news to Grandpa that his son was quite ill. She came with me to school. She told Mamselle she might need to fetch me before time for school to be over. Gabby looked at my face and immediately came out of her chair and squeezed herself into mine. We did our lessons together.

Late morning, Gabby poked my side. "Look, Hortense!" She pointed out Félicité scurrying across the field from my house to Grand-Mère Mémé's.

"She's come about Papa. I know that's it," I whispered to Gabby.

A few moments later Grand-Mère Mémé came to the schoolroom to fetch me. Gabby gave me a hug and I went with Grand-Mère Mémé. At the door, I looked back and saw tears on Gabby's cheek.

Grand-Mère Mémé gathered the three of us—myself, 'Tiste, and Camille—into her arms. "The doctor came, my dear ones. Too late for your Papa. Just as the doctor put the worms on his arm, your Papa stopped breathing. Your Maman and Félicité were right there with him. Your Papa has gone to heaven."

We all cried. Grand-Mère Mémé took my hand. Félicité held Camille on her hip and held 'Tiste's hand. We walked across to our bungalow.

Maman's wailing pierced our ears as soon as we set foot on the gallery. Maman came out of the bedroom and met us in the hall. She hugged us for a long time, tears pouring onto my shoulder. She crumpled to the floor. Félicité set Camille down and dropped 'Tiste's hand. She pulled Maman to her feet and coaxed her past the bedroom door to the parlor, leaving us standing stunned in the hallway. After some time, Félicité came back to us.

"Is Papa still in the bed?" I asked her.

"Yes, but—"

"I want to see him."

Félicité took my arm. "No, no, my dear. Your Papa's spirit has gone to heaven. When the spirit leaves the body, there is nothing to see."

"Yes, there is. Papa's still there. Félicité, I'm going in to see him."

Gabby was right about Félicité. She was small but strong. She had me by the arm and was winning the struggle. The boys began to whimper.

Right at that moment, Grandpa came in the front door. He took in the scene and bellowed at me.

"Stop it, Hortense. Stop it right now! Go to the parlor with your mother."

The words stunned me. I'd never before heard Grandpa Bérard speak like that. I started to cry, but I obeyed him. Félicité took the boys by their hands and led them into the parlor behind me. She put us on the sofa and sat with us until we got our tears under control. Through it all, in a chair on the other side of the room, Maman seemed to be sleeping.

Too late in the day to make a trip to St. Martinsville before dark, they shuffled us back to Grand-Mère Mémé's for the night. I couldn't sleep. I closed my eyes, but Papa's grey face stayed in my sight.

In the morning, Félicité packed us up and settled us in the wagon. Étienne drove us to St. Martinsville. I held Camille on my lap, and we both slept most of the way. We moved into Grandpa's house, not into our bungalow but into the main building. Félicité set up me and the boys in two rooms that opened into each other. She moved Maman into a different room.

Grandpa, Uncle Baptiste, Aunt Abigale's and Aunt Christine's husbands, and a couple cousins had long meetings in the parlor.

"That's the family meeting," Félicité explained to me. "When a Papa dies, the family meeting makes all the decisions for a widow and children.

"Just the men?"

"Yes, just the men. Women have no legal standing."

In sympathy for our loss, the men always lowered their eyes and scratched their beards as they passed us in the hall on their way to discuss what they called "our situation." They alone would decide where we would live and what we would do.

The next few months of my life remained a blur. Nothing at Grandpa's seemed the same as it had on our visits. We lived in a house of mourning. We ate our meals with Grandma and Grandpa. They hardly spoke. We had family dinners on Sundays, but Grandpa didn't tell stories. Grandma sat in her chair watching the slaves bring in the food, but she didn't smile. Sometimes Grandpa and Grandma went back to their room before the guests left.

I saw little of Maman; she mostly stayed in her room while Félicité took over our care. When Maman gave birth to my third baby brother, they named him Achille after our Papa. Maman turned him over to a wet nurse who also came to stay in the house.

Who tried to explain the situation to us? Who consoled us? Félicité. "You loved your Papa so much. I know how you hurt. It's like at first when you get a really bad cut. You will heal, but you will have a scar. Your Maman will be better in time."

"What about Grandma and Grandpa?" I asked her. "They are so sad."

"The loss of a child is the hardest. They are old. I hope they have time to heal."

Remembering those days seized my stomach. We had nothing to distract us from our grief. No school, of course, no Mamselle, and no Gabby. Except for Sunday dinners when I saw my friend Henri and my not-friend Dutch, my only companions were my St. Martinsville cousins. They told me they were sorry for me, then turned back to their embroidery and gossiped about people I didn't know.

I worried terribly about my Maman. Her hair hung limp, and her eyes dulled. She had a faraway look in her eyes and often seemed confused. After a while she tried to play games with us, but she didn't remember the rules. If 'Tiste pointed out her missteps, which I knew not to do, the torrents of tears returned. And I worried about baby Achille. At three weeks old, when he began to look around and seek a familiar voice, the sight and sound of Maman brought no reaction. To him, Maman was a stranger.

My spirits lifted when the family meeting at long last decided we could go back home to La Nouvelle-Ibérie. We did so, but after just three weeks in familiar surroundings—our own house, school, Gabby, and my other friends—we were packed up again and told to return to Grandpa's. A herd of longhorns from Texas had come to town. Maman, already precariously holding herself together, had taken to her bed in fear of the cattle drivers.

A few days before, sitting on the front gallery doing her needlework, Maman had looked over the railing to see ten Texas longhorns clattering down the road in front of our house. She called out to one of the herders and, in the course of their exchange, learned he was merely a scout. More than two hundred head waited in a pasture north of town ready to follow behind him. They came on the established route from Liberty, Texas, were coaxed to swim across the rivers on the border with Louisiana, and then driven to pasturelands north of town to await transfer to market in New Orleans. Nothing unusual about cattle coming from Texas and passing through our town. We'd had cattle drives come to town before. When they were in the area, Maman always made sure we stayed clear of the places the herders might congregate. Cattle drivers, free and slave, were a tough bunch, everyone said.

The usual route to take the herds to New Orleans was north of town and over to Butte LaRose to catch a barge. Cattle barges traveled down the Atchafalaya River to Bayou Plaquemine, then to the town of Plaquemine to catch another barge down the Mississippi River to the city. The scout told Maman the plan for this herd was different. They would not go to Butte LaRose. They would be driven on the levees down to the mouth of the Bayou Teche and across the lower Atchafalaya to the town of Vacherie on the river. At Vacherie, they would catch a barge to the market in New Orleans.

"Does that mean they'll come right in front of our house?" I asked Grand-Mère Mémé.

She said yes, and that's why we had to leave.

"Couldn't we just stay inside until they go by?"

Grand-Mère Mémé rolled her eyes at such a foolish question. I guessed we couldn't avoid the herd or the herders if they streamed a few feet from the front gallery on what we called the Old Spanish Trail. Although their house sat farther back than our bungalow, Grand-Père and Grand-Mère Mémé had the same concerns. They closed their house and the school. With summer just around the corner, they took Gabby and Mamselle down the bayou ahead of the herd. We packed up and fled back to Grand-pa's in St. Martinsville even faster than we had after Papa died.

After three weeks in St. Martinsville, the family meeting met once again to consider "our situation." For once, we were consulted about what we wanted to do. With summer hard upon us, there'd soon be no school and no Gabby. We all agreed to stay with Grandpa until fall.

Staying in St. Martinsville was a fortunate decision. Maman got slowly better. Grandpa resumed telling us stories after Sunday dinner. Best of all, Papa B came into our lives.

CHAPTER FIFTEEN

I don't know exactly when or where Maman first met Baron Benoit Bayard, but a year after Papa died, I became aware of a tall, smiling man who always seemed to be with our family for Sunday Mass. When I looked down the pew, I would see a pile of blond curls floating over my Maman's red hair. A big man, he stood a foot taller than my Papa had.

"You're right, my dear," Papa B told me later. "During his sermon, Father Isabey may have thought me transfixed by his descriptions of hellfire awaiting sinners who strayed from the straight and narrow, or even worse, failed to attend Mass on Holy Days of Obligation, but to tell the truth, my attention totally focused on being as close as possible to a beautiful young widow with long auburn hair, sparkling green eyes, and an adorable family—especially ten-year-old Hortense!"

Maman introduced us to Monsieur Bayard at the social event of the year—the wedding of Antoine Philippe Fournet and Carmelite Ami. 'Tiste and I giggled mightily over the name Baron Benoit Bayard—so many Bs! The following Sunday, Grandpa used the story of Antoine Philippe Fournet and his bride as the topic of his post-dinner entertainment for the children. I had this story written down in the notebook I kept of Grandpa's performances. That notebook might be lost, but I remembered the story well.

"Has anyone heard about the bloody revolution precipitated by Toussaint L'Ouverture that took place on the island of Saint-Domingue?" Grandpa asked the children gathered at his feet on the Sunday after the Fournet-Ami wedding. No one spoke up. If someone had, we'd have hooted him down. We wouldn't allow anyone to stop Grandpa from recounting his version of any event. A story about a bloody revolution would be especially exciting to hear. Grandpa provided drama and juicy details, even if, as I later learned, his stories were not always historically accurate.

"Many years ago, a lot of our friends and relatives grew sugarcane in the Caribbean, including on the island of Saint-Domingue. As you know, sugar work is done by slaves and is hard, hard. For years, overseers successfully dealt with slave unrest on the plantations in Saint-Domingue by prompt application of the lash, but some slaves managed to escape from the plantations and hide out in the mountains to the east.

"One day, without warning, a band of escapees under the leadership of a slave named Toussaint L'Ouverture came running down from the hills and began a wholesale slaughter of the white sugarcane farmers and their families. Really, all white people, whether they were plantation owners or not. The bandits honed their cane knives as sharp as any sword and lopped off heads right and left. Whack, whack."

Grandpa reached for the sword he kept over the fireplace and held it in his right hand. He danced to the right and to the left, demonstrating the whacks by slicing the air with his sword.

"Every white person who could manage to run, ride, or travel headed to the harbor at Cap-Français to find a ship to take them away to safety. One man who did so—actually a rancher not a sugarcane farmer—was Antoine Philippe Fournet, the man who was married at our church yesterday afternoon. Antoine Philippe Fournet,"—Grandpa loved the ring of the name—"found berth on a ship bound for New Orleans. He left Saint-Domingue in such a hurry he still wore his gold-tipped boots!"

"Real gold on his boots?" Dutch asked.

"Yes, indeed. Antoine Philippe Fournet escaped the slaughter, but he did not escape adventure. As bad luck would have it, his ship didn't make it to its destination. A dreadful storm blew the ship west. The ship wrecked on rocky shoals off the coast of Galveston. Still wearing his gold-toed boots, Antoine Philippe Fournet leapt into the raging sea and swam to shore."

"No way! Swim in heavy boots?" Dutch again. A chorus of hisses told Dutch to be quiet. Grandpa didn't miss a beat.

"You saw him yesterday, Dutch. A powerful man, he is. All that happened almost fifteen years ago. It took Antoine Philippe Fournet fifteen years to put his life together, acquire a herd of longhorns of his own, and drive them across the rivers and into Louisiana. On the way to St. Martinsville, he passed through the town of Natchitoches and met the woman who would become his bride: Carmelite Ami. They came to St. Martinsville to be married at our church, L'Eglise des Attakapas, and settle among us. He is a brave—and now very happy—man."

Grandpa's stories were always worth the wait.

During this period in my life, Félicité stepped into a different role in the family. Maman, first immobilized by her grief and then besotted with her new love (neither of which conditions put her children at the front of her mind), hardly noticed us. Félicité was our slave of course, taking instructions from our grand-mères, but whatever she was doing, she listened to our concerns. When I knelt at my bedside to ask the Blessed Virgin to protect my family, I included Félicité in the list—because she was the one at my side. Following Gabby's advice, I didn't share my thoughts about her importance with anyone, except Gabby.

"I know, Hortense," Gabby said. "Remember my warning. You'll get in trouble if you even bring up the subject of slavery." I remembered.

When we returned home, we had almost a dozen girls in our school and harder lessons. I wrote my stories. We continued to visit St. Martinsville most Sundays and always seemed to be in the company of Mr. Bayard. When he sat next to Maman in church, her eyes sparkled the way they had when my father had been alive. I told Gabby about what I saw, that I thought I was seeing that emotion I'd heard about—love. In my mind, I thought when love happened it came out in the eyes.

With Papa gone, we were a family of five: Maman, 'Tiste, me, and two little brothers. Two years later, when Maman told us she and Mr. Bayard planned to marry, I had a tinge of pain that he would be taking the place of my Papa, but only a twinge. I had warmed to him from the first day we met. My brothers and I decided we would call him Papa B because of all those Bs in his name. He came to live in our house in La Nouvelle-Ibérie next to Grand-Père and Grand-Mère Mémé. He and Maman made plans to build a bigger house next door on family land. And they started to add to Maman's crop of babies; another baby boy came a year or so after they married. Félicité came to our house every day now, but she continued to spend most nights in her cabin at Grand-Père's.

I remembered what Félicité said at the time. "Your Maman is very lucky. Not everyone has a second chance at happiness."

There was a story there. I hoped one day I'd hear it.

Félicité didn't hug me the way she used to when there was no one around. She started to call me "Miss."

* * * * *

Félicité was right about loss. The wound of my Papa's death healed, leaving a scar. But I soon had to take another wound. Two years after Maman married Papa B, Gabby returned from a holiday in Plaquemine with an announcement that knocked me back on my heels. I didn't need a journal to bring back the memory of how I felt. I recalled every detail. We were sitting on the back gallery watching my new baby brother when she made a declaration.

"Hortense, I'm going to be married."

"Of course you will, Gabby. One day we will both marry. We won't be able to spend all our time together the way we do now, but we'll have husbands. And we'll have children. Do you think our children will know each other, maybe be friends like we are?"

"No, Hortense. I'm not talking about some way off time in the future. I'm going to marry soon."

"What? What are you saying? You're way too young to marry."

"Not *right* away. When I'm sixteen. My parents have arranged for me to be married when I'm sixteen."

"Arranged?" Gabby had talked about being married. We both hoped to marry when we fell in love with somebody.

"Yes. They've talked to the Dumond family and they all agree that I will marry their son Gerard when I am sixteen."

I did some quick calculations. Gabby wouldn't be sixteen for over a year. This was just some thought she had about sometime in the future.

But then she finished her declaration.

"I won't be coming back to school after the summer. I'm going to live with my mother for a year and be married after my birthday the following fall."

At that news, the reality sank in. I burst into tears and threw myself into her arms. "You can't do this, Gabby. I've never heard you say you loved somebody. You can't marry someone you don't love." I was sputtering incoherently.

"I think I will love him, Hortense. I've known Gerard Dumond forever. He's older than I am—not very old or anything—ten years older. He's handsome. Everyone in Plaquemine thinks he's a great catch. His family has a plantation on the river, and——"

"Stop it! This is madness. A plantation? He's a cane farmer? Who will you talk to about books and everything?"

Gabby laughed out loud. "He reads as much or more than we do, Hortense. He went to school with the Jesuits in New Orleans. I know you will like him a lot. We've talked about you. I will miss you so much, of course, but after we're married you can come visit and stay as long as you like."

I had never been able to visit Gabby and that always bothered her. I knew she wanted me to visit, but she didn't seem to have one home. Sometimes she lived with her mother and sometimes with her father.

Gabby seemed totally happy with her plan. I took those deep breaths Maman had recommended so many years ago as a way to come back from the edge. Gabby had been sent to live with her Grand-Mère for most of her life. Finally, she would have a chance for a permanent home. I'd heard talk that Grand-Mère Mémé and Grand-Père weren't well and were talking about spending more time with Aunt Thérèse in Plaquemine. Maybe Gabby was doing this because she didn't have any place to go.

"You know you can come live with me anytime you want. My parents would love to have you."

Gabby hugged me very hard. "No, I really want to marry Gerard."

I swallowed to get a grip on my emotions. "Then that's exactly what I want also." I began to say a few of the things I should have said when she first made her announcement.

That night I talked with Papa B for a long time. I was going to lose one confidante, but with mother's marriage, I had gained another. Papa B and I talked a lot.

"I know of the Dumonds, Hortense. Very good people. The family has a large plantation, maybe close to a hundred slaves. It's not far from the Andry plantation where they had that dreadful revolt and retribution, but people tell me the Dumonds have a kind overseer. There's never been any trouble there."

A hundred slaves?

"But Gabby pretty much admitted to me she doesn't love him. She says she will. That doesn't make sense."

"Love comes in many forms, my dear. Not every person gets as silly as I am about your Maman."

Yet, years later, I did fall in love—with Fréderick Duperier, the most charming and handsomest man on the earth. I saw love in his eyes and I'm quite sure love showed in mine.

PART III

September 1839

CHAPTER SIXTEEN

"**D**o you have the pony yet," Little Fréderick called out to me as Papa B's new skiff pulled up at the dock. "Remember? You promised!"

Papa B returned Aphonsine and little Fréderick after their visit at his house while our household recovered from our all-night effort to save Patrick. Yes, I had promised, in a moment of weakness, and Little Fréderick thought I'd had nothing to do except shop for a pony! That was being a six-year old-boy. I threw up my arms in surrender.

"Give me time, son. We'll see what we can find next week. No pony as yet, but I think you'll find a surprise under the back gallery."

"What is it?"

"Go see for yourself."

Little Fréderick tolerated a hug and scampered up the path. He shrieked with delight when he found his dog Ghost under the house with three puppies nursing on her teats, two pure white like their mother, the third coal black. Blessed events in our animal yard happened frequently, which is one of the reasons I needed Jacques, especially for the big animals. One of the puppies would go to Papa Bs to help with the herd.

Alphonsine climbed out of the skiff more slowly, carrying a cloth bag I didn't recognize. She lingered at my side.

"What do you have there, my girl?" I asked.

She opened the bag and pulled out a square of stiff cloth. Stitches filled the holes three inches by three inches in the center. She dipped her chin. "Grand-Maman is teaching me how to sew."

I examined the cloth back and front. "This is very fine work! Do you like to embroider?"

A shy smile. "I love it."

My arm encircled her shoulders. "My dear, Alph! I believe you've saved the throne!"

"Throne? What throne, Mama?"

"I'm sorry, dear. That's just an expression. I'm a disappointment to your Grand-Maman because I never could do what ladies are supposed to do—embroider and tat. Grand-Maman tried so hard but I just couldn't master the technique. At ten years old, you do better work than I ever did. Grand-Maman must have loved your visit."

"She said so, many times." Alphonsine tucked her work back in the bag. "I want to show Félicité."

Alphonsine did a couple skip-steps crossing the gallery to the kitchen.

Today, I felt confident that we had escaped from the clutches of that scourge Félicité called yellow jack. Yesterday, the second morning after Patrick's fever broke, I was still reluctant to have the children come home. I had Jacques take me down the bayou to join them at Maman's for lunch. I saw for myself that what Papa B and Maman had been telling me was true. Freedom from chores and lessons with the tutor, along with the company of eight- and nine-year-old Hypolite and Alfred, and their pony, more than made up for being away from home. Especially the pony.

Little Fréderick said he'd be begging me to come home if we had a pony. I'd find one somewhere. It was hard to resist that little fellow.

"Tell me if I'm interrupting anything, Hortense," Papa B said as he tied off the skiff. "I want to congratulate you again on your accomplishment—and show off my new boat. She's bigger than the old one, but I can still manage her by myself."

I leaned over the gunwale to look into the belly of the skiff. "And now you can carry two mostly grown children and more tools from your house to mine. Come on in. The coffee's waiting."

Together, we started up the path. "Everyone at your house is still healthy, right?" I asked.

"Yes, indeed. Your Maman, our children, and everyone next door, including the slaves in the quarters. By the way, I've sent word up the bayou to your Alfred's school. We may not know how yellow fever passes from one person to another, but we're certain rumors fly through the air. If he hasn't already heard about the sickness down here, he soon will. And at thirteen years old, he knows enough to worry. I told him we're all well and haven't had any new reports of fever."

"Thank you for thinking of Alfred. Every day I'm feeling more confident about what Félicité told us about how fever spreads. She says it just skips around, and is not spread by being close to someone with the disease. We physically cared for Patrick and we have no symptoms. That proves it. By the way, I wish Fréderick could have seen me." I saw Papa B raise his eyebrows. "Okay. I know what you're thinking. If Fréderick were still here, I probably wouldn't have been so bold. I've just gotten in the habit of doing everything."

Papa B laughed. "No one, not even I, could have imagined a matron of La Nouvelle-Ibérie joining a band of slaves to nurse another slave through yellow fever."

"I don't know how God moves in our lives, Papa B, but I believe He was with me on this journey. I'm happy to be running the household again, but I won't forget that night—ever. You know we're expecting all your family for a celebration supper Friday night."

"Maman told me. Around five thirty, I understand, so we can catch the last ferry across the bayou to go home. There'll be too many people for my new skiff." Papa B lowered his eyebrows with a question. "How is the celebration going to work out?"

"You'll see. I have some ideas."

Papa B appeared to be in no hurry to leave, so I took advantage. If anyone could give me counsel, it was my stepfather. I'd been turning something over in my mind since I woke up the morning before.

"Do you have a few minutes?" I asked. "Perhaps you can help me think through a situation that is troubling me."

"I have time, my dear. Today we took the herd to a patch of prairie close to the house. I just have to be home in time to get them back in the corral. First, let me make a pass by the addition to drop off some tools for Jacques."

"Don't hurry. When you're done, meet me in the front parlor where we won't be disturbed."

"This time I'll sit on the divan. I don't want to crack another of your little French chairs!"

"Please stop apologizing for that, Papa B. That must have been a year ago."

When we were settled in the parlor, I took a deep breath. "I think I want to do something more for Félicité."

"Really?" His bushy eyebrows rose a finger width. "Because of how she helped you with Patrick's illness?"

"Yes, and for other reasons. I care about Patrick, of course, and the loss of a slave who'd been sold, even an old one, would've been a hard hit financially. I can't afford to buy a replacement. You can imagine how scared I am about an outbreak of the bad fever in the quarters. So often the buyers are given time to pay and sometimes they arrange to pay in installments. It just depends on what they agree to, but once the hammer goes down the seller is responsible."

"I understand. You're fortunate Félicité knows what to do for fevers."

"Félicité is amazing. This is the second time she's pulled me through a tough situation. Do you know how she stepped in after my father passed?"

"I know some, but not a lot. Your Maman doesn't like to talk about that time, which I can understand."

"She wants to forget those dark days." I took Papa B's hand. "Usually Maman doesn't worry about thinking before she speaks. She's impulsive. I'm glad she has the discretion not to tell you about what a devastating blow she suffered when she lost her husband. That's all history now. I'm sure you're aware you've given Maman the happiness she never thought would come her way again."

"I feel the same. Your mother is a second chance for me too. We are two lucky people. I thank God every day for our good fortune. But tell me whatever you want about the time Félicité saved you before."

I gave Papa B a condensed version of how, for over a year after my father passed, Félicité not only took care of us, she became like our mother.

"It's apparent I don't treat her as I treat the other slaves. She has her own cabin. I don't give her heavy work to do. But is that enough?"

"Enough? What are you thinking about doing for her?"

I moved up to the edge of my chair—and the edge of the topic my childhood friend Gabby told me never to talk about. Did Papa B suspect what I might be considering? What would he think about it? I studied what I could see of his expression beneath his forest of facial hair. I couldn't tell. I took a deep breath.

"I think it grossly unfair for someone like Félicité to be a slave. I'm thinking about giving her freedom."

A smile crashed through the barrier of Papa B's *grande moustache,* as Alfred called the thicket around his lips that seemed to grow more luxuriant every year. "Well, my dear, you've surprised me there!"

"I would have to support her, of course. She's probably sixty years old. She could hardly be expected to earn a living out in the world. Without education and training, even young slaves who are freed are at a terrible disadvantage. I've done a lot of thinking these past six months, Papa B. The whole system of slavery is a problem."

"My dear Hortense. You'd be in a terrible fix without slaves to help you operate your household."

"I know, I know. I've already asked you to help me keep Jacques. With fall around the corner, I'm worrying about the physical work involved in cutting enough timber to keep us in a supply of charcoal. I may have difficulty with some people owning others, but I am, in fact, no different from the cane farmers whose economic existence depends on slavery. I need my slaves."

"I was trying to think of a way to say the same thing to you without hurting your feelings."

"Don't hesitate to tell me anything, Papa B. I'm grateful to have someone to talk to. I can't discuss this with Maman."

"Because her first thought is to see to it you have everything you might need for your security."

"I know. Maman truly puts the interests of her children first. She drilled into us from the beginning to be kind always, but is that enough for someone who has done as much as Félicité for my family? I can't even discuss this topic with my best friend Susanne. Their plantation depends on the backbreaking labor of a large number of slaves in their sugarcane fields. Gabby and I used to talk about the subject, but she married a man with three times as many slaves as Susanne and Max have. I worry about that. Occasional rumors of problems on the big plantations over there on the river drift our way, and also the violent measures planters take to nip trouble in the bud. I know long ago you told me Gabby's husband's family had a reputation for being kind masters, but when trouble begins, it spreads."

Papa B struck his forehead with his fingers. He reached into a pocket in his jacket and pulled out a battered-up envelope. "I totally forgot, my dear. The postmaster gave me a letter for you from Gabrielle."

I clutched the letter to my chest. "Thank you! Oh, how I miss her. I feel so cut off from my friend. We write often, but it's not the same as talking. She wrote me after Fréderick passed and said she would come visit me soon, but she never followed up. I haven't heard from her since. I've wondered why. That was six months ago now." I looked at the postmark before I set the letter on the end table. I shook my head. "This letter has been traveling for five weeks. Gabby probably knows nothing about the fever."

"Go ahead and open it now, if you'd like. I don't mind."

"No. I'll curl up and savor hearing from her later. I would rather talk to you about Félicité."

"Do you know if Félicité would want to be free?" Papa B asked.

"Wouldn't anyone rather be free than be a slave?"

"Perhaps not. It's scary out there. Have you ever heard her talk about freedom?"

"No, I haven't."

Papa B pulled on one drooping end of his mustache. "There are a couple other considerations for you to think about."

I sat back in my chair. "Tell me."

"You know you'd be criticized. Some people feel threatened when a prominent person such as yourself demonstrates objection to the system. You've probably noticed most acts freeing slaves come in people's wills, when the owner will no longer be around to hear what people have to say."

"I appreciate you putting that on the list of what I should think about, but unlike Maman, I'm not going to take any notice of what people might think."

"Okay. Last consideration. A legal problem. You may not own Félicité."

"What? I may not own her? She's been with me forever. I thought Grand-Père and Grand-Mère Mémé gave her to me when I married. She'd always lived at Grand-Père's, but when I moved into this house, she came with me."

"We all thought you owned her, but I can't find any record to prove that. Here's all I know. Grand-Père died shortly after you and Fréderick married. The inventory of his succession listed Félicité as one of his slaves. Your Uncle F. C. bought Félicité at Grand-Père's succession sale, the price to be paid in two installments, one the first of April, and the second on April 1 of the following year. You know, of course, that slaves are property that has to be accounted for."

"I know, but she has lived with us since we married. She must be mine, and I've told her so. If not me, who else could own her?"

"The list of your grandfather's property is not the only recorded document concerning Félicité. After the sale to your uncle, the rest of the family filed a paper in the courthouse saying that if Uncle F. C. didn't make the payments due each of the following two years, they'd stand good for her price."

"What does that mean?"

"For one thing, it means they realized Félicité's value. They wanted to be sure she didn't leave the family."

"I'm happy about that."

"Your Maman and I had only been married a couple years then, and I don't remember paying attention to any of the discussions. I do know the family didn't make any such commitment about any of the other slaves who were sold. Here's the problem. We don't know if Uncle F. C. paid her price. If he made the payments, he owns her. If he didn't make the payments, perhaps she still belongs to Grand-Père Boutté's heirs. That would be Maman, your Aunt Thérèse, and your Uncle F. C. We don't have a record of anything legal having been done since."

A crease dented the space between Papa B's eyebrows.

"Considering her long service, I think Aunt Thérèse and Uncle F. C. would cooperate in what you want to do, but I can't be certain. We'd have to ask them. I don't want to ask any questions until you've made up your mind about what *you* want to do—and until we know if Félicité would want to be free."

"I guess I'd first have to tell her I have no record saying she's mine. She is so attached to my children, this news will be very upsetting. Before I do that, is there a way you could find out if Aunt Thérèse and Uncle F. C. would be willing to free her? I think Maman would agree."

"Right off, I can't think of a way without telling your aunt and uncle they might own her. Thérèse's husband would make the decision for her, and I think he would cooperate. Who knows what your Uncle F. C. or one of his creditors would do with the information."

I felt a flush. "Is it possible they might want to claim her? Could they do that?"

"Smart girl, you are. I suppose they could."

"That would be devastating."

Papa B folded his hands on his chest. "Let's both give all of this some more thought."

"Yes. We can talk more. You know, without Fréderick to talk to . . ." I swallowed hard to keep control of the lump in the back of my throat.

Ready to go back down to his boat, Papa B hugged me for a long time. And he had a few parting words about the fever.

"I should tell you that the postmaster says there are a couple people in town who say they have headaches."

"Psht! There're always people having a headache. Nervousness, that's what I think. Nobody's come down with fever for at least a week."

"Right. But we do need to be vigilant. Remember Félicité gives a lot of the credit for your success with Patrick to starting treatment early."

"Oh, yes. I know. I think everyone here is tired of me asking them how they're feeling."

"At my house too. My sassy Hypolite starts each day by giving me a salute and a health report."

* * * * *

After Papa B left, I retrieved Gabby's letter and tore it open to see what she had to say.

> *My dear, dear Hortense,*
>
> *I have very sad news. The darling little girl we named after you passed away a few days after her second birthday. Until then, I had been so blessed. I have six healthy children, Gerard and I are well, the crop is good. But it is very hard to count your blessings when you bury a child, especially one born so long after the others. I think mothers love best the child who needs them the most. A month has passed. I am just now going out and able to write these sad words.*
>
> *She was so sweet. I still see her in every corner of this house. As you know, she was sickly since her birth. The doctors told me she would outgrow her problems. She learned to walk and seemed on the mend, then she came down with a bad cough. She had no breath. In the last few months she could hardly leave her bed, which is the reason I didn't make a trip to visit you after you lost Fréderick. Gerard promises to take me to see you soon.*
>
> *Pray for my little Hortense. I know she is one of the angels. I am sorry you never got to know her.*
>
> *You would not recognize my children. The twins are men! After two years with the Jesuits in New Orleans, Louis-Claude decided to come home to help on the plantation. Charles will stay in the city to study medicine. He is very interested in the new methods being taught in France. He may go there next year. Marie and Thérèse are both engaged to marry. The "little" boys are with a tutor here on the plantation. Right now, I cannot bear to have them go away. How can I call them little when they are almost six feet tall?*
>
> *There have been problems farther up the river but everything has been quiet around Plaquemine. I still have the same opinions, but I keep them to myself—especially now.*
>
> *I love you.*
> *Gabby*

I understood why I hadn't heard from her and succumbed to sadness.

CHAPTER SEVENTEEN

"What are you up to Jacques?"

From the gallery, I saw Jacques pushing a wheelbarrow out to the pecan grove next to the house, and I noticed a rope strung between two of the trees. I came out to check.

"I thought up a game, mistress."

"A game? For the children to play?"

"For everybody, mistress. I'm makin' a clear spot. Pecan trees are messy. I can get up the branches, but not all the nuts."

"Explain the game to me."

Jacques picked up a bedraggled looking round object from the ground. "I found a ball in the play yard and wrapped it in cloth to make it soft. We can have two teams, one on each side of the rope."

"Okay. What do the teams do?"

"Hit the ball over the net."

"How do they do that? Show me."

Jacques held the ball in one hand and struck it with the other fist. The ball soared over the rope and hit the ground on the other side.

"And then what?"

"The other team got to catch it before it drop. If not, one point for the striking team."

"Oh, I think I understand. I guess then a striker on the other side gets a turn."

"Yes, mistress. First team to six points wins the game."

"I like it!"

"You think we can do this?"

"Let me give it a try." I needed three attempts to get the ball over the rope. "If I can do it, anybody can. I think the boys will love the game. They play ball all the time. Wonderful idea, Jacques."

I didn't think I'd ever before seen a smile on Jacques's face that showed every one of his big white teeth.

"Let's go to the gallery and help Louisa finish setting up for supper."

Jacques put out six tables of varying sizes.

"Scatter some chairs and all the barrels you can find, Jacques. Close, but not against the tables. There'll be no special seating."

Louisa set out plates, utensils, and cups. Later she'd bring lemonade and platters of food, all portable: fried chicken (always reserved for special occasions because the children were allowed to eat with their hands), corn on the cob, and biscuits. Caroline, Félicité, Patrick, Eliza, and her children joined us on the gallery.

"I do believe we're ready. We're lucky. The first touch of fall has cooled off the day."

We finished just in time. Papa B, Maman, and their family came around the house. Their oldest son Benoit brought his wife and their two little children, the littlest one only walking for a few months, and a nursemaid. Little Fréderick came up to the house with them. He'd been waiting on the dock for their arrival. Alphonsine came out of the house to the gallery, carrying her sewing bag.

After the family hugged each other and greeted the slaves, Caroline and Louisa served lemonade. Papa B lifted his cup in a toast.

"I raise my glass to the fever team, and to Patrick who fought bravely through the scourge! Congratulations to you all!" Everyone cheered.

Just when I thought things might start to get awkward, Eliza's children and Benoit's children broke the ice. They took off running together, Eliza in pursuit. Caroline joined the chase and turned the romp into a game of tag. Maman and Benoit's wife found chairs to sit on. I took the opportunity to take Papa B aside. I needed him to help explain the game.

"Okay everybody," I said to the group. "See that rope between two pecan trees? Jacques has created a game for us to play. Jacques, give us a demonstration of how to hit the ball over the rope."

"Yes, ma'am." Jacques held up the ball and socked it over the rope, more softly than he'd done for just me, I noticed.

"Now we're going to need two teams of players," I continued.

Papa B took over the team selection. "Let's start with my Alfred and Little Fréderick on one side of the rope. Hyppy, you go to the other side. Take your places, boys. How about you Caroline? You be with Hyppy."

"Yes, sir." Caroline jumped up and stood with Maman and Papa B's middle child, Hypolite, or Hyppy, as he was frequently called.

"We need more players, sir," Jacques announced.

"Of course, we do. Hortense, you go to Alfred's team."

"Sure, Papa B."

Papa B asked Benoit's wife to be my opposite and go with Hyppy. Both sides wanted Jacques to play. Papa B said, "Jacques to Hyppy's team and I'll be opposite him with Little Fréderick."

Papa B continued running the show. "Okay, everybody, let's each take a turn trying to strike the ball. We know Jacques has been practicing."

I was surprised how quickly everyone got the hang of it.

"Alfred, your team strikes first. Let the game begin!" Papa B called.

Alfred gave it a whack. Hyppy went scurrying. Too late. The ball hit the ground on the other side. "One point for Alfred's team. Your team's turn, Hyppy."

The same result. I went after the ball, but it hit the ground right next to me.

"Oh dear," I said. "I think the strikers will always score. Let's add a rule. Both teams back up a couple feet and we'll say the ball has to go over the net and hit the ground *behind* the first two players on the other side for a score."

Better. Most of us had trouble getting our strikes to go that far. I believed Jacques and Papa B held back.

When the score reached four to four and everybody had a chance to strike a couple times, I could see Benoit and Eliza itching to get into the game.

"Can we have substitute players, Jacques?" Benoit asked.

"Yes, sir." Even Maman took a turn. Everyone except Alphonsine. She sat on the edge of the gallery swinging her feet, bent over her sewing. Patrick, instructed by Félicité not to over-exert, sat next to her. We had a rest time and started the game all over again.

During and after the game, the guests picked up a dinner plate and served themselves. Papa B's Alfred, the youngest and taller than his older brother, must have devoured a whole chicken by himself.

"I swear," Maman exclaimed, "that boy of mine needs to eat enough to fill up each of those long legs every day!"

Papa B understood what I wanted to do with the celebration. He told me he had a little trouble getting my mother on board. She still worried about what people would say. Papa B assured her no one in town would know the details. He'd instruct his family to be vague if anyone asked. I'd do the same.

After the meal, Louisa and Caroline cleared the tables, pushed them aside, and I asked everyone to find a spot to sit. I tried my hand at what I had not done for years, and never before to a mixed group. "Let me tell you a story, a true story my grandfather told me about living on the bayou long ago.

"When my Grandpa Bérard first came to the colony of Louisiana, he and a handful of other young men from France made their way up the Mississippi River and across the Atchafalaya swamp. They set up camp on the banks of the Bayou Teche. They'd heard Indians lived in the colony, but they hadn't seen any on the whole trip. They'd been camped just a few days, sitting in their tents thinking about how to go into the woods to hunt for fresh meat to eat, when they had visitors. A band of Attakapas Indians rode up to their camp, one dressed fancier than the others. Attakapas is the Indian word for man-eaters, you know. That was the general belief—that the redskins ate both white and black people."

I told the group that although the Indians made Grandpa nervous, he smiled and gave the chief a salute. The chief saluted back and rode off into the woods.

I told them about how years later, the Indians came again, led by a young Indian dressed like the chief who came before. Grandpa figured this one was the first Indian's son and new chief. He and Grandpa got to be friends. Although other people had trouble with the Indians, Grandpa and these Indians never had any trouble with each other.

Everybody applauded when I finished my story. Yes, I was moralizing, but I was wrapping a lesson about friendship and trust in a package of adventure.

Before sunset, we walked down to the dock to send the guests off on the ferry. The two ferrymen looked wide-eyed at the sight of our group laughing with one another. Our family had never had a celebration like this before, and probably would never do so again. After all, I thought, the reason for the celebration was also a once-in-a-lifetime event.

*****

The following morning, we were still smiling as we returned to our routine. We smiled all day. Mid-afternoon, my friend Susanne came to visit. Still feeling like celebration, I had Caroline brew tea and serve us in the parlor. Tea was a treat. Coffee we had aplenty, but tea leaves traveled a long way to reach Louisiana. I saved my supply to share with a good friend.

Toward sunset, we heard something. Was an animal scratching at the front door? I called Caroline and asked her to check it out.

We heard the door bolt slide. A thump and a thud resounded in the foyer. Caroline cried out, "Mistress! Come quick!"

I found Dr. Neal splat across the doorsill, his man Charles kneeling beside him. Two long black fingers pressed into the pale skin at the base of the doctor's neck. Caroline stood to one side, biting the knuckles of her fist.

Charles sat back on his heels and raised his head. "The doctor's passed right out. We need to get him into a bed."

The narrow staircase, which the doctor had used to get to his room upstairs for the past three nights, presented an insurmountable challenge. The only available bed I had at ground level was in the overseer's cabin on the path to the quarters, an accommodation sure to invite Mr. Gordon's ire. *Tant pis!* Too bad! Mr. Gordon wouldn't return from New Orleans for weeks, and perhaps, if the family meeting approved my plan, he wouldn't come back to me at all.

"Caroline, go fetch Jacques from the addition. Tell him to bring us the litter he used to carry Patrick to the sick cabin."

I spun the ring of keys attached to the pocket of my day dress, separated out one of them, and called for Félicité. When she came from the kitchen, I unhooked the key from the ring and handed it to her.

"Open the overseer's cabin and freshen Mr. Gordon's bed. We're going to put the doctor in there."

Charles still knelt by Dr. Neal. "Do you know what ails the doctor?" I asked him.

"No, ma'am. He's complained of a headache a few times during the past few days. Perhaps it was worse today. He squeezed his eyelids together off and on, but he wouldn't stop making calls. He said we still had patients to see. When he couldn't go on any longer, he asked me to take him to your house."

"Jacques will be here with the litter in just a minute. You two carry Dr. Neal to the overseer's cabin behind the house and stay with him right there. We'll get whatever you need for the doctor's care."

"Yes, ma'am."

"Should I contact the doctor's family?" I asked Charles. "They live in Opelousas, I believe. My friend Susanne Decuir is here. Her wagon is out front. If you know the address, her driver could ask the ferryman to have the livery send a courier to tell them the doctor is ill."

"I have the family's address, but I want to hold for now. The doctor gave me instructions in the event of something like this. I'm checking a few signs."

Still on the floor at the doctor's side, Charles placed his ear on the doctor's chest, on the right and on the left. Rolling him on his side, he listened on the doctor's back. He pressed his finger to the doctor's forehead and, on release, counted the seconds out loud until the depression disappeared. He made a notation on a pad from his pocket. He pulled down the lower lid of each eye and peered inside. He prodded the doctor's stomach. His examination complete, Charles stood up and nodded to Jacques.

Jacques and Charles wrestled Dr. Neal onto the litter and placed his medical bag at his side. They carried him through the house, out the back door, down the steps, and across the yard to the overseer's cabin. In a few minutes—which seemed forever—Jacques came up to the gallery where Susanne, Félicité, and I waited for news.

"Mistress, the doctor asks for you."

Félicité and I crossed the yard and stepped into the cabin together, immediately dizzied by hot, stuffy air. The cabin had been closed tight since Mr. Gordon left for New Orleans almost a week ago. We found Dr. Neal in a nightshirt. He lay on the covers, face flushed, eyes closed, beads of sweat on his brow. Charles brought over a chair and placed it a few feet from the head of the bed. He indicated I should sit. I backed the chair up a bit before I sat down. Félicité said yellow jack didn't transfer by breath, but . . .

"How are you feeling, Doctor?" I asked.

The doctor's eyes cut to me. He exhaled but didn't answer my question. How stupid of me! Obviously, he felt dreadful.

"Shall I send to St. Martinsville for a doctor? It doesn't look to me as if you should travel."

"No, ma'am." The doctor whispered. He drew in breath to continue. "Charles knows what to do. He can do it by himself." With force I didn't know he had, the doctor turned his head to Charles and issued a command. "Get started!"

I stood up, taking the order to Charles as permission for me to leave. Félicité followed me. At the door, I asked Charles what supplies he might need.

"I have the medicines, but I need a cup and three basins, one filled with water. And I'd like some clean rags or towels, ma'am." Félicité nodded acceptance of the assignment. "And I want Jacques to assist me for a short while."

"Well-water for drinking or water from the cistern?" I asked.

"Water from the cistern will be fine."

"You can open some shutters—"

From his position on the bed, Dr. Neal cut me off with a firm negative. "No!"

Charles set to work. He moved the chair from the bedside and replaced it with a table. He opened the doctor's medical bag and pulled out three bottles of medicine, a thumb lancet for performing a bleeding, and an enema pipe, all of which gave me a pretty good idea the doctor had instructed Charles to treat him with standard medical practice—quinine, calomel, bleeding, and purge. And maybe a bit of laudanum to ease the doctor through tough patches. The doctor wasn't going to get fresh air or water from the well to drink.

Charles drew the notebook from his pocket and tore out a page. He handed it to me. His large dark eyes hooked mine.

"You can send word to the doctor's family, ma'am." Charles said. "Tell them the doctor suspects he has contracted yellow fever."

Both Félicité and I took long, deep breaths as soon as we were a decent distance away from the overseer's cabin.

Susanne dispatched her wagon driver to cross the bayou and ask Burke's livery to send the message to Opelousas. She accepted an invitation to join me at dinner while she waited for her driver to return. Believing Dr. Neal would be eating with us this evening, Louisa and Caroline had prepared a fine meal, but we had no appetite. I asked Caroline to take two plates to the overseer's cabin; most of the food would go to the quarters. With fever again on the place, I doubted the slaves would enjoy their unexpected bounty.

"Is there no way we can interfere with what Charles does for the doctor?" I asked Félicité as she cleared the table.

"Charles has been Dr. Neal's assistant for years, mistress. He does all the procedures: examinations, bleedings, dressing wounds. Dr. Neal said Charles knows exactly what to do. Charles has his orders."

"Charles thinks he's a doctor. When I first met him, he said we—not the doctor but we—have been examining patients."

"Right, mistress. He probably did every examination today."

"You still don't believe in their ways?"

"No, ma'am."

"Neither do I." My voice quavered as I gave Félicité her next assignment. "I think we should prepare for the possibility we'll need to care for our people, using your ways of course. What are we going to need?"

"We'll need the ingredients to make fever tea and poultices, mistress. I have some supplies, but if the fever spreads, not near enough."

"Where can we get you more supplies?"

"I'd like to see the herb shop you told me about, mistress."

"Oh, my, yes. I said I'd take you there and I haven't done so. I've been distracted. We must repair my omission right away."

Félicité turned to my friend Susanne. "I understand you have a big garden, Madame Decuir. Do you grow herbs?"

"I have some for cooking, but the slaves have planted a large section for themselves. You may know what's growing there."

Félicité smiled. "I probably do, ma'am. May I come see?"

"Absolutely."

I told Félicité we'd go to the herb shop first thing tomorrow. No, not first thing. I first needed to arrange for Alphonsine and Little Fréderick to have another visit with Maman and Papa B. After going to the herb shop, I'd have Jacques hitch up the wagon and take us up the bayou road to Madame Decuir's garden.

Dr. Neal had apparently been feeling bad for at least two days, but we'd had no reports of other victims. We'd be prepared just in case.

CHAPTER EIGHTEEN

Having no idea how much the herb shop might charge for supplies, I filled my purse with *piastres* and tucked it into the pocket of my dress. I rattled like a baby's toy. Concerned the noise of my cache might attract a thief, I sought out Jacques to ask him to come with us. Caroline intercepted me on the path to the overseer's cabin.

"Jacques is in there helping Charles perform a purge, mistress. I'm tending a pot of boiling water to soak the soiled towels. Messy business. You don't want to go anywhere near."

Messy and smelly.

The report settled a question. For now, I needed to shut down the building of the addition. Jacques had enough to do helping Charles with Dr. Neal, making sure the animals stayed properly cared for, and generally keeping the household in operation. No one would want to come live with me right then anyway.

I clung to the belief we were coming to the end of this sick spell and would be through with yellow fever in just a few days. We were shopping for herbs only as a precaution, I told myself. I remembered what my father said so long ago, don't worry about what might become a problem and it'll be less likely to happen.

Félicité and I crossed the bayou on the ferry and walked the block and a half to the herb shop. I'd never met the proprietor and was surprised to find him a black man. He introduced himself as Gabriel Fouchard, *un homme de couleur libre*, a free man of color. He and Félicité opened a rapid-fire exchange in Creole. While I could usually understand Félicité, this was too fast for me. After five minutes of the chatter, Mr. Fouchard offered me a chair. I sat for almost an hour while he and Félicité assembled a collection of bottles of liquids and packages of powder. When they were done, Félicité swept her hand over the display, nodded her satisfaction, and turned to me.

"We've a lot here, mistress, but we'll be prepared. When news about Dr. Neal spreads, I expect people to panic. Mr. Fouchard will be cleaned out in a snap. Will you spend eight *piastres* on fever supplies?"

"Yes, I will."

I expected to be charged much more. In the days when our quarters were fully occupied and Fréderick had ordered drugs to come on the steamboat from New Orleans, he had laid out as many as forty *piastres* for a season's supply of quinine, calomel, camphor, and castor oil. I hadn't bought any drugs since Fréderick passed.

Félicité produced a bandana from the pocket of her dress. Mr. Fouchard wrapped up the bottles and packages of powders. I lightened my purse.

"While we're in the neighborhood, Félicité, could we stop in at the houses of a couple friends of mine? They were interested in what we did for Patrick."

"Of course, ma'am."

We ended up giving lessons on fever tea and the importance of water and air. When we left each house, someone was on the way to the herb shop.

Félicité shook her head as we walked back down to the dock to catch the ferry home.

"Mr. Fouchard had no mahogany bark, mistress. He says the winters here are too cold to grow the tree. He had everything else, and a few potions I'd forgotten about. He's very good. He came from Saint-Domingue. He uses the same rituals my mother did when she made the remedies we used in New Orleans."

This is the first I'd heard from Félicité of rituals to prepare the remedies. Had I signed on for voodoo?

"Do you believe in the power of special rituals?" I asked.

"Not the way you're thinking, mistress. I don't count on supernatural forces to make good mixtures, but the mixing chants have a purpose. The instructions for our potions are not written down. Chants help the preparer remember the proper proportions, especially important when working with the bits of poison." Félicité poked out her lips and raised her eyebrows, but she didn't smile. "Mind you, I don't turn down an extra bit of help from the beyond."

"Do you know when Mr. Fouchard left Saint-Domingue?" I asked. "At the time of the revolution, perhaps? You know that's when the master lost his father." And maybe was himself taken out of there as a baby, if one of the family stories was actually true.

"Before that, I think. Probably when my mother left with me. By the time of the revolution, they wasn't letting any of us into the city of New Orleans. They said we made trouble and brought fever."

"Your mother was a healer, wasn't she?"

"Yes, ma'am."

I stopped walking and looked at Félicité. "You know, I'd like to hear about Saint-Domingue one day, and about your family."

Félicité bowed her head. "I'll tell you one day, mistress. What I can remember, that is. Most is gone out of my head. When you try hard to forget things, you do."

After lunch, Jacques hitched up the wagon and we traveled up the road to Belle Place to see Susanne's herb garden. We interrupted her saying goodbye to her son Eugene. He'd taken a job helping set up a sugarcane operation for a newly arrived Englishman down the bayou in St. Mary Parish. Tears filled my friend's eyes as her son threw his leg over the saddle and rode away.

"I hate to think of Eugene down there among the English," Susanne mumbled. "A young man always thinks the grass is greener somewhere else. There's work for him right here, but he'd have to take orders from his older brother. Lucien already works with Max. One good thing, Eugene's getting away from the fever. I haven't heard of anyone down there who's sick."

Before we went out into the garden, Susanne wanted a report about Dr. Neal.

"He's set up in our overseer's cabin being cared for by his man Charles. In fact, his illness and one report of someone in town with headache are the reasons we're stockpiling ingredients for Félicité's traditional remedies. I believe we're at the end of a bout of yellow fever, but I want to be cautious. I prefer Félicité's methods to those of the doctors."

Susanne picked up a basket and a pair of scissors and led us around to the back of the house.

"We once grew indigo, you know. We shipped the leaves north for making dye. Some of our slaves thought they could make the dye themselves—a tragic notion. They boiled the leaves and got very sick from the fumes. A couple slaves died. Max gave up the crop and turned entirely to sugar. The slaves asked if they could use some of the area where we pulled out the indigo."

Félicité's eyes opened wide at the sight of a variety of small plants and aromatic shrubs growing in well-tended beds.

"I know these plants, ma'am. You say your slaves planted them for you?"

"For themselves. In Saint-Domingue, they grew herbs they'd used in Africa, but when they got here, they couldn't find what they wanted. They asked the master if they could have a section of garden. Max was happy to oblige. Cheaper than buying them medicines, he said. They planted seeds they'd brought to Louisiana in their hair. The slaves take turns tending the patch on their Sunday break. Max still orders drugs from New Orleans, but only for the family. The slaves rarely follow any doctor's suggestions."

"Does the man at the new herb shop know about this, ma'am?" Félicité asked.

"Oh, yes. He buys from us. Take what you want. And when you need more, just come back again. We're reaching the end of the season and many of these plants will die back during the winter."

When we returned home, Félicité asked if she could use one of the unoccupied cabins to hang her harvest to dry. I gave permission, of course.

After dinner, I sat on the back gallery with a little glass of blackberry wine, waiting to be sleepy enough to go to bed. Félicité passed by on the way to her cabin. I invited her to sit with me.

"Keep your lamp lit, Félicité. The flame keeps away the mosquitos."

A great horned owl in one of the large oaks called to his mate. *Who cooks for you? Who cooks for you? I do, I do*, came the response.

"Hear the owl, Félicité?" I thought fancifully about telling the owl Caroline and Louisa cook for us.

We'd been sitting quietly for a while when Charles came out of the door of the overseer's cabin. He saw the glow of our lamps and walked up the path to us.

"Thank you for dinner, ma'am," he said.

"You're welcome. I sent enough for two. Did the doctor eat anything?"

"No, ma'am."

"Is there any change in his condition?"

"No, ma'am. He still has fever. I'm watching him close."

Charles returned to the overseer's cabin.

"I stay busy all day, Félicité, but I'm lonely when night comes. I get to thinking about Fréderick. I miss him, especially when I have to cope with situations I've never faced before. You know how I was. I took care of my babies, put on wonderful dinners, and didn't worry about a thing. He was so good to me."

"He was good to us, too, mistress."

"Do you remember when I first met him?"

I couldn't see her face in the darkness, but I heard her giggle. "Do I remember, ma'am? Lordy, yes, I remember!"

"Oh, dear. Was I so ridiculous you'll never forget?"

"I won't answer that, mistress."

"Papa B tells me I was ridiculous, but he liked Fréderick from the first. Well, not really from the *very* first time they met. He saw Fréderick when the lad was just a stock boy working for Tante Hester at Pintard's store. Fréderick's Tante Hester and Mr. Pintard brought Fréderick down from Philadelphia after his parents died, you know. A few years later, Papa B came home from a dinner at Leonard Smith's talking about an impressive young man who had a lot of dreams about the future of La Nouvelle-Ibérie—didn't think it right we should have to check everything we did with those fancy people in St. Martinsville. He thought they took advantage of us. Pretty bold talk for a young fellow. Papa B agreed with him."

"You met the master at church, I believe."

"I did. Fréderick rode up on a beautiful bay mare. Handsome as can be, he was. And charming! After Mass, he chatted up everybody. I know I came home talking of nothing else."

"We joked about your newfound devotion to religion at your Grand-Mère Mémé's, mistress. You wanted to make the trip up the bayou to Mass no matter the weather."

"I must've been impossible."

"No, mistress, just wrapped up in your infatuation."

"Maman had her doubts about Fréderick at the start. She had in mind for me one of the St. Martinsville French, maybe even Dutch Grevemberg for heaven's sakes! But she warmed up to Fréderick when she learned his family was as distinguished as any around. His mother's family owned a plantation in Saint-Domingue. Fréderick was orphaned when the rebels killed his father and then his mother died in Philadelphia. At least that's one of the versions of his story!"

"That's not the story I heard, mistress. Alfred told me his father was in Saint-Domingue with *both* his parents when the revolution came. The rebels cut off *both* their heads and a slave who was his nurse smuggled him out in a blanket."

"Alfred claims his father told him that. Either one of them—Fréderick or Alfred—might have added a bit more drama to the story. It may be true, but I can't imagine a mother taking a very young child to that place, or going there when about to deliver a baby with what they knew was going on. When we married, Fréderick wrote in the church records that he was born in Philadelphia. If so, he and his mother must have stayed behind while his father went down to sell the plantation. There is no one alive now who knows for sure."

"Stays a mystery, I guess, mistress."

"Maman took more notice of Fréderick when Tante Hester died and Fréderick got all that land in our town. When he started to talk about building a brick home on Tante Hester's property for his bride, Maman thought him a great catch!"

Félicité laughed. "She wanted you to have a secure future, mistress."

"Maman tried hard to make me keep my feet on the ground. Do you remember the day I got dressed down for my behavior toward you?"

"No, ma'am. When was that?"

"Fréderick told me at church he was going to come to our house that afternoon to ask Maman and Papa B to give permission for us to marry. On the way home from church, Papa B stopped our wagon to point out a magnificent bald eagle perched on a tree over the road. I was so anxious to get home to redo my hair, I screamed at Papa B to keep moving. When we got to the house, I *ordered* you to get me my green silk dress *immediately*. Of course. I wanted to show off my eyes! That was the last straw. Maman made me go to my room and said she was going to refuse to receive Fréderick. I had a tantrum. I believed Maman had destroyed my one chance for happiness."

"She gave in, didn't she, mistress?"

"Yes, she did. Fréderick asked them for my hand, wisely including my stepfather in his request. Eventually Maman said yes, but not that day. It was torture. She made us wait."

"The master built you a grand house, mistress."

"Yes. There were no brick buildings in our town then, and Fréderick began to build one for me. Grand-Père Boutté came every day to supervise the construction. His nephew in New Orleans, an important architect, had a lot to do with it. He made sure the pilings went deep into the ground. Two stories, big rooms, galleries front and back. Solid as can be, my house. Fréderick had the bricks made from a clay pit right back there." I indicated the area on the bayou next to Félicité's cabin. "I think the Weeks family used the same bricks for the Shadows."

"May I ask you a question about the house, mistress?"

"Of course. What would you like to know?"

"There's a trapdoor in the floor of the room in front of the kitchen."

"Yes, there is."

"What's down there?"

"A tunnel, Félicité. An escape tunnel that goes to the bayou."

"To escape from what, mistress?"

"Pirates. We still had pirates around here when Fréderick built the house, or so Maman thought. You know, Maman still gets upset when people talk about pirates because of the story that her father and Jean Lafitte were related. She's irrational on the topic, thinks it's shaming the family. I think she half believes it's true, and it makes her afraid. Maman told Fréderick I had to have a way to get out in case any came to get us. I think there are several houses down the bayou in Franklin that have escape tunnels, but ours was the first one in town."

"Have you ever been down the tunnel, mistress?"

"Oh, no. And I don't want to. I've forbidden the children to open the trapdoor."

I heard a chuckle from Félicité. "You know, mistress, Alfred opened it up."

"He did? Did he go down in there?"

"He pulled up that square of floor and took three steps down into the darkness. Just three steps. The top of his head stopped dead, and he came scrambling out! I don't think he ever lifted the trapdoor again."

"Good."

"I have another question, mistress."

"Go ahead."

"Could someone go into the tunnel from the bayou and climb up into the house?"

"No. One time, I had Jacques take the skiff and look for the opening in the bayou bank. He couldn't find it. I think maybe when they cleaned snags out of the bayou they dumped them on the bank and closed the opening. And anyway, you notice that heavy table sitting on the cover? No one could move it from underneath."

"Good, mistress."

We sat quietly for some time. I slipped into memories about Fréderick. I heard rustling from where Félicité sat. I didn't want her to go.

"Did you ever marry, Félicité? I mean, did you ever have someone?"

A deep sigh. After a moment, "Yes, ma'am."

"Will you tell me?"

"It's painful."

I didn't speak. We sat in the dark, I heard her voice crack as she started to tell me her story.

"He wasn't the first man I knew. I was fourteen when your Grand-Père Boutté bought me. I went to the quarters where I had to put out for any man, white or slave, who wanted me. That's the way it was. Animals, I thought, as they used me. They grunted with their pleasure, not mine. Years of that."

She sat quiet. I didn't speak either.

"One man came to me like all the others, but after he had his way, he rolled over on his back, sat up, and said he was sorry. He took my little hand in his great big one and kissed my fingers. He stroked my arm. For the next little while, he just sat silent. He asked me—yes, he asked me—if he could have another beginning. I can't talk about this except to say he treated me different, delicate like.

"The next day he went to the fields and I went to the big house as usual. When the plantation bell rang for supper for the slaves, he was waiting at my door. He led me to a whole half-cabin just for us. He was a big, strong man. Nobody messed with him. Anyone who looked at me was sorry. I loved him, and he loved me."

"How long were you two together?" I asked.

"More than four years."

"Did you have children?"

"No, ma'am."

"Four years. How did it end?"

Félicité waited a long time before answering this question. "One day, the men came back from the fields and he wasn't with them. The overseer told me he got sold."

This time, I waited before asking another question. "What was his name?"

"The overseer called him Andrew, which wasn't his name."

"What did you call him?"

"I called him Tonja, what they called him in Senegambia where he came from. Why you want to know his name?"

"So, I can pray for him."

Another long pause and I spoke again. "I want to ask you a favor, Félicité."

"I do what you ask, mistress."

"Will you come sleep in the house?"

"If you want, ma'am."

"When the children are gone, I'm nervous in there by myself, rattling around upstairs. I'd feel a lot safer with someone else there."

I heard a smile in her voice. "I'll bring my pallet to the hall, ma'am. Like I used to do when the children were sick. I'm okay about coming now you say no one can get into that tunnel from the bayou. Tell me when you're ready to retire, mistress."

Chapter Nineteen

Whatever treatment Dr. Neal received the following day took place quietly and without any assistance from Jacques or Caroline. His man Charles rarely came out of the door of the cabin. Jacques brought meals to the cabin door, but Charles made no conversation with Jacques other than to say thank you. I didn't know if Dr. Neal improved or sank lower. I regretted that I had tied myself up with a stranger while my children had to stay away. But what could I do now? Nothing. How long would this situation go on? After supper, which again I ate without enjoyment, I summoned Jacques.

"Come to the overseer's cabin with me, Jacques. I need to know how Dr. Neal is coming along."

We walked down the path. I knocked on the door. Charles took some time to answer. He didn't ask us inside. Thank goodness. A stink like a dead animal rotting in the sun wafted out around him. How could Charles stand it in there?

"I'm about to retire for the night, Charles. I need information about Dr. Neal. What can you tell me?"

My throat felt dry and tight, the words barely squeezing through. Charles didn't notice, or if he did, he didn't care.

"He's quiet, Madame Duperier."

"Has the fever broken?"

"No, ma'am. His fever continues."

In contrast to Charles's measured words, I spoke rapidly, the pitch of my voice rising. "Is he improving in any way, even in enduring the difficult course toward recovery from the illness?"

"I fear he is not."

"Are you telling me his condition is worse?"

"Perhaps so, ma'am.

"Damn it, Charles. What are you doing for him?"

Charles drew himself up. "Madame, I am doing exactly as Dr. Neal instructed me to do. I give him the medicines the doctor prescribed and at the times he prescribed them. If the fever continues past forty-eight hours, I will administer a second bleeding and purge. That will take place tomorrow morning. I have asked Jacques to assist me in doing so, and he has agreed. Until then, I watch and wait and give such comfort as I can."

I swallowed my annoyance and repeated my offer to do what I could. I wished Charles a good night. He turned back into the cabin. Jacques and I started up to the house. Jacques spoke before I did.

"Dr. Neal gonna die, mistress."

"God bless his soul." Jacques and I both made the sign of the cross.

I continued. "Unfortunately, the poor man may live long enough to endure the torture of another purge. I keep thinking about Dr. Abbey. After the bleeding and purge administered by the doctor from Opelousas, he lay quiet for twenty-four hours, a quiet probably induced by a dose of laudanum—*for the patient to gather strength to overcome the rigors of fever break*, the doctor said. Then came crazy talk. Dr. Neal has a way to go, but we can anticipate the direction. Down!"

I walked faster and faster. Jacques's long strides kept up with me, but he stopped when we reached the house.

"Go to bed, mistress," he said "Tomorrow may be a hard day. I'll tell Félicité you're retiring."

"Goodnight, Jacques."

Félicité stopped at my bedroom door to wish me good night. I didn't have one. I twisted in the covers and woke every few hours. Before dawn, I went down to the kitchen and picked up a glass of juice Caroline set out on the counter for me to drink should I need something in the night. I couldn't identify what she had found to squeeze. The problem might not be an unfamiliar fruit but the churning of my stomach. I saw no sign of activity from the direction of the overseer's cabin.

Caroline and Louisa came to the kitchen to prepare breakfast. Félicité reported as well.

"I gather no one has news from the overseer's cabin."

"No, ma'am," they chorused.

"Coffee, Louisa. That's what I need first. And when you have it ready, take a cup to the cabin for Charles. See if you can put your head in far enough to get an idea how the doctor is doing."

Louisa did as I asked. She learned nothing. Returning from the privy, Charles passed right by her, she said, lips pressed tight together, eyes fixed on the ground. "No coffee, thank you," Charles said to her.

When Jacques appeared in the kitchen, Louisa had a breakfast tray ready for the cabin. Jacques picked it up, and we watched him go to the door of the overseer's cabin and knock. The door opened; he disappeared inside. Caroline, Louisa, and I lined up on the back rail of the gallery watching for him to reappear.

"Nothing good to report, ma'am," Jacques told us a few minutes later. "I heard mumblings from the direction of the bed, but Charles didn't want me to stay. He made sure I'd be available for the treatments later this morning. As I walked out, the doctor let out a stream of curses."

Delirium?

Papa B came around the back of the house. He walked up the back steps and turned left into the kitchen. I threw myself into his arms.

"Okay, okay. What's going on?" he asked. "I looked for Jacques at the addition, but he's not there. The beams we raised two days ago stand upright but bare. The cross boards to frame the rooms are stacked, waiting for attention."

"I took him off the project, Papa B. First things first. Are Alphonsine and Little Fréderick okay?'

"Oh, yes. Happy as can be."

"Are you still comfortable with them at your house?"

"Indeed, yes. I came to tell you so. Just let them stay. I stopped at the landing. The postmaster told me Dr. Neal returned here sick."

"As you know, he came in the night before last—fell in, actually. We set him up in the overseer's cabin. Yesterday, his man Charles gave him a bleeding and a purge. Charles kept him shut inside all the rest of the day. I don't know how the doctor is this morning. Charles plans to administer another treatment, but—coffee, please, Caroline. We'll be out on the gallery."

"The postmaster had some other news, Hortense. We've had another death from fever. A friend. Joachim Etie."

I fell onto a chair and dropped my head into my hands.

"I didn't even know he was sick. He came to dinner with Fréderick many times. He and John Fitz Miller got the incorporation papers through the legislature."

The door to the overseer's cabin opened, and Charles came sprinting up the path to the gallery. He dispensed with the usual greetings.

"It's time to call the priest, ma'am." He turned and scurried back down the path.

"Jacques!" I called into the kitchen. "Charles says the doctor needs the priest. Can you handle getting a message to the church?"

"Yes, mistress."

"We sent word to the doctor's family night before last, Papa B. I guess we can wait now until . . ."

"Yes. They're probably on the way."

Louisa came out on the gallery with two cups of coffee, a plate of biscuits, and a message.

"Mistress, a wagon from the Decuir house is out front. The driver has urgent word for you. Madame Decuir's son Eugene has come home sick. Very sick. Perhaps the fever."

That news knifed into me. I felt faint.

Papa B swallowed his coffee, picked up a biscuit, and stood up. "Go to your friend, Hortense. Your children are fine with us. I'll let you know immediately if they're not."

"As long as you and Maman can care for them, I'm comfortable. I'm in charge at this house and you need to go be in charge at yours. Do you think . . . ?"

"Don't think ahead, my dear. We've done all we can to be prepared. Do what has to be done at the moment. Courage and calm."

His face expressed both.

"Is the wagon from the Decuir house still outside?" I asked Louisa.

"Yes, ma'am. The driver's waiting to hear from you."

"Good. Tell him I'm coming. I'll leave our wagon for you people here. With the way things are going, no telling what Jacques might need to do. Wait a minute. Where's Félicité?"

"She's putting together a package of the remedies she would like to take—if you will allow her to go with you, that is."

"Yes, yes. Tell her yes. I need her, and I need her remedies."

Papa B walked with me to meet the wagon from the Decuirs.

"Susanne hated to see Eugene go to that plantation in St. Mary Parish, Papa B. At least they didn't have fever down there, she said. What is this crazy sickness anyway? Is it everywhere? I've been trying to convince my-self it was coming to an end."

"Still possible, my dear. And you must remember that many people who get it recover. Patrick did."

The trip up the road to Belle Place seemed twice as long as it had two days ago. The road twisted with the bayou. As we rounded the last curve and came in sight of the Decuir house, my heart sank. Wagons scattered haphazardly along both sides of the road. Not a good sign. No one summons this many friends to a vigil for the sick, I thought.

Our driver threaded his way through the wagons and turned off the road onto a path around the near side of the house. He pulled up at steps leading to the end of the front gallery. I climbed down from the wagon. Félicité watched me, but remained seated.

"I'll accommodate Félicité, ma'am," the driver said. "Miss Susanne particularly asked me to bring her."

I would be using the front door; Félicité, the back entrance for slaves.

Susanne's oldest son Lucien spotted me and came to my side, his lips clamped tight together. I hugged him.

"My brother Eugene has passed. My mother is asking for you. Come with me."

"I'm so sorry, Lou."

"Mother's in her bedroom. She instructed me to take you and Félicité to her as soon as you arrived."

"Your driver has Félicité coming in the back way."

"Yes, ma'am. I'll fetch her."

I found Susanne sitting on a chaise, weeping. Her daughter Celemine made space for me by her mother's side.

"Oh, Hortense, they say he died on the way home to us. They'd pulled a blanket over his face, but I made them show him to me." She choked, drew in short breaths and squeezed out her words. "He was yellow, his eyeballs the color of a lemon. There can be no doubt . . . My poor boy. His face was all twisted. He suffered . . ."

I held her tight and said something, I'm not sure what.

"Just twenty years old. His whole life ahead of him. Why, why, why did I let him go down there?"

I thought I said she let him go because she was a wonderful mother who allowed her children to make their own choices. I wasn't sure what else. There was no way to ease the pain of the loss of a child. Why wasn't her husband here with her?

"Max . . . ?" I couldn't get my question out of my mouth.

"Max went to the church with Father de St. Aubin and the sexton. And with . . ." She choked. "They have to do the burial as soon as possible because of what they think it is. You'll be there, won't you?"

"Of course, I'll be there. And I'll stay with you now as long as you'd like. Here's Félicité. You asked for her to come."

"Yes, I did." Félicité said her words of sympathy. "Thank you, Félicité.

I want to tell you that I grilled the driver who brought Gene home about what they had done for my boy. He *proudly* told me they called a doctor who did what he called 'everything.' Everything the doctor's do, that is. They didn't send Gene home, where we could do what *we* thought right. I got angry, I know."

Sometimes finding someone to blame helps. Susanne was entitled. She continued.

"I want you to know Max is of as strong a mind as I am. If we have an epidemic on our hands, and I very much fear we do, we want to be ready to help our own family and all our people who might get this scourge. We need you, Félicité, to tell us what to do."

Astounding! My friend Susanne had just lost a child, and she already thought how she could help others.

"Do you have anyone sick in your house or in your quarters, Madame Decuir?" Félicité asked.

"Not that I've heard of, but . . ." Susanne's voice trailed off.

Félicité spoke up. "If you'd allow me, ma'am, I could talk to your overseer. I could tell him the signs to look for, and perhaps prepare him just in case. Beginning treatment early is very important."

"Very good. I have no idea where Mr. Dart could be. Maybe he's in the fields supervising planting." She called to her daughter. "Celemine, can you have François find Mr. Dart so Félicité can talk with him? I want Dart himself on this, not one of the assistants. Make it clear your father and I need to be told as soon as anyone shows a sign of the fever—not just fever itself but bad headache also. And Mr. Dart needs to have a full discussion with Félicité about steps we can take right now to prepare. Can you do this?"

"Yes, Mother. I can."

Susanne squeezed my hand.

More people came by to extend sympathy, but we kept the places next to her on the divan occupied. When the people thinned out, Susanne leaned back and closed her eyes.

"I have to believe God has a plan, Hortense, and that Eugene is a part of His plan. The loss of him may save others."

* * * * *

Max returned in the early afternoon and took over my position at his wife's side. I found a place deeper in the room from which Susanne could still see me. Max announced that the service would be at ten the day after tomorrow. Father de St. Aubin told him he had already scheduled two services for tomorrow morning and two in the afternoon. At St. Peter's, Max said. Burial would be in the new cemetery a block away.

Fréderick would never have imagined the church and cemetery he so recently made possible now served our town for this dread disease.

I sat quietly. Celemine brought sandwiches for lunch. Mid-afternoon, Lucien came to tell me Jacques had arrived with our wagon. My family was fine, he hastened to tell me, but they needed me at home. I left Susanne, telling her I'd be by to see her the next day. I had them find Félicité.

Félicité reported she had a good session with Mr. Dart. He'd identified two caring women. Félicité trained them how to recognize the symptoms of yellow jack and care for a patient with the fever.

"That's how we can be helpful, mistress," Félicité said. "I explained what we did for Patrick. People need to know what to look for and how to set up if the signs appear. And they need to realize they can beat the fever."

A lesson I needed to remember. We climbed into the wagon.

"What is it, Jacques? Has something happened at home?" I asked, although I guessed what news would cause them to summon me.

"Yes, mistress. Dr. Neal passed right after you left this morning." Félicité and I both made the sign of the cross. "His family came at about the same time and took over. The sexton took the body. We waited as long as we could to call you, but we need to get into the overseer's cabin to clean up."

"Yes, we must do that. Is it bad in there?"

"It's bad, ma'am."

"There's more, mistress. The overseer from the Miller place is here. He wants to talk with Félicité. They got someone in their quarters with a bad headache. We hated to take you away from your friend, but—"

"You did right, Jacques. My first responsibility is our household, but if Félicité can help other people, her people, we need to make that possible. Early treatment is critical. How is everyone at home?"

"We're well. And at your stepfather's house also. He sent word."

"Thank God!"

Félicité packed up a fresh basket of her remedies. She came to me on her way to the door.

"The overseer promises he'll have you home to me by dark," I said.

CHAPTER TWENTY

I dragged my weary body up the stairs to the bedroom and lit the oil lamp on the table by my bed. The vision of Eugene leaping onto his mount—hair tousled by the wind, his face glowing with anticipation of adventure—haunted me. How could he be gone? Seeing Susanne's family in mourning thrust the scourge smack back into my face. My belief we neared the end of the epidemic washed away like a levee of sand in a spring flood.

I knelt at my bedside, a prayer position I hadn't taken since childhood. I recited every prayer I knew. I begged the Blessed Mother to hold my family in her heart. I called on every saint I'd ever heard of and the souls of Fréderick and all my departed loved ones to put my family before the eyes of God. I promised God I would keep faith, seek hope, and hold fast to both. I didn't crawl up onto the bed until my numb knees sent daggers of pain into my back.

Wait! Félicité said yellow jack could take a week to appear and more days to run its course. That was it! Eugene could have taken the fever with him to St. Mary Parish. I grabbed back onto the hope we were indeed nearing the end of the epidemic.

No. To do so, I needed to discount reports of more people with symptoms. I had to accept reality to cope with it.

"Excuse me, mistress." Félicité's voice came from the direction of the door.

"Come in, Félicité. I didn't hear you out there."

Félicité had probably left her shoes at the back door and come up the stairs barefoot.

"Mr. Miller wants me to thank you for letting me come to his quarters."

"Sit with me a minute. I hope you had some dinner."

"Oh, yes. Mr. Miller made sure."

"How's is it going over there at the Miller house?"

169

"No one has fever, as his overseer told you. One man in the quarters has bad headache."

"Was Mr. Miller's overseer receptive to your ways?"

"Yes, ma'am. He found several women who wanted to know how to help. I explained what we did for Patrick. They set up a sick cabin, moved their man in, and got started giving him fresh air and water to drink. I showed them how to make fever tea and left some supplies. Mr. Miller came by and approved what we were doing. He says if anyone has headache or fever, he'll have his overseer take him off work and put him to bed. They're boiling water to have on hand."

"This is good."

"Yes. Mr. Miller brought over a neighbor who wanted to hear what I was saying." Félicité shrugged her shoulders. "Mr. Miller says they might as well use my ways. They don't have any doctors in town anyway. I don't know whether he'd feel the same if one of his family got sick, but so far, they're all well."

"Mr. Miller is a good man, Félicité."

"Yes, ma'am. Not everyone's like that. I hear tell there's some slaves fallin' down in the fields, the owners not willing to stop the harvest."

"Mr. Miller's done a lot of good for the town. When the government changed the price they'd give for raw sugar at the market in New Orleans, he helped many famers over the hump."

Félicité looked up quickly. "Is that when the master got poor, mistress?" she asked.

"The master didn't get poor. He couldn't meet his debts right away. The sugar business is like that. You borrow to get the crop to market and pay off the creditors when you sell. The problem was Fréderick got sick. Another year and we would've been fine."

"But you stopped raising sugarcane."

"Yes, I did. The family meeting made the decision. I couldn't have managed a sugar operation, and I didn't want to anyway. I have the landing, the town lots, and my family. We're going to be fine."

"But the sale . . ."

"Yes, yes. I know. There's good news about Jacques, Félicité. He can stay to finish the addition, and perhaps after as well. Papa B has a plan. I'm hopeful."

Félicité started to stand. I dug for words to hold her.

"Mr. Miller did a lot of good for the town. He came to the meetings when Fréderick gathered his friends to draw up the papers to put us on the map. I'm trying to remember all the men who were there at the final dinner: Mr. Miller, John Wilkins, Henry Peebles, Judge Paul Briant, Dr. Leonard Smith, Joachim Etie. Joachim's gone now."

"Dr. Peebles, too, I think."

"Yes. Mr. Henry Peebles *and* Doctor Peebles. I remember it was a beautiful evening. Jacques set a table under the trees. You and I mostly stayed in the kitchen while Louisa and Caroline served the food. Jacques kept everyone's wine glass full. No blackberry wine that night. Fréderick put a Red Bordeaux on the table. Someone could do a painting of the scene."

"Yes, ma'am. I'm happy to see you smiling at the memory."

"Yes. I'm thinking of what Fréderick said about Mr. Miller that night. He wouldn't stay on the subject of the incorporation. He wanted to talk about his new racetrack in the country and his horse named Sorrow. He told Fréderick to place a bet on a sure winner. I'm afraid Fréderick took his advice and found the horse's name appropriate. Sorrow came in dead last!"

"The master did like to wager, mistress."

"That night, Fréderick had a mission. If he kept Mr. Miller and Mr. Etie focused on the incorporation, he knew he could count on them to get the papers through the legislature. When Fréderick came down from Philadelphia with Tante Hester and Mr. Pintard, we were just a handful of houses between the Smith plantation at one end and the Weeks land on the other. A tannery, a bakery, not much else in the so-called town. When I was a little girl, the landing was a couple of boards crumbling into the bayou. We went to St. Martinsville for everything we needed, even to go to church. Now look at us. The fact we're as big as we are is because of the master."

I stopped speaking, driving down thoughts of what might happen to our town if the fever took hold. Already no steamboats came up the Teche from Franklin or down from St. Martinsville. Neither town had any fever and they didn't want to get it. That was the way the fever could be. When New Orleans had the last bad epidemic, the disease didn't cross over the city limits.

"It's good to think of happy times, mistress. I'm glad the master got to know we were a real town before he passed."

My tears welled up again. "The last conversation Fréderick and I had, we talked about the incorporation going through. After that . . ."

We sat quietly. The present threat crept back into my mind.

"I guess you know we're hearing of more people with signs of the fever."

"Yes, ma'am. I can't tell you it's nothing. Mr. Miller's overseer says he knows of a death in the Darby quarters. They burying their own dead over there and keeping quiet about it."

"I'm scared. If it comes, a lot of people will die. Maybe everybody."

"No, no, mistress. No matter how bad, not everybody gets it, and many who do get it recover. You've got to remember."

"Yes, but . . ." I thought back to a conversation this afternoon. "Maybe we lose only some, but as my friend Susanne's daughter Celemine told me, when you lose one of your own, it's everything. I'm so afraid for my family."

I kicked myself for saying *my family*. Félicité didn't have any family to start with.

"I should say our family. You're a member of our family. Tell me, Félicité, are we as prepared as we can be?" Stupid question. We've had this exchange a half dozen times. I didn't want her to leave.

"For now, mistress, although I wish we had mahogany bark."

"I sent a letter to Aunt Thérèse in Plaquemine to see if she can locate any. But even if she finds a mahogany tree, when they hear about what's going on here no one will want to cross the swamp to bring it to us. We can't get anything directly from the islands. Not even New Orleans has contact with Saint-Domingue anymore. Do you suppose there's an herb shop in New Orleans that might have some left over?"

"I asked Mr. Fouchard about that when we went to see him. He said he already sent a request to a friend. My mother thought mahogany bark an important ingredient in fever tea, but above all, she told everyone to keep patients drinking water. Water's the best. She thought people under doctors' care dried up."

"You're thinking of your mother a lot these days, aren't you?"

"Yes, ma'am. I'm trying to remember her ways."

I chanced a question. "When she was in Saint-Domingue or when you were in New Orleans?"

"New Orleans. I suppose she did the same in Saint-Domingue, but I don't know. I was little when we left."

"Was your mother a saltwater?"

"Yes, ma'am. She said she came on a ship"

"Did she tell you about that?"

"Not much. She wanted to forget. She did say that when she had bad dreams, she could hear the moaning."

"Do you know whose plantation she came to?" I hoped I wouldn't hear the name of Fréderick's mother's family, Longier or Laugier, or something close to that.

"No, ma'am. She said she worked in the house of a *petit-blanc*. Her real owner lived in France. In fact, that's how she got to New Orleans.

The *grand-blanc* in France heard rumors of trouble long before the big revolution. He sold the plantation—practically gave away the land—but picked the best slaves and sent them to a place he owned in New Orleans. Good thing. Later on, they wouldn't let anyone from the islands into the city. I was too young to remember any of that. I do remember living in New Orleans."

"And you helped your mother with her healing?"

"Yes, ma'am. I mixed powders and went with her to treat people. That's what I'm trying so hard to remember now. Exactly what I did."

"But then you left New Orleans?"

Félicité looked down at her hands. "Yes, ma'am. The owner in France died, so the overseer took us to the market. Your Grand-Père Boutté bought me."

"Grand-Père didn't buy your mother?"

"No, ma'am. I was over 14 years old, so I got sold separate. Code Noir allowed that." She must have seen distress on my face. "It's okay, mistress. I was luckier than most. He and your Grand-Mère Mémé were always kind."

"Do you know what happened to your mother?" I asked.

Félicité waited a good while before she answered this question. When she did speak, I could hardly hear her words.

"No, ma'am. Last time I saw my mother, she stood naked on the block at the market, men pokin' at her. She was crying my name when they led me away."

I closed my eyes. "I'm so sorry, Félicité."

I thought she might get up and leave my room. I wouldn't have blamed her if she did. I'd dug into a sore. She stayed.

"What about your father? Where was he?" I asked.

"I never knew him. He died in Saint-Domingue. My mother said he fell down in the fields. They worked him to death."

I heard once about how things were down there. The most profitable colony in the Caribbean, but they didn't take care of their slaves the way we did. Or mostly did. If a slave got sick or worn out in Saint-Domingue, it was cheaper to just go buy a new one.

Félicité stood up. "I go to bed now, mistress."

"Good night, Félicité. Thank you for keeping me company."

The owner in France died, so the overseer took us to the market. Félicité's words stayed in my head and brought back what happened to me when Fréderick died with debts I knew nothing about. The big sale. Papa B said Uncle F. C. might still own Félicité. What if Uncle F. C. died, or even if he was living and his creditors—he always had plenty of those, now maybe even more since he wanted to go into sugar—found out he owned another slave? Would someone come get her? I needed to talk to Papa B before we opened up the subject.

And I needed to think hard before I considered worrying Félicité with a proposal that might have dire consequences for her.

* * * * *

The next two days were all about funerals. I put on my black clothes, ate breakfast, and had Jacques row me across the bayou to Pintard's Landing to meet Maman and Papa B for the services. I went home with them for lunch, visited the children, and then went back to church. The bells tolled most of the day.

Our priest, Father de St. Aubin, said we weren't burying everybody who died. Some country families never transferred to our new church. They buried their dead in St. Martin. How many? He didn't know. And, of course, he knew nothing about any slaves who passed. The plantations had their own ways. Buried them on their land. I heard about a few people sick in the country, and one person in town who died, but not anyone we knew well. Sometimes, I even had hope this would all pass.

The third day, everything about our town changed.

Crossing the bayou to go visit the children, the ferryman looked at my shopping basket and shook his head. "There's a sign on Murphy's store, ma'am. They won't be open until noon, and then only for two hours."

"What? Why is that?"

"Everybody's gone inside, ma'am. Joachim Etié's widow passed, the first time two deaths in the same family. Now people are scared to be close to anybody. The town's shut tight."

I saw the change. Empty streets, closed shutters. I was lucky to find a wagon to take me to Maman's. She confirmed the news.

"I know Félicité tells us yellow jack doesn't spread by contact," she said. "But with the Widow Etié gone, people don't want to take a chance. And we've had two more pieces of bad news. William Burke is down again, and there's another death in the country."

"Whatever shall we do, Maman?"

"I'm thinking."

"What *can* we do? Félicité tells us yellow fever is totally random. It's going to go wherever it wants to go and we can't stop it."

"Doing something is better than shutting ourselves inside waiting for the worst. There must be some way we could be of use."

Maman hardly uttered a word all day. After dinner, when the children left the table, she signaled me and Papa B to stay.

"I have a thought. A few days ago, Félicité went to some houses to give them supplies and tell them what you did for Patrick. We could go back to see those people and see if they need anything. At the least, we could be sure they have supplies."

"I like the idea, Maman. My friend Lody Smith sent word she'd be interested in learning how they can prepare. I don't know about her mother, the Widow Darby. You know she still lives just past the Smiths on the way to St. Martinsville. We could go talk to Lody. I'm sure Félicité would want to go too. We could start in the morning. If the ferry's running, Félicité and I could cross over and meet you at the landing when the church bell strikes. Could we use your wagon? If we have no ferry, I'll get Jacques to cross us in the skiff."

Papa B's mouth hung open.

Papa B stood up. "I wouldn't stop you, if you're of a mind to do that. It'll be dark soon. Hortense, you need to get on home. Go tell your children good night. I'll get the wagon to take you to meet the ferry."

"You know I could walk this short way," I told Papa B as we drove the bayou road.

"I know, but the way things are going, maybe the ferry won't be coming. Anyway, I wanted to tell you I haven't forgotten our conversation about Félicité."

"Nor have I, and I wanted to talk to you about that. I have second thoughts. Uncle F. C. seems to have forgotten all about her. Probably everyone else has forgotten also. Everyone like his creditors. We couldn't talk to Félicité about freedom without telling her there's a possibility that reminding Uncle F. C. could cause him or his creditors to make a claim."

"Good thinking, my dear. Yes, it's risky. Anyway, we have too much on our plate right now. By the way, tonight I'm damn proud of your Maman."

A week later he was even prouder.

CHAPTER TWENTY-ONE

W e found the Leonard Smith house closed up tight. My friend Lody answered our knock and threw up her arms at the sight of us.

"Come in, come in. I'm going crazy shut up like this."

Maman and I went inside; Félicité and Maman's driver stayed in the wagon.

"I don't see the point of locking ourselves in the house," Lody said. "Yellow jack is a crazy disease. It strikes or not, no matter what anybody does. There's not anything we can do about it."

She called to the kitchen for coffee. I got to the point of our visit as quickly as good manners allowed.

"You're right, Lody. We can't stop yellow fever, but there's a lot we can do to deal with it when it comes—*if* we're prepared and get started at the first sign. My Félicité has had experience. If you and Leonard will permit her, she'd like to talk to your overseer about being ready."

"How can we be ready? We don't even have a doctor in town to do the bleeding."

I took a deep breath. "There are treatments other than bleeding and purge. Perhaps you've heard how we treated our slave Patrick."

"But he didn't really have it, they tell me."

"I assure you he did. If you'll agree, Félicité will teach a few willing slaves how to recognize the signs and nurse someone using her traditional methods. She'd leave your overseer some of the remedies like the ones we used for Patrick. And some for you, if you'd allow her."

"It can't hurt, I guess. The overseer's in the field. I'll send word for him to come talk to you. And Leonard will be home shortly." She put her hand over mine. "He speaks of Fréderick often, Hortense. We all miss him."

The overseer reported they did indeed have a slave who complained of headache. That got Leonard's attention, and he agreed to hear what Félicité had to say.

"We can give these methods a try," he said when Félicité had finished her explanation. "We can always go to more drastic treatment if fever develops."

We had a foot in the door. The overseer agreed to move the slave with headache into a separate cabin and have Félicité talk to a few women who were willing to be nurses. The overseer and Félicité started to walk to the back door to go to the quarters. I got up to go with them. Leonard stopped me.

"No, no, Hortense. You don't want to be back there."

"Yes, I do," I said.

Although I explained how I'd helped with Patrick, Lody and Leonard wouldn't let me go. Neither would Félicité.

"I'll tend the plantation slaves, mistress. You serve by explaining our ways to the owners."

Maman rolled her eyes. "Hortense, I think before this day is over, you and I'll be drinking a lot of coffee."

A half-hour later, Félicité returned to the house. I could tell from the calm look on her face that she believed the designated nurses understood her methods.

"I left them an ample supply of fever tea, Madame Smith. We'll check back with you in a few days. We've heard a slave at the Widow Darby's has died," she said. "I'd like to go there to see if we might help."

Lody's eyes popped open. "Somebody died at my mother's? Nobody told me that."

"I saw no need to worry you, my dear," Leonard said.

"Please go to my mother's. I didn't know slaves were dying."

Back in the wagon, we headed up the road. Félicité had a compliment for me.

"You were a help there, mistress, talking with Madame Smith. Your job will be a lot harder if it's owners who are sick."

When we were almost at the Darby plantation, Félicité spoke again. "You showed your grit with Patrick, mistress. We'll need a good bit more of it before this is over."

As at the Smith house, the overseer took Félicité back to the quarters. She left fever tea and instructions for the care of anyone who might have symptoms. Maman and I visited with the Widow Darby, as everyone referred to her. I hated when people called me the Widow Duperier. They only did it behind my back.

We returned to town, checked in with the postmaster for messages, and picked up a new recruit for our mission: Josephine Hayes, a lovely young woman. She'd been introduced to traditional medicine by a slave from the islands who nursed her babies through childhood ailments. When she learned what we were doing, she asked to join us.

We stopped at the livery to ask about William Burke. In her Irish brogue, Ellen Burke turned down our help.

"I know you have our interests at heart, Hortense. I appreciate that. But Dr. Neal cured William the first time, almost three weeks ago now. He left behind a bottle of calomel. He told us to give it to William if he should have a relapse, and to use it for anyone in the family who might come down with fever. Calomel works for William," Ellen said. "I'm sticking with it. I've given him a dose."

We already knew she had done so from the barnyard odor seeping out to the front porch!

"Did Dr. Neal say anything about drinking water?" I asked. "Félicité's experience has found water very important."

Ellen frowned and shook her head. "The doctor was clear. No fluids!"

"Pray for him," I told our little team when I got back into the wagon.

At the end of the day, we'd been welcomed at four more houses. At three of them, we found slaves who said they didn't feel good, but at two of the houses the owners thought the slaves were just trying to get out of work. I tried to persuade the owners to give them a day off to see if the headache got worse or a fever developed and, in the meantime, to be sure they drank a lot of water. I wasn't certain I succeeded. Not everyone thought we were of use. We'd been flat turned away from two doors.

On the first day, other than William Burke, we had only encountered slaves who had symptoms. Most owners took our remedies, if only because it was something to do that cost nothing. We didn't know if they would be as willing if members of their own families went down. We all felt better for being busy.

When Félicité and I returned home, Caroline had a message from Belle Place. Susanne's husband Max had been by our house. He said Susanne heard what we were doing and wanted to join us—and bring along her cousin Felonise Broussard. Everyone who lived out there on the big oxbow of the bayou seemed to be a Broussard or be married to one. Broussard was Susanne's maiden name. Max said he persuaded Susanne to rest at home, but the next day, when the church bells sounded eight o'clock, she and Felonise would be at my house to cross the bayou with Félicité and me to join Maman and Josephine for the visits.

We were a group of six. The postmaster collected messages for us—three houses, none of whom had been prepared by Félicité—sent word asking us to come. They each had someone with symptoms and wanted the ingredients for fever tea. By the time we reached the third house, neighbors had gathered asking for some also. By afternoon we had to split up, dropping Félicité and Maman at one house while the rest of us checked in with a house nearby.

White people started to complain of headache.

"Félicité, do you think—?"

"Don't think, mistress. Remember what your Papa B said. Deal with the situation at hand."

When we met at the landing on the third morning, we had a message from the Millers. The slave who had a headache had awakened with a raging fever.

"I want to go to him, mistress. Could you drop me off and keep going?" Félicité asked.

"Yes, of course. I think I should try to find a second wagon. There may be more times when someone needs to stay at a house."

Later, when we checked back at the Miller house, we learned that Félicité had set up a crew of four to work the routine of wet cloths and fanning to bring down the fever of the slave.

"It's bad, Hortense," John Fitz Miller said. "Félicité wants to spend the night. Are you seeing it all over town?"

"Yes, we are. We have to face what's going on, John. Tell Félicité we'll check back first thing tomorrow."

* * * * *

The next morning Josephine's husband David sent a second wagon and driver for our use. We needed it. We split up to cover all the calls. We were being summoned by people we hadn't prepared or even seen in the early stages. We ran two wagons hither and yon, bearing advice, encouragement, and packets of fever tea.

Sweet Josephine was the first of us to get caught in a serious situation. We'd left her at a house with someone who had low fever. We were delayed getting back. When we returned to pick her up, we found her sitting on the edge of the porch, her head in her hands. I ran to her and smelled her from five feet away.

"My, God, Josephine. You're a mess! Tell me!"

"They took me back to the patient. When I leaned down to touch his forehead, he exploded all over me. I didn't handle the situation very well."

I helped her into my wagon and took her around the corner. Her turn to vomit!

"I'm taking you home," I said

A wan smile. "I do need to clean up, but I'll be fine in the morning. Don't you dare leave tomorrow without me!"

I returned to the house Josephine fled and took over care of the patient. Thank goodness I'd seen Dr. Abbey when he was ill. Even so, when delirium came, my stomach rolled. The end was bad. The thrashing about ceased abruptly. The patient's hand turned cold in mine.

That day, three people died. We stayed well, but yellow jack took a toll, particularly on my dear friend Susanne. She saw Eugene's face in every patient. Not one of us voiced the conclusion clear from the set of our lips. Epidemic.

The slave Félicité had tended at the Millers' came through the high fever. The patients in two houses we had prepared turned the corner. I dared to think that the bad results were only because some people failed to use Félicité's methods in time.

"It won't always be like this, mistress," Félicité warned. "Sometimes we start early, do everything the way we should, and yet patients succumb. It's gonna happen."

Before another day passed, her prediction came true. We went to a home of someone well trained in Félicité's ways. The family started treatment at the first sign of headache. When the fever came, they used the fever tea, plenty of water, and wet cloths to bring down the fever. Yellow jack marched on undeterred. The patient went through every stage of the disease and died in delirium.

We were devastated. I felt personally responsible and stayed at that house until the dreadful end. I couldn't mourn with the family; we had two more houses asking for our support. I told them I would be at the funeral, one of the few services I took time away to attend.

Then we received word that William Burke had died. And that Eloise DeBlanc passed as well. I knew her from church, and we had given her family instructions.

"I closed her eyes at six this morning," said Josephine. Now as strong as any of us, she had spent the long night.

Our wagons were alone on the streets. No boats came up the bayou or went down. The postmaster closed himself inside the landing, only opening the door to insistent knocking from someone he knew. The tavern and store stayed shut. Those who were not physically sick were grey with worry about their families and friends—and what would become of our town.

"How many slaves are dying?" I asked Félicité.

"Probably twice as many as white people. They're dropping in the fields, some overseers not willing to idle the work force in the middle of harvest. They might as well. The mills in Franklin refuse our wagons."

To embrace my children and stave off the panic of thinking we were all going to die, I slept at Maman and Papa B's at night. Yet, still I worried. Rent for the post office would eventually come from Washington, but how could I deposit a check? I'd have to forgive rent for the store and tavern. No one would move here and buy one of my town lots.

"What's going to happen to New Town?" I asked Papa B.

"I won't deny we're taking a blow. No ships have come in or out for weeks. The fire in the foundry is cold. Even if the fever should disappear tomorrow, we'll be months getting back to normal. If it goes on another few weeks . . . We *must* fight despair, Hortense. God knows, it doesn't help. The cattle keep my mind on the moment. Every day, they have to be taken out to graze."

Does one get used to death? I hated to admit, but yes. Numb, really. I thanked God our family stayed healthy, prayed for everyone who didn't, and got back in the wagon to continue the mission.

Not everyone of us went every day, but Félicité always. Susanne and Felonise came across the bayou in the morning, sometimes carrying a basket of fresh herbs for Félicité's potions. When two Decuir slaves fell sick, Susanne stayed home. That had been agreed. Family came first. She gave Jacques instructions on gathering herbs. He went out to harvest and sent them with Felonise.

I went to William Burke's funeral and saw his boys holding up their mother. Father de St. Aubin buried Louis DeBlanc and Jerome Monjean on the same day. Three days later, the bells tolled for Marie Boutté—a Boutté, but no relation to me. The three lived in different areas of town.

"We have full Requiem Mass for every victim," Father said. "All I can do is call on God for mercy."

I noticed that children who got the fever usually recovered. I asked Félicité if that was usual.

"Yes, ma'am. Chances are better for the young."

Again, we saw the end for a patient whose family had followed all our recommendations, but more of those who died were shriveled and grey from dehydration. Even if there was no doctor to do a bleeding, some families tried to do it themselves, and they administered purges. The families we'd trained had better results.

The day came when I thought we had fewer patients to visit. I dared voice optimism. "Are we coming to the end of it, Félicité?"

"Quite possibly we are, mistress. I'm not seeing many new cases in the quarters either."

And then yellow jack hit home.

Ten days after we started making calls, Maman and I came home to hear her son Alfred, he of the voracious appetite, say he didn't feel like dinner.

"What is it, Alf? You don't feel well?" I heard the edge in Maman's voice.

"My head kind of hurts."

The words knifed my gut. Maman turned pale. We threw ourselves into action. By God, we'd sure had practice.

We set Alfred up in a separate room and plied him with water and fever tea. At first, he protested.

"I'm not really sick, Maman. I just feel like taking a nap."

Maman was firm. "Fine. Take your nap, but drink water. We're coming in every few hours to be sure you do."

The next morning Alfred felt too bad to give us an argument. And he felt warm. One of us stayed at his side day and night. Two days after the headache, his fever spiked. We started wet cloths.

The wagons kept up the visits without us. Félicité stopped in first thing in the morning, every night, and a few times during the day.

Papa B repeated his mantra—do what has to be done at the moment and do not think about what might come—but his face set hard.

After three days of fever, Maman, who knew Alfred best, of course, said he looked different.

I stopped breathing. "How different, Maman?"

"Good different, pet. Look at his eyes."

"Maman, how can I look at his eyes when they're closed?"

"The lids are softer, relaxed."

I thought she was imagining things, but I had hope. A few hours later, Alfred's eyes opened, and he spoke. "Is there any food around here, Maman? I'm starving."

Maman and I fell on each other and wept.

As we did with every patient, we made Alfred rest in bed for two more days. Maman stayed with him, but I returned to the nursing crew.

As it turned out, Maman and Papa B's Alfred was one of the last to get sick. For five days in a row, no one died. Félicité reported good news from the plantations as well. Slaves were weak, but they were coming through. Our little band of nurses kept up our rounds. We went to all our patients for another week, urging them to rest.

Seven weeks after the body of Raphael Smith came to New Town pickled in rum, we dared speak the good news aloud. The fever had ended.

Our job had not. We heard of people in town and out in the country who were hungry. Our band of nurses had more work to do. We made the rounds to find who had supplies to spare and shared the bounty of one family with another that had nothing. We were weaker, thinner, but smiling on these rounds.

Still no boats came to replenish the shelves at Murphy's. No one came down the bayou from St. Martinsville or up from Franklin.

After two weeks without a death, a great storm passed through in the night. In the morning, the sun came up in a gorgeous blue sky. Papa B stood on the front gallery and looked up and down the bayou. He called us all out to see the sunrise.

"I feel like Noah, my dears. If I had a dove, I'd send him out. Failing that, I'm going to go myself."

He mounted his horse and galloped up the bayou road to St. Martinsville. An hour later, he reappeared, passed up the house, and galloped down to Franklin. He spread the word. New Town had been washed clean. Yellow jack had vanished.

EPILOGUE

On the afternoon of New Year's Day, 1852, a steady trickle of wagons pulled up at the corner of the Duperier property on the Bayou Teche in the town now known as New Iberia. Well-wishers came to the Duperier House for a birthday celebration. No one knew the actual birthday of the honoree, but in the fall of 1839, shortly after John D. Wilkins, unofficial mayor of the town, sent word to the *Attakapas Gazette* that yellow fever had vanished, there was one person everyone wanted to thank for the town's survival: the Duperier slave known to all as Félicité.

Yes, she was still legally a slave. She herself decided to leave it that way.

At the suggestion of the Widow Duperier, Félicité had chosen the day for her yearly birthday celebration: New Year's Day, appropriate to commemorate a new life for the town of New Iberia. Since January 1, 1840, grateful townspeople came to the Duperier House on this day bearing sweet cakes, which the honoree loved, but more importantly, deep gratitude from the many who would see the new year because of her ministrations during the period of the scourge.

Clear to all, this would be the last year Félicité could be present at her celebration. She used two canes to rise from her chair to greet her guests. Always of slight build, today she could have been taken aloft in a high wind. A woman of few words, she now had breath for even fewer. Before the end of the month, Félicité would lie in rest in the Duperier family plot, leaving behind on this earth gratitude for her unfailing dedication to the care of others and the memory of her coal black eyes.

Acknowledgments

I thank the descendants of the French settlers and those who keep the memory of Félicité alive and shared their family lore with me. Special thanks to James Akers, Michael Bell, Henry Clay Bienvenu, Jane Buillard, Robert Derouen, Sandra Egland, Gladys and Gerard Fournet, Dr. Phebe Hayes, Dr. Thomas Kramer, Al Lasalle, Patrick Onellion, Patricia Watters, and Penny White.

I thank the staff of the clerks of court of the parishes of Iberville, St. Martin, and St. Mary who dug in crumbling records to find answers to my questions. I am grateful for the expert guidance of Patty Gutekunst, genealogist at the St. Martin Parish Library, Shane Bernard, PhD, historian for McIlhenny Company, and Linda E. Sabin, PhD, professor emerita, Kitty DeGree School of Nursing, University of Louisiana at Monroe, an authority on nursing in the nineteenth century.

I thank the current owner of the Duperier house, Herman Schellstede, who opened every corner of the house, and his records, for my inspection. I thank Jerome Weber for his cover painting of the house as it was in 1839.

I thank my readers, Ann B. Dobie, PhD, professor emerita, University of Louisiana at Lafayette, Bette Kolodney, MA, Stamford, Connecticut, and my friend Tom Carruthers. My family encouraged me at every turn, especially my daughter-in-law Margaret G. Simon. I would not be writing today without the seed she planted and continues to nurture.

I thank the team at the University of Louisiana at Lafayette Press, especially Mary Duhé and the managing editor Devon E. Lord, for their skill, dedication, and patience. How fortunate I am that the director of the UL Press, Josh Caffery, hired a trained historian just in time for my work.

Finally, I am ever grateful for my friendship with the late Glenn Conrad, who introduced me to the complexity of the history of the bayou country fifty years ago.

Front inscription on obelisk of the Duperier family grave

Rear inscription on obelisk of the Duperier family grave

The Duperier family grave with Félicité's marker (bottom center)

The Duperier House (2019)

Bibliography

Attakapas Historical Association. *Attakapas Gazette 1966-1994*, Lafayette, Louisiana, Acadiana Manuscripts Collection, University of Louisiana at Lafayette Library.

Bergerie, Maurine. *They Tasted Bayou Water: A Brief History of Iberia Parish*. New Orleans: Pelican Publishing Company, 1962.

Bernard, Shane K. *Teche: A History of Louisiana's Most Famous Bayou*. Jackson: University Press of Mississippi, 2016.

Brasseaux, Carl, and Glenn R. Conrad. *The Road to Louisiana: The Saint-Domingue Refugees, 1792–1809*. Lafayette: University of Louisiana at Lafayette Press, 1992.

Carrigan, Jo Ann. *The Saffron Scourge: A History of Yellow Fever in Louisiana, 1796–1905*. Lafayette: Center for Louisiana Studies, University of Southwestern Louisiana, 1933.

Conrad, Glenn R. *New Iberia: Essays on the Town and its People*. Lafayette: Center for Louisiana Studies, University of Southwestern Louisiana, 1980.

Crete, Liliane. *Daily Life in Louisiana, 1815–1830*. Baton Rouge: Louisiana State University Press, 1981.

Follett, Richard. *The Sugar Masters: Planters and Slaves in Louisiana's Cane World, 1820–1860*. Baton Rouge: Louisiana State University, 2005.

Hall, Gwendolyn Midlo. *Africans in Colonial Louisiana: The Development of Afro-Creole Culture in the Eighteenth Century*. Baton Rouge: Louisiana State University Press, 1992.

Jackson, Jim Bob. *They Pointed Them East First.* Houston: John Kemp & Company, 2008.

Scott, Julius. *The Common Wind: Afro-American Currents in the Age of the Haitian Revolution.* London: Verso, 2018.

Stein, Robert Louis. *The French Sugar Business in the Eighteenth Century.* Baton Rouge: Louisiana State University Press, 1988.

Tanner, Lynette Ater, ed. *Chained to the Land: Voices from Cotton and Cane Plantations.* Winston-Salem: John F. Blair, Publisher, 2014.

Wood, Peter H. *Strange New Land: Africans in Colonial America.* New York: Oxford University Press, 1996.